What the critics are saying…

4 stars "Totally entrancing…" ~ *Romantic Times Magazine*

"These authors know their stuff, and I enjoyed every minute of these three captivating and erotic love stories! The heroines are fantastic and posses wonderful traits and powers. All of the heroes are super sexy, and I simply couldn't get enough of them. Any paranormal romance fan is bound to fall in love with these well-written stories of magic and love. Authors *Wilder, Midnight and Adams* will leave you breathless and craving more." ~ *ecataromance.com*

"These stories were HOT." ~ *coffeetimeromance.com*

"A delightful trio of magickal tales." ~ *PNR Reviews*

"Talk about mesmerizing, *Full Moon Magic* is a romantic story that will certainly bewitch readers. *Ms. Wilder* writes a heated, sensual tale of good old fashioned lust mixed with love. Esme is a sweet, innocent woman who wants to know a man's touch. Hawk is powerful, gentle, and understanding when it comes to his bride-to-be. All in all, a fascinating read." ~ *Romance Reviews Today*

"*In Moonlight* shows how an anthology should be done." ~ *Fallen Angel Reviews*

JC Wilder

Liddy Midnight

Elisa Adams

In Moonlight

ELLORA'S CAVE
ROMANTICA PUBLISHING

An Ellora's Cave Romantica Publication

www.elloriscave.com

In Moonlight

ISBN # 1419953540
ALL RIGHTS RESERVED.
Full Moon Magic Copyright© 2004 J. C. Wilder
Half Moon Magick Copyright © 2004 Liddy Midnight
Wishful Thinking Copyright © 2004 Elisa Adams
Edited by: Kari Berton, Briana St. James, Martha Punches
Cover art by: Syneca

Electronic book Publication: July, 2004
Trade paperback Publication: December, 2005

Warning:

The following material contains graphic sexual content meant for mature readers. *In Moonlight* has been rated *S-ensuous* by a minimum of three independent reviewers.

Ellora's Cave Publishing offers three levels of Romantica™ reading entertainment: S (S-ensuous), E (E-rotic), and X (X-treme).

S-ensuous love scenes are explicit and leave nothing to the imagination.

E-rotic love scenes are explicit, leave nothing to the imagination, and are high in volume per the overall word count. In addition, some E-rated titles might contain fantasy material that some readers find objectionable, such as bondage, submission, same sex encounters, forced seductions, etc. E-rated titles are the most graphic titles we carry; it is common, for instance, for an author to use words such as "fucking", "cock", "pussy", etc., within their work of literature.

X-treme titles differ from E-rated titles only in plot premise and storyline execution. Unlike E-rated titles, stories designated with the letter X tend to contain controversial subject matter not for the faint of heart.

Contents

Full Moon Magic

Dedication:

To Kari Berton, Christina Brashear and Tina Engler three divas who possess a magic all their own.

Chapter One

Esmerelda Proctor stared at the wedding gown in absolute horror. The white silk and tulle creation was nestled in a bed of ivory tissue paper in an oversized cardboard box closely resembling a coffin. The bodice and long fitted sleeves were covered in delicate seed pearls, glittering crystals and yards of Brussels lace. The voluminous tulle skirt was barely restrained by the yards of tissue paper wrapped around it. At the bottom of the box, her mother's wedding tiara was nestled in its own bed of tissue paper next to dainty silk slippers.

Her eyes slid shut and a feeling of impending disaster washed over her. Maybe it was a mistake and she'd imagined the gown on her bed. A half-laugh, half-sob escaped and her hands fisted. She took a deep breath and slowly released it before allowing herself to open her eyes.

The gown was still there.

"Drat."

Fashioned for her great-great grandmother, the original Esmerelda, the gown was fit for a princess and, despite its age, was as pristine as the day it was first worn. Her great-grandmother, Angelina, had worn the dress, as had her grandmother, Brianna, and finally her mother, Carolan. It was part and parcel of being the seventh Proctor daughter of a seventh Proctor daughter legacy. She, Esmerelda Julianna Proctor, was the last of her line and destined to wear this dress.

Only she'd been hoping it wouldn't be this soon. Her lips twisted. Not to mention the fact that the dress would never fit her without magical assistance. Carolan had been a sleek size eight, while Esme was a sturdy size sixteen. She sighed again, poked at a sleeve and felt something stiff tucked into the edge of the box.

A thick cream linen envelope peeked out from the layers of cloth and paper. She picked it up and her stomach plummeted. The paper was obviously expensive and on the back was her father's seal, a raven with a dagger clutched in its claws.

She broke the scarlet wax with a fingernail, tipped the envelope over and a cassette tape fell out. Her hand trembled as she picked it up and hurried to her stereo to shove it into the player. She pushed the play button.

"Esmerelda." Her father's voice sounded from the speakers. "The day has come for you to fulfill your duties to your family and marry the Montgomery heir as was set forth in the betrothal contract. By now you've received the wedding gown and everything you'll need for the ceremony. The car will pick you up Saturday morning at 10:00 a.m. and the ceremony is set for 10:45 a.m. sharp. If anything is missing or does not fit properly, have Shani contact my assistant and they will take care of the issue." There was a slight pause and the sound of a heavily indrawn breath.

"Do not disappoint me."

The tape whirred, then fell silent. Esme stared at the player in total disbelief.

"This can't be happening." She crumpled the envelope in her hand and her stomach cramped with betrayal. The message hadn't contained even the slightest hint of affection that a father should have shown his daughter. Instead, it had been a cold and impersonal message, as if he were speaking to a complete stranger.

Her lip curled. Edward Barrows-Proctor hadn't even granted her permission to contact him. Instead she'd been directed to go through her guard, who in turn would contact her father's assistant. She bit her lip hard to prevent the sob that threatened to erupt.

My father doesn't give a damn about me.

Her knees wobbled and her eyes stung. Less than a week ago, she'd sent her father a message through her guard, asking him one last time for release from the marriage contract. She'd been only five years old when the contract had been signed and she'd been forbidden to see her fiancé during the intervening twenty years. Even though they'd religiously exchanged cards and gifts at Yule and on birthdays, she knew no more about her future husband than she had as a child.

The past few days had been tension-filled as she'd waited for a response to her request. Tonight, when she'd returned from her evening walk, Shani had notified her that she'd received a package from home. Thinking, mistakenly of course, her father had relented and had sent her a token of his change of heart, she'd raced upstairs to find the dress on her bed.

Her father hadn't even acknowledged her request.

Her lips twisted and a cry locked in her throat. Her body shook and the envelope, still clutched in her hand, burst into flames. Cold blue flames devoured the paper, yet left her skin untouched. She flung the burning paper into the fireplace. She wouldn't let him get away with this.

She was through being a pawn to a father who didn't love her. She wouldn't be forced into marriage with a stranger she'd met only once. Edmund had kept her on a short leash, thinking only of the riches her famous name and magical lineage could bring him rather than her ultimate happiness.

Esme stalked to the bed and struck out at the box, shoving it across the bed so hard, it slid off the other side and spilled onto the floor. She ignored the pile of white silk and tulle when she strode past it to her altar.

All of her adult life had been spent hidden away at Hill House like a freak of nature. Her heritage of being a Proctor daughter, combined with the fact that she was the seventh daughter of a seventh daughter, made her a valuable commodity to her father. As far as she knew her six sisters hadn't been imprisoned as she had, but she had no doubt they'd also been sold to the highest bidder. That was her father's way. She rubbed the back of her hand across her forehead.

Where are you guys and why won't my father speak of you?

She snatched her mother's silver Goddess bowl from its honored place on the shelf above her altar. Esme had become betrothed to the Montgomery boy on her fifth birthday, two days after they'd buried her mother in the cold, damp earth. She'd been too young to understand what had occurred the day the contracts were signed. She vaguely remembered meeting several men and a tall, dark-haired boy with stormy eyes and a serious expression.

She set the bowl on her worktable with a thud.

With the air still heavy with the scent of flowers from Carolan's funeral, she and her father, along with the Montgomery family, had attended the impersonal ceremony that had concluded with the signing of the betrothal contract. Nothing had been asked of her, not even what she'd wished for her future, not that she'd have been able to answer then. One minute she'd been a grieving child trying to escape the curious gazes of a group of strangers and the next, a promised bride.

Betrothed to a stranger before she could even spell her full name.

She draped a purple silk cloth over a wooden serving tray. As if anyone was still betrothed in this day and age. It was the new millennium and women weren't supposed to be treated as property, yet her father still intended to hand her over to the highest bidder. She clearly remembered the fat envelope that had changed hands when the contracts had been completed. She had no doubt now that it had been filled with money, the agreed upon price for her name and her precious virginity.

She placed the Goddess bowl in the center of the tray. At the arrival of her menses, her father had imprisoned her at Hill House with Shani, her eunuch guard, and Ivy, a deaf woman, as her cook and housekeeper. As a final insult, Edmund had cast a spell over the property that prevented her from walking more than a mile from the house in any direction.

For the past eleven years, she'd lived a life of near silence and utter loneliness, her precious virginity intact. As the years had passed, she'd thought for sure she would've been able to sway her father from this path. On the rare occasions she'd had contact with him, she'd done her best to convince him to release her, but he'd staunchly ignored her pleas.

Esme moved to the narrow shelves next to her altar and picked through containers of dried plant materials. According to lore, the seventh Proctor daughter could only yield her maidenhead to a male witch of pure blood in order to secure the strongest of powers in their offspring. Her father professed to believe that if she were to squander her only possession of worth upon a lesser mortal, it would spell the end of the exalted line of Proctor women. In reality, he was looking to line his own pockets.

Esme snorted and pulled a few dried hyacinth flowers from a jar and dropped them on the cloth. The son of one of the most powerful magical families on earth, Ethan was probably as coldly ambitious as his father, Kiergan. The elder Montgomery was rumored to be ruthless in his determination to increase the already impressive magical talents of his family.

Those were the stories passed around when she was a child. Unfortunately, she'd heard little new information over the years, secluded as she was. Only the tidbits her father had passed on had left her in no doubt that, if she tried to thwart their plans, he and the Montgomery family would make her pay for the rest of her life, however long that would be.

Well, she would just see about that.

She selected a handful of dried white rose petals and added them to the tray. With her last message, she'd given her father one last chance to grant her the freedom she craved and his response had been to deliver the wedding dress and move up the date a few months. He'd forced her hand and now it was time to put her backup plan into action, a plan that would either gain her freedom or hasten her death.

She reached for the bulging book that contained her spells. Now, what else did she need? A soft wave of calm slipped under her skin when her fingers brushed the worn leather of the oversized tome. Held by the Proctor women for centuries, it was well known that the book wouldn't reveal its secrets for anyone other than a true Proctor daughter. She'd seen this in person when her father had tried to open the book shortly after her mother's death. Instead of opening, bolts of bright blue electricity had shot from the silver latch and knocked him on his generous backside.

She smiled when the cover turned easily and the familiar scent of dust and dried plants rose from its pages. Filled with spells written by many hands, bits of dried herbs, feathers, and extensive drawings of sacred rites, the grimoire was a feast of information for any practicing witch.

Esme scanned the crowded pages until she found the rite she'd marked with a scrap of white ribbon. She'd come across the spell several months ago while in search of something to heal the wounded sparrow she'd found in the woods.

Her gaze moved over the pale brown scrawl.

Summoning a Lover

She was going to conjure a lover to take her virginity. Once the deed was done, her father would have no choice but to set her free, as the marriage contract would be breached.

Or she hoped it would be that easy.

She reached for a container of bay leaves. She knew very little about engaging in the sex act or even dealing with the opposite sex. Just the thought of taking a man into her bed made her a bit queasy. The only thing she knew for sure was that she needed to lose her virginity to a non-witch, and since her father had seen to it that no men could get near her, her only option was to conjure one.

She looked at the list of ingredients.

R-O-S-E

Next to the word was a small picture. Definitely a rose and shaded with white chalk. White rose petals. Check. The next picture was a tuft of bushy, white, star-shaped blossoms. That would be the white hyacinth flower. She already had those arranged.

She frowned. But what was this next ingredient? Her gaze moved over the meaningless jumble of letters. While she recognized the letters, the arrangement didn't mean anything to her.

M-O-R G-O-R

Frustrated, Esme shoved the book away. If only she weren't so stupid. Her father had given up on her ever learning to properly read. He'd sent the tutors away when she was eleven and still unable to read at even a second grade level.

Stupid, stupid Esme, he'd ranted.

Luckily, what few magical abilities she possessed were ones she'd been born with and they were more or less intuitive. Her grimoire was filled with many drawings and, in general, she did fine with the simplest of spells. She could light a candle in the blink of an eye, turn water into wine, wash dishes in a flash and set the broom to sweeping the floor. Those were certainly worthy talents that would've made her mother proud.

Of course, there was the time she'd accidentally turned Ivy into a rat and it had taken a whole week to return her back to normal. Esme sighed. She didn't like to remember that incident. Years had passed before Ivy had become comfortable around her again.

Then there was the unfortunate incident with the fruit pies…

She shook her head. No, no, she couldn't bear to even contemplate that one. She'd had to use three layers of paint to cover the mess on the walls and the white table linens had had to be destroyed. Who knew raspberries could stain like that?

She pulled the book toward her. She wouldn't screw up this spell, not this time. Her entire future depended on it working correctly and, for once, her magic would perform as she'd intended. She was sure of it.

She glanced at the drawing next to the garbled entry. It looked like a morning glory blossom and next to it was a small seedpod. Did she use the dried flower or the seed? Did it matter? Surely they were of the same plant and their powers would be similar.

She selected a jar of the black morning glory seeds and placed a small amount on the tray, then added dried petals for good measure. She retrieved several rosemary sprigs and a pinch of lavender petals before adding the sage bundle to indicate the goddess should send her a man.

Esme stifled a giggle. Wouldn't it be a tragedy if she'd forgotten the sage and the universe sent her a woman instead?

After double-checking the book to ensure she had everything she needed, she retrieved her wand. The wooden handle was smooth and familiar against her palm. The wand had been the last gift she'd received from her mother and it was her most cherished possession. She laid it across the Goddess bowl.

Now she was ready.

She picked up the tray and carried it outside to the spacious stone terrace. The unseasonably warm evening air smelled of damp earth and decaying leaves, while overhead the waxing moon was high in the sky. Autumn was approaching and the moon was several days away from being full. It was the perfect night for casting a spell.

She placed the tray on a wrought iron bistro table before hurrying back into her room to retrieve three white candles and the Book of Shadows. After arranging them near the tray, she lit the candles with a single breath. Their flames flickered and danced in the slight breeze and the scene was set. She smiled.

Magic was afoot.

Taking a deep breath, she tilted back her head to gaze at the swollen orb of the moon. It was almost midnight, the witching hour, and time to cast her spell.

She ran her finger around the rim of the bowl and tried to ignore her suddenly queasy stomach. She took another deep breath and her mother's words whispered through her mind.

"Esmerelda, it isn't the content of the spell, it's the intention behind your words. The business of magic is never to be taken lightly. Be succinct about how you phrase yourself and above all, be careful what you wish for as you just might get it…"

"Mama, I wish you were here," she whispered.

Ignoring the pang near her heart, she turned her attention to the open book. Some of the letters and words of the spell were jumbled into an illegible mass. She could pick out most, but the rest were a mystery to her.

She rubbed the back of her hand across her forehead, then turned her attention from the book to the tray. As her mother had always said, it wasn't the words that were said but the intent behind it. She was sure her intent was clear and hopefully she'd gotten all of the ingredients correct.

Clearing her mind, she closed her eyes for a few moments of quiet reflection. Her heartbeat slowed, and when she concentrated on the soles of her feet and the solid feel of the terrace beneath her, she experienced the familiar rush of power from the earth as it entered her body and expanded through her limbs.

Steady now, she opened her eyes and reached for the dried rose petals. Sprinkling them into the bowl, she spoke out loud while adding each ingredient.

"Silent night,
Cast in white,
With all my might,
I ask you make it right.

Hear my words, mighty Hecate,
Save me from my father's plan,
Grant me my most urgent wish,
And send me a man.

Fair of face,
With kindness and grace,
A smile so bold,
And a heart of gold.

In the dark of night,
Mighty Hecate, make it right
Under this full moon,
Save me from my father's doom."

With the last line, she picked up her wand and stroked its tip along the edge of the silver bowl. A soft breeze licked her dark curls and the dried plant materials began to swirl as if an unseen hand were mixing them.

She stepped away from the table and the air currents increased. Her gaze remained fastened on the twirling herbs and dried flowers as the enchanted breeze eased the ingredients out of the bowl in a circular swirl of warm air to be swept into the evening sky.

A feeling of inevitability settled over her shoulders as her offering vanished in the distance. What was done was done and for better or worse, her spell had been cast. Now all she had to do was wait for her lover to arrive.

A sharp twinge struck her in the chest near her heart. She was bitterly disappointed that her first lover was to be a man of her own making. He would be a magical creation rather than a mortal man with a family and hopes and dreams of his own. He could never be a real lover and there could be no chance of a future between them.

She shook away that sad thought and gathered her things together. She had to do whatever was necessary to gain her freedom. Once she'd accomplished that, she'd be able to seek the man who was destined to be her one true love.

Chapter Two

Ethan "Hawk" Montgomery glared at the crystal ball in the center of his desk. In the smoky depths of the orb, his fiancée moved about her chamber, replacing the items from her altar. Her usually animated face was solemn.

For her sixteenth birthday, he'd gifted Esmerelda with a special set of crystal globes with the explicit instructions that they be placed around her sanctuary. Unbeknownst to her, he'd spent a lot of time watching her through those years and he'd seen her do many things he didn't understand. Then again, who truly understood women to begin with?

He'd seen her charm birds from the trees, dance in the moonlight and spend quiet evenings painting or knitting. He'd watched as she'd cast spells to cure sick animals and wax her bedroom floor. He'd been watching the time she'd completely botched a simple offering spell, the outcome of which perplexed him to this day, but he'd never seen her do anything like what she'd done this evening.

She'd asked the Goddess to send her a lover.

With a growl Hawk lunged to his feet. He'd just received a note from Edmund stating the wedding date had been moved up several months due to an illness in the family. In a few days she was destined to become his wife and it was a complete mystery to him as to why Esmerelda would make such a request. He'd never seen a man enter her sanctuary and her father had assured him that she'd never had sexual contact with any man.

He snorted. If this were true, then why would she have chosen to conjure a lover? Virgins did not conjure lovers. Only a woman of experience would do so.

Irritated, he stalked to the wide windows overlooking the valley. There was no way he'd allow his woman, his Esmerelda, to accept another man into her bed and her body. She was destined to be his and had been since the time they were both but children.

The Proctor women were known for being a little eccentric but, thanks to their limitless magical abilities, most people had a tendency to overlook their odd habits. They were powerful and uncommonly beautiful and they exuded both mystery and sensuality. It was said that a man only had to spend a few minutes in their company and he'd be ruined for any other woman.

He couldn't attest to that personally, as he'd met Esmerelda only once when she was but five years old. She'd been a sad-eyed imp traumatized by the recent untimely death of her mother. A dark-haired angel in a misshapen black dress, she'd paid little attention to him, preferring to hide behind her father as the marriage contracts had been reviewed and signed.

He regretted that he'd never been permitted to spend time with the woman she'd become. It hadn't been from a lack of desire on his part, rather her father had forbidden any contact between them from the moment they'd been betrothed. In the contract, Edmund had stipulated they be kept apart until the morning of their wedding. His reasoning was that the consecration of their union needed to happen after the proper bonding ritual to ensure the purity of their bloodline. Edmund had been afraid that youthful passion might cause them to forget themselves and she'd lose her virginity too soon.

Hawk raked his hands through his hair. That excuse was a load of manure. The bonds of a traditional marriage did nothing to ensure the purity of their blood, and though the bonding ritual itself was important, it was not completely necessary. The most important aspect was the phase of the moon coupled with the loss of her virginity. As long as the moon was waxing, if not completely full, the magical powers of their children would be secured.

He turned away from the window. Was there another reason her father had wanted them kept apart? He dropped into the leather desk chair and his gaze landed on the globe. Was it possible his blushing bride-to-be was no virgin at all? Was this the reason her father wanted to keep them apart? To hide his daughter's lost virtue?

In reality, when it came to casual sex, Hawk preferred an experienced woman in his bed. Shrinking virgins were not his style, but Esmerelda wasn't just any woman, she was his future wife and the mother of his future children.

To join the Montgomery and Proctor bloodlines was to ensure the survival of two legendary lineages of witches. The old knowledge, which was passed verbally from parent to child, was falling by the wayside, and it was essential to attend to the needs of future generations. While this alone was reason enough to marry her, there was a larger, more important reason.

Hawk was in love with her.

The same year he'd sent his gift of the gazing globes, he'd dared to approach her secluded home, which was protected by various spells and enchantments designed to prevent her from leaving the grounds and he from entering. He'd sat at the edge of the spell field and waited for her to appear.

It hadn't taken long before a beautiful girl had emerged from the woods. Clad in an oversized blue dress smudged with dirt and torn at one shoulder, she'd carried a wounded animal in her arms.

She hadn't even glanced in his direction as she'd hurried toward the house, all the while murmuring a healing spell over her damaged charge. Tall and curvy with her feet bare and her long, dark hair barely restrained in an untidy braid, she'd been the loveliest thing he'd ever seen. Her expression, a mixture of concern and serenity, had captured his attention as well as his heart. He knew then that Esmerelda was destined to be his and his alone.

Hawk leaned forward and laid his hand over the globe. Her image shifted as if reflected upon water. His woman wanted a man, did she? He released the ball and her image dimmed.

He reached for the Montgomery family grimoire. Her wish was his command, but first he had to find a way around that confinement spell.

* * * * *

Something wasn't right.

Esme stretched, enjoying the sensual slide of crisp cotton sheets against her bare calves. She opened her eyes, just a slit, to catch a glimpse of the sky through the open French doors. The moon was no longer peering in her door and the sky was now a velvety black and liberally sprinkled with stars. She smiled into her fluffy pillow, relishing the comfort of her bed. Autumn would soon be upon the land and the doors and windows would have to be locked against the night air. For now she was enjoying the unseasonable warm spell—

The spell!

The rush of memory had Esme catching her breath and anticipation zinged through her body. When would the Goddess grant her wish? She had so little time to accomplish her goal before the day of her wedding. Maybe she should have stipulated a time frame. She frowned. Was there even a way to do so?

She rolled into a more comfortable position and smashed the pillow beneath her cheek. She stretched out her legs then started when her foot brushed against something hard and unfamiliar.

What in the world?

She prodded the obstacle with one pointed toe. It was warm and covered with a layer of coarse hair and when she prodded again, harder this time, it shifted. The sound of human flesh sliding across sheets sent a ripple of alarm down her spine.

She couldn't have…not already…

Holding her breath, Esme scooted toward the edge of the bed, excited and terrified at the same time. Her heart thudded in her chest as she slid her leg off the side of the bed when an arm snaked around her waist to prevent her escape. A squeak erupted from her mouth and she was hauled into the shelter of a warm male chest.

"Where do you think you're going?" A sleepy male voice rasped in her ear, sending her nerves into full alert.

What the ---

She did!

She had!

Oh joy!

The Goddess had answered her spell in record time.

Esme barely managed to muffle a squeal of delight by pressing her fist against her mouth. Her spell had worked. Maybe she wasn't such an incompetent witch after all.

The thrill of victory turned to nervous sweat as reality set in and her stomach bottomed out. Now that he was here, what should she do with him? Should she introduce herself? What was the protocol for such a situation?

She swallowed audibly. "Who are you?" Her voice was faint and she was acutely aware of warm male flesh searing her back and buttocks through the thin cotton nightgown.

"Who do you think I am?" Amusement laced his words and his arm tightened around her waist. He nuzzled her shoulder and she shivered.

"I-I-I have no idea," she lied. One of his big hands flattened against her side and his thumb strayed perilously close to her breast. She held her breath. She wasn't used to being touched in such a familiar fashion. Heck, she wasn't used to being touched at all, for that matter.

"You didn't send for me?" His chest rumbled against her back and his voice had a sleepy, sexy tone that made her feel warm all over. "How soon you have forgotten," he chuckled.

A jolt of glee rocketed down her spine.

Yes! She'd done it!

Tamping down her excitement, she fought for a calm tone and failed when her voice came out as a squeak. "Well, of course I didn't forget, I just didn't think you'd arrive so quickly."

Esme started to turn but her head connected with his chin, hard. He grunted and ducked. She tried to move away but his arm tightened to prevent her escape.

"Mmm, don't move," he purred.

The stranger cuddled even closer and his clean masculine scent surrounded her. Her heart raced and she could hardly breathe. She'd never been this close to a man and she was finding it to be an overwhelming experience. She felt oddly warm and her chest ached. Did other women experience these feelings when they were close to a man?

She closed her eyes. How she wished her mother or one of her sisters were around so she could ask them some questions. One of the first ones would be, now that she had him in her bed, what exactly did she do with him? Just how did a woman ask a man for sex? Did she simply tell him she wanted to make love — no, have sex with him? Should she try to seduce him? She didn't know the first thing about seducing a man. Was it enough to take off her clothes?

She caught her lower lip between her teeth. Would he think her too forward if she merely blurted it out? Her eyes popped open. Then again, did it matter what he thought? He was her creation after all, and while he was a living, breathing male, he was here at her command.

Summoning her courage, she asked, "Are you really who I sent for?"

There was a moment of heavy silence before he spoke. "You doubt your own powers?"

She shook her head, unwilling to admit her incompetence when it came to witchcraft. If he thought her to be a great and powerful witch, what was the harm in allowing him to believe for a little while longer?

"Of course not." She injected a note of confidence into her voice. "You see, this is the first time I've ever asked for such a boon. Having never performed this spell, I was uneasy with regards to its outcome."

"I see." Judging from the tone of his voice, it sounded as if he didn't see at all. "Do you care to explain why you sent for me?"

She shook her head. "It's very complicated and I'd rather not go into it right now."

"Complicated…" he muttered.

Suddenly Esme was free, and for a split second, she mourned the loss of his warmth. Clutching the sheet she rolled in time to see his shadowy form as he moved to the foot of the bed. He positioned his back against the footboard and faced her.

In the darkness she couldn't see him very well, and he was little more than a shadow among the shadows. He stretched out his long legs and crossed them at the ankle. He didn't appear to be wearing much in the way of clothing, just a pair of dark shorts.

Her gaze moved over his indistinct form from the top of his dark head to his large feet. Whoever he was, he was a big man. She shivered and forced her gaze away to focus on her pristine sheets.

"Since you don't want to talk about why you sent for me, how about we simplify things?" His voice was a deep rumble. "Why don't you simply tell me what you want?"

She shot a quick glance at the shadow that was his face then looked away, suddenly uncomfortable. How could she verbalize that she wanted the freedom to make her own decisions and live her life how she saw fit?

Esme sat up and scooted to the head of the bed. Stuffing several fat pillows behind her, she propped herself against the headboard.

"That isn't easily defined." She carefully tucked the sheet under her arms. "I want a lot of things and you're only the first step."

"First step of what?"

"Well…"

There was no way to put into words the burden her heritage had placed upon her, especially to a man who had no conception of her world. One thing was for sure, there was no way she would spill any details of her life to a man whose name she didn't know.

"What shall I call you?" she asked.

She caught a flash of white teeth when he grinned. "What do you want my name to be?"

She shook her head. "I'm serious, what's your name?'

"You can call me Hawk."

"Is that a nickname?"

"Yes."

"Hawk." She rolled the name across her tongue and decided she liked it. Hawk was a strong, confident name for such a big man and it implied everything she wasn't feeling right now. "Well, Hawk, you're in the unique position to do me a favor."

"And what would that be?" She heard a hint of impatience in his tone.

The words hovered on the tip of her tongue like gold nuggets, hard, emotionless and cold. Her palms grew damp and she rubbed them on the sheet. If there was ever a time she was going to take control of her life, she needed to muster all the courage she had to get through the next few minutes. Her freedom, her dreams and her very life lay within her grasp.

She took a deep breath and blurted, "I want you to have sex with me."

* * * * *

Hawk jerked as her words struck his flesh like pellets of ice. It was one thing to know she'd cast a spell to bring a lover to her bed, it was quite another to hear it from her lips.

Images of his fiancée nude flooded his mind. Blood rushed to his cock and he stifled the growl that threatened to erupt as visions of her naked and wet beneath him surged through him. Her lush body would be sweet and tight, her breasts soft and ample, every man's perfect fantasy, only he was the lone man who'd ever touch her.

"You're a beautiful woman, why would you need to conjure a lover?"

"Well, that's the complicated part." Her face was a pale oval at the other end of the bed. "And it's one that I won't talk about right now." She scrunched down in the bed and hunched her shoulders. "Can't we just get on with this? We can talk afterward."

Hawk glanced out the French doors. If she was still a virgin, he couldn't make love to her, not yet. The moon had almost set, so its position was all wrong. But tomorrow— tomorrow evening between eleven and midnight would be perfect. The full moon would be on the rise, and in the light of that moon he'd claim her.

He shook his head and reached for her leg beneath the sheet. "You're in a hurry. Some things in life are to be savored and this is one of them."

Through the sheet he located her ankle and she twitched when he touched her. The pale blur that was her face turned away, and he sensed her discomfort. His thumb zeroed in on the sensitive flesh above her anklebone and he began stroking her in a lazy, soothing caress.

"What's your name? Or shall I just call you Enchantress?" He wanted to hear her speak again. Her voice was soft and melodic, and he knew he would never tire of hearing her speak.

"Esmerelda, but you can call me Esme." Her words were faint.

"Esmerelda." He savored the name on his tongue as if it were a rare vintage of wine. "That's a beautiful name."

"I-i-it's a family name."

He already knew that. For the past four generations, there had been an Esmerelda Proctor, though none as lovely as his Esme.

He slid his hand up her calf a few inches and felt her tense. She was way too uptight and the first thing he needed to work on was getting her to relax.

She was almost cowering behind the sheet, and he wasn't quite sure what to make of her behavior. Had he been mistaken? His jaw tightened. It wasn't possible. Why would a virgin send for a lover?

Chapter Three

He released her leg and tried not to smile when she moved a safe distance away.

"Relax, Esme, I'm not going to bite."

Yet.

He rose. "I need some light."

Sheets rustled. "It's here on the bedside table."

Hawk found a silver candlestick with a fat, white candle and, out of habit, he started to light it with a wave of his hand but managed to stop just in time. For now, it was probably better if she thought he was mortal.

"I'll need some matches," he said.

"I can do it."

She propped herself on her elbow and leaned toward the candle until the wick was several inches away from her mouth. With a soft exhale, sparks danced along the wick before it burst into flame.

He squinted against the glare, and after a few moments his vision adjusted and he caught the first good look of his future wife. His heart stuttered when he realized the cold crystal of the gazing globes didn't come close to doing her justice. Esmerelda Proctor was the loveliest woman he'd ever seen.

Her long hair was as black as night and bound into an unkempt braid that allowed a few silky tendrils to frame her heart-shaped face. Her sooty brows arched over wide, brilliant green eyes that were slanted ever so slightly, giving them a cat-like appeal. Her cheeks were tinged a delicate pink and her lush scarlet lips were enough to tempt any man into kissing her.

"Do I have something on my face?" She rubbed a finger over her nose and the candlelight winked off an amethyst ring on her middle finger.

"No, not at all." He sat on the edge of the bed and his hip nudged the soft curve of her thigh. "You're more beautiful than I'd ever imagined." The moment the words left his mouth, he realized his error. She believed he was her creation and at her command, consequently he wouldn't have seen her before this very moment.

She tilted her head to the side and her brow knitted. "What do you mean, more than you'd imagined?"

Seeking to stop her from asking questions he didn't dare answer, he leaned forward and pressed his mouth to hers. She made a soft sound and her hands came up to his chest. For a split second he thought she meant to push him away. Instead her nails scraped his skin before she went still as if waiting to see what he'd do next.

He cupped the back of her neck and gently tipped her head to the side before letting himself slide into the kiss. Heat shafted through his body when she crowded closer. He licked at the seam of her mouth and her lips tightened then opened a fraction, and it was just enough. He slid inside and the taste of her, rich and womanly, rocketed through his system and set his nerves on high alert.

She made a sound low in her throat, her nails digging into his chest as his tongue sought her secrets. He took her by the shoulders and pulled her closer until her soft breasts were pressed into his chest and he could feel her hardened nipples. Esme was a soft, fragrant armful and he longed to lay her down on the bed and suckle her ample breasts, to tease the thatch of dark curls between her plump thighs—

The soft, musical sound of bells jerked him from the pure carnality of the moment. He raised his head and listened. Somewhere in the depths of the house, a clock tolled the time.

It was five a.m.

"Wow," she whispered.

He gazed into her beautiful face in disbelief. With a simple touch of her lips, he'd forgotten the reason he was here. Her gaze was soft and blurry, her creamy skin flushed with desire. He wanted her more than his next breath, and still he forced himself to push her gently away. Her kisses were potent and, if he weren't careful, he'd have her flat on her back within minutes. No matter how much he desired her, it would not be a smart move.

"That was only the beginning."

Her eyes widened. "So what comes next?"

He smiled. "You'll have to trust me, Enchantress. Your wish is that we become lovers and I would like this as well, but I do have a condition to that agreement."

Looking distinctly uncomfortable, Esme crossed her arms over her chest. "What would that condition be?"

He reached over and tucked a stray lock of hair behind her ear. "I need to be in charge in the bedroom."

"In charge? What do you mean, 'in charge'?" He caught the note of suspicion in her voice.

"It means I like to call the shots in bed."

Her eyes narrowed. "What if I don't want you to?"

"I'd never hurt you, Esmerelda." He gave her an encouraging smile. "Am I not your creation? How could I hurt or frighten she who summoned me?"

She smoothed the sheet over her lap. "Indeed, you have a valid point." She lifted her head and their gazes met. "Very well, I agree to your request."

He smothered the surge of triumph. Catching her hand he raised it to his lips. "You won't regret it." Her skin was warm beneath his mouth and his tongue snaked out for a quick taste before he released her. "Now roll onto your stomach. I'm going to show you how to relax."

"What are you going to do?"

He laid his fingers over her mouth. "I think you've forgotten our agreement already. I'm in charge here, remember? We have time, Enchantress. Why are you trying to rush me?"

"We have a little time," she amended.

Under his guiding hands she stretched out on her belly and propped her chin on her crossed arms. He eased the thick braid to the side, taking only a second to enjoy the feel of it against his palm. It was so long he wondered if she'd ever cut it.

"You have beautiful hair," he said.

"Thank you." Her voice was little more than a whisper.

He eased the sheet away from her body. She was clad in an enveloping white cotton nightgown that covered her generous curves from neck to toes. To say that it was modest would be an understatement. All she needed was socks and a stocking cap and she'd be completely covered.

"Do you have scented oil I can use?" he asked.

Her head popped up. "What for?"

"I'm going to give you a massage."

"Oh." She started to rise and he stopped her by gently pushing her back down on the bed. "Don't move, just point."

She indicated the dim corner of the room near her altar. "On the second shelf, you'll find some essential and carrier oils."

Hawk rose and picked up the candle before he moved toward the shelves. As he drew closer, his nose detected the scents of dried herbs and a myriad of essential oils. On the shelf indicated were several neat rows of small brown bottles. None of them were marked or labeled but around the neck of each bottle was a colored ribbon. What kind of system was this? He picked up the first bottle.

"Do you have a preference?" he asked.

"Almond oil is in the large bottle on the far right. As for scents, I have lavender in the small bottle with the lavender and green ribbons."

Hawk selected the requested bottles then found a small dish he could use to mix them. When he returned to the bed, Esme still lay on her stomach and her cat eyes were fixed on him. His gaze slid over her face.

They were going to have beautiful children.

He set his burden on the bedside table. "You'll need to slide your gown off your shoulders."

She hesitated before reaching for the bodice. She undid a handful of the tiny pearl buttons at her throat before shimmying the garment off her shoulders. She pulled her arms out of the sleeves then immediately lay flat in order to conceal her nudity from him.

With her gown pooled at the middle of her back, the pale curve of her shoulders was exposed. Heat pooled in his groin.

"So tell me something about yourself, Esme." Hawk poured a small amount of almond oil in the shallow bowl before adding a few drops of the pungent lavender. The rich floral scent teased his senses.

"What do you want to know?"

"Everything." He picked up the bowl and moved it out of her line of sight before trailing a finger around the rim and the oil began to swirl, mixing itself. "What do you like to do when you're alone? Do you read?" He touched his pinky to the blend and added a small jolt of heat to warm the liquid until he judged it ready to be worked into her skin.

"I usually listen to books on tape. I don't have a lot of time to sit down with a book."

"Why is that?" He sat on the edge of the bed and gently eased her gown lower to expose the curve of her back before dribbling some of the warmed oil into the delicate furrow of her spine. The moment the oil touched her skin she flinched.

"I-I have too many things to do during the day to just sit around with a book so I use a headset instead and I can take my books out in the woods as I work." Her rapid speech betrayed her unease with the situation.

He dipped his fingers into the oil and began smoothing it over her skin, enjoying the supple feel of her flesh and the slick oil.

"What do you do in the woods?" He glanced at her well-stocked shelves. "Gather herbs?"

"Yes, and I have a vegetable garden as well as my herbal garden. If I'm careful, I have fresh lettuce until late in the fall."

He didn't miss the hint of pride in her voice. "That's a talent." He worked the oil into her skin, concentrating first on her shoulders until her skin was slick and pliant. He knew he'd never again smell lavender without associating it with this moment.

"My mother was an excellent gardener."

"And she taught you?" He kneaded down her spine.

He felt her nod. "She'd just started when she died. She taught all of her daughters how to tend a garden and how to heal with herbs." There was a sense of loss in her voice that was impossible to overlook and his heart ached for her. His mother was very much alive and eagerly awaiting his wedding day.

"You miss her," he said.

"Very much." Her voice was low.

"Where are your sisters? Do they live here?"

"No, they don't."

He'd never seen any of her sisters via the gazing globes and her short tone told him all he needed to know. Esme had little to no contact with any of her six sisters and he made a mental note to figure out why. He continued massaging his way down her spine. "Don't you get lonely living here in the woods?"

"I'm not alone." She shrugged, and if his hands weren't on her back he might have taken her at her word if he hadn't felt the slight hesitation. "I have my guard—um—assistant Shani, and Ivy, the cook and housekeeper. I have my work so I don't have time to be lonely."

"It sounds like you have a very full life." He ran his hands down her sides, making note of how much more relaxed she'd become.

"I do." She nodded vigorously. "My life is very full and I'm happy."

He didn't buy what she was trying to sell him. She was lonely and he'd bet his wand on it. Via the gazing globes, he'd seen the many hours she'd sat on the terrace, simply staring into space with her heart in her eyes and a sad, faraway look on her face.

He leaned over her and whispered into her ear, "But do you have love?"

She gave a soft, heartfelt sigh. "What is love really? Does a mother love her child because that is her child and it's what she's supposed to do? Does a father love his daughter more if she's perfectly well-behaved and marries well?"

Hawk remained silent, not quite sure how to answer her. In his family, love was about acceptance no matter how one acted. It had nothing to do with expectations, either meeting or falling short of them. It simply was what it was.

He slid his fingers down her spine. "Love is about accepting faults and enjoying each other's company. It's about wanting to see your loved ones achieve all they can with their talents and abilities, and to reach their dreams."

He finished massaging the oil into her back and urged her to roll over. She clutched her gown and her eyes were wide when she stretched out. His hands closed over hers and he looked deep into her emerald eyes.

"It's about bringing pleasure to another human being by just breathing." He coaxed her to release her death grip on the gown, his eyes never leaving hers. "And receiving pleasure as well as giving it."

Esme gulped audibly and his gaze dropped to her exposed flesh. The candlelight kissed her pale skin with gold. Her perfectly rounded breasts were crowned with fat, rosy nipples.

They quivered as she drew in a shaky breath and he burned with the need to take one into his mouth and suckle her until she forgot her unease. But he didn't act on that thought because he sensed that if he rushed things too much, his beautiful Enchantress might bolt from the bed and he'd have a tough time coaxing her back into it.

Instead of reaching for her, he picked up the bowl of massage oil from the bedside table.

* * * * *

Esme's breath caught when he leaned closer. For a moment she thought he'd kiss her and she really, really wanted him to do so, but he reached for the bowl of oil instead. Her breath left in a rush and she wasn't sure if she was relieved or disappointed.

She was so far out of her element, she was unsure about what to do next. She was half-naked in front of a stranger and she fought the urge to squirm. Thanks to the fashion magazines she read each month, she knew she was plump, much plumper than the models on the glossy covers. It didn't seem to matter what she did, as she could never manage to lose the thirty pounds or so she wanted, and the weight just stubbornly stayed where it was. She glanced at Hawk's handsome face. He didn't seem to mind her mature curves. In fact, he seemed to enjoy them.

One thing she did know was that she'd gotten what she'd asked for, a lover like no other. Who knew he'd be so handsome? His hair was black with bluish tints and his features were strong, masculine. His thickly lashed eyes were a greeny-gray that seemed to be oddly familiar, though she was sure she'd never seen this man before.

He was big, well over six feet tall, and his shoulders were broad. Clad only in black shorts, his muscular chest was bare to her avid gaze. She'd seen Shani without his shirt once, but her eunuch guard looked nothing like Hawk.

He dribbled oil over her shoulders and she flinched at the intrusion upon her intimate thoughts. Then his big, warm hands came down and he began massaging the oil into her skin.

She wanted to groan at the warm sensuality of the act. For a woman who'd hardly been touched in her life, she reveled in the unfamiliar feel of male skin against hers. Her eyes narrowed to slits as he continued the sensual massage down her right arm. His strong fingers kneaded the muscles in her biceps before working his way to her hand until her arm was completely limp.

"Tell me, Esme, what of passion?"

His gaze was fixed upon her hand and his expression was curiously intent as if he were truly interested in the answer to his question.

"What do you mean?"

"Have you ever had passion in your life?" He switched to her other arm. "Have you taken a lover before now?"

She curled her toes. She didn't want to admit she was still a virgin because it would tell him how empty her life had truly been. Surely, in the outside world, a woman wasn't still a virgin at the advanced age of twenty-five. Since she'd conjured him, who said she had to answer his questions anyway?

"That's a rather intimate question." Her tone was stiff.

His gaze met hers, then he shot a pointed glance at her exposed breasts. "And this isn't?"

She fought the urge to cover herself. "Physical intimacy is one thing. Prying into my brain and private life is completely different."

"Ah, I see." His suddenly cool tone told her he didn't see her point of view at all. "So I can fuck you, but not talk to you? Is that what you're saying?"

She flinched at his use of the crude word. "I—"

"So I can do this…" He rose and yanked the covers off the bed. Before she could draw a breath, he grabbed the neckline of her gown and tore it from her body, leaving her completely exposed.

Stunned, Esme sat up and scrambled for something to cover her nudity when he caught her arms. She made a sound of protest when Hawk lowered his big body over hers, preventing her from covering herself. He forced her thighs apart and insinuated his hips between them, pressing his cock against the apex of her thighs.

His impressive cloth-covered erection ground into her exposed mound, setting off warning bells along with a slithering feeling of something pleasurable that shocked her to her core.

"Hawk…" Her words died when his big hand landed on her breast and began to manipulate it. Shock and arousal sang through her system as he expertly teased her nipple into full awareness.

Her gaze flew to his face and his expression had gone hard, angry. Where had her tender lover gone?

"Hawk, please," she whispered. "Not like this." Her hand covered his upon her breast and she shook her head. "Never like this."

He stopped his erratic movements and braced his upper body on his elbows, then allowed his head to drop forward. His big body trembled and his breath raged in his lungs.

"I don't know what came over me." He spoke without looking at her. "I'll leave…" He started to move away and she grabbed his shoulders and held him in place.

"Please, I don't want you to leave," she said.

Still he didn't look at her. "I…"

She caught his chin and turned his face toward her. Confusion and remorse warred with desire in the depths of his eyes. She ran her fingers along the strong line of his jaw and the prickle of his beard teased her fingers. She decided she quite enjoyed the sensation.

"Please," she whispered. "Don't walk away now."

His gaze dropped to her mouth and he raised his right hand to brush stray curls away from her face. She sensed the leashed tension that lurked in his dark eyes and hovered beneath his skin. He could be gentle, he'd proven that, and judging from the look in his eye coupled with his erection, he was also very aroused. He was just the man to take her virginity and teach her the art of sex.

Hawk ran his agile fingertips over the contours of her face and she held her breath. He followed the line of each brow, the curve of her cheek, lower lip then the tip of her nose. Everywhere he touched, her body sang with joy and her nerves came alive for the first time.

His head dipped and just before their lips met, he hesitated. Anxious to kiss him, she grabbed the back of his head and pulled him the rest of the way.

Their lips met and this time, without his urging, she opened beneath him. His breath was hot and when his tongue touched hers she moaned and her grip tightened. Their tongues caressed and she took the sweetness he offered and lost herself in his effortless sensuality.

Hawk cupped her breast and she moaned when his thumb stroked the hardened tip and the kiss grew darker, more heated. Reality faded and her fingers tangled in his hair. He gentled, then slowed the torrid kiss, and her ears were buzzing by the time he raised his head.

"You have perfect breasts," he said. His palm plumped the sensitive underside and her breath caught in her throat when he teased her nipple with his thumb and forefinger. "They're made for my hands."

He gently squeezed her breast and a raw moan escaped her. She'd never dreamed such feelings had even existed. Even when she lay in her bed alone, touching herself under the cover of darkness, nothing had aroused such feelings of heat and excitement as did a few moments with Hawk in her bed.

"For my tongue."

He took her nipple into the heated warmth of his mouth. Esme's stomach flopped at the sight of his dark head lowered to her breast. His tongue seduced her, lapping at her hardened nipple before taking it deep for a long, leisurely suck.

Her grip tightened on the back of his head as he worked his magic on her body. The sensations were heady and rich as he moved from one breast to the other, subjecting each to the same tender torment.

He released her nipple and without missing a beat began working his way down her stomach, lavishing her flesh with wet, open-mouthed kisses that made her go weak. The flesh between her thighs went warm and liquid.

She knew what he was about to do, she'd managed to order a few explicit romance novels on tape before her father had caught on, but still she hesitated when he moved to open her thighs.

"Esme?"

Hawk sat back on his heels with his big hand covering her knees. He gave her a reassuring smile and her stomach fluttered then flipped over. His smile was devastating. It should come with its own warning label.

"Trust me," he said. "Let me pleasure you."

* * * * *

Hawk released a breath when Esme relaxed her knees. He ran his hand over her smooth skin, the gentle curve of her knee and up the inside of her thigh. At the apex was a neat thatch of soft dark curls. He covered her with his hand and she jumped and tried to draw her knees together, but he prevented her movement by leaning forward and blocking her with his body until he was sitting on his heels between her spread thighs.

"Let your mind go." He drew his hand up her thigh to her knee and then down again. Judging by the dilation of her pupils, his touch was arousing to her. "Just let yourself feel what I'm doing to you."

He continued stroking her thigh, massaging each tender inch of her skin, until she relaxed and her leg fell limp to the bed. Then he switched his attention to her other leg lavishing the same attention upon it until she was trembling and completely open and vulnerable before him.

Hawk cupped her, sliding one finger into the prize that awaited him. With a light touch he caressed her clit and was rewarded with a strangled cry. He wanted to see her, all of her, now. He wanted her completely bare beneath him as she came.

His erection lunged against the thin material of his shorts and he wondered for a second if the garment could contain him for much longer. Wincing, he shifted and tried to find a more comfortable position but quickly learned there wasn't one, short of burying himself inside her.

His breath huffed out. The only other way to relieve the discomfort was to strip off his shorts, and if he did that he would take her here and now and nothing could stop him. But this time wasn't about him, it was about her and her alone.

Pushing his discomfort aside he caressed the silken curls that covered her pussy. Her hips shifted forward as he slipped his finger into the well of slick heat awaiting him. A cry from Esme was hastily muffled as he cautiously inserted one thick finger into her vagina. A groan escaped him as her muscles clasped around him, welcoming him and urging him onward. She was so tight he knew that when he did bury himself in her he'd be lucky to last more than a few strokes. He rose over her with his finger still buried in her.

"What do you desire, Esme?" he whispered. His voice sounded oddly strained and unlike himself.

Her aroused gaze met his. "You."

"You're mine, Esmerelda." He shifted into position so that her spread thighs were draped over his parted knees, leaving her completely open to his gaze and his touch. "Mine and only mine." Pressing his finger deeper within her, he stroked her damp flesh with long even strokes as she writhed on the bed.

Within seconds she peaked and her cries surrounded him as her nails clawed at the mattress when she convulsed around him.

No matter what happened, Hawk knew in that moment no man would ever have her, not like this. She was his and it was important to him that she admit his possession of her, body and soul.

Stretching from his cramped position, he settled himself between her thighs, bringing his face level with hers. Lightly he traced her lips with his damp fingers, parting them with her essence as he memorized their shape, their fullness.

"Say it," he whispered, gently nudging her lips, forcing her to taste her own arousal. He groaned as her soft, warm tongue touched his fingertip. "Say you're mine."

She reached for his hand and pulled it away from her lips. "I'm yours, Hawk."

He swallowed a shout of triumph. Their lives were hopelessly tangled now, even more so than before. Silently, he dipped his head to kiss the woman beneath him, putting into his kiss what he couldn't begin to express just yet.

Chapter Four

"Miss!"

Esme's teaspoon struck the bone-china teacup when Shani's strident voice broke into her daydreams. She winced at the resulting clang. All she needed was a lecture on the proper care and use of delicate china.

"Yes, Shani. Did you need me?" She laid her spoon down.

"I've been calling your name for the past few minutes, Miss Esmerelda." Her guard stepped in front of her, then leaned down to peer into her face. "Are you feeling well?"

Esme fixed a placid smile on her face and gave Shani a languid wave. "Of course. I was mentally running through a list of things I need to accomplish in the next few days. I'm getting married, you know."

"Yes, Miss." He didn't look convinced and his broad, olive-skinned face reflected his doubt. "Ivy would like to know if the Dijon Salmon will be an acceptable substitute for dinner this evening. She'd planned on your requested steak salad and it appears the grocer neglected to include the steak in the delivery."

Esme nodded. "Sounds lovely, thank you for asking."

Shani started for the door then stopped to hover by her side. His thick, pudgy fingers knotted against his round belly. "Miss, is there anything you'd like to talk about?"

She was startled by his unexpected question. Never had Shani extended any friendly overtures. Their relationship was cordial, almost painfully so. She was aware anything they'd discussed would be reported to her father. She'd learned the hard way many years ago and consequently she was very careful to keep him at arm's length for her own sake.

"Of course not. It is a beautiful day and I'm soon to be a bride." She pasted on a guileless smile and gave him a wink. "What more could a woman want?"

A remote expression dropped over his homely features and he gave her an abbreviated bow. "As you wish, Miss."

She listened for the sound of his footsteps and the soft snick of the door closing. He was gone. She exhaled noisily and sank in her chair, thankful the prying eyes of her guard were finally gone. It wouldn't do for her father to receive word that she'd been acting strangely. She wouldn't put it past Edmund to send a contingent of guards to keep an eye on his wayward daughter. She had two days until the wedding and her father must never know something was afoot.

And something was definitely afoot.

Esme stretched out her legs and laced her fingers across her stomach before she allowed her eyes to slide half-closed. She was tired but completely relaxed from the top of her head to her polished toenails. Hawk had shown her physical delights she'd only heard about on her audio books and the writers hadn't done them justice.

A soft smile played about her lips. Hawk knew how to touch a woman and make her melt into a boneless puddle. Did all men know how to do that? A shiver of excitement ran under her skin and her nipples began to ache. Who knew when she'd conjured a lover that she'd end up with Hawk, a man handsome enough for every woman's dreams?

She rubbed her stomach. But he'd failed to take her virginity last night and that was her top priority. After he'd shown her the sensations her body was capable of, she'd thought for sure he'd take her, but he hadn't. Instead he'd forced a declaration from her that, in retrospect, hadn't been smart to make. She wasn't his and she never could be. This entire exercise was designed to gain her freedom and she didn't want to belong to anyone but herself.

She couldn't deny the odd sense of familiarity she'd felt with him, but it didn't change the fact that she was looking for her freedom, not a relationship with a man she'd conjured out of thin air. He might be a flesh and blood man, but he wasn't for her no matter how handsome he was.

She stirred in her chair.

No matter how well he kissed.

She sighed. As if she'd had anyone to compare him to since she'd never been kissed before Hawk. But she couldn't get his taste out of her mind — dark and sensual, heated and male. She shivered in the full afternoon sun.

He was due to return a few hours after sundown. He'd left her a short note on her pillow and, while she couldn't read all of it, she'd understood the gist of his imminent return.

A yawn came out of nowhere and threatened to split her jaw. She had just enough time to grab a nap and take a long luxurious bath before Hawk would return, and this time, she was determined he'd make love to her.

* * * * *

The moon had risen by the time Hawk climbed the steps to the terrace outside of Esme's room. Now that he was an older and more experienced witch, the confinement spell had been ridiculously easy to outmaneuver. It was designed to keep humans away, but it had lacked any such restrictions upon animals. All it had taken was a simple transformation into animal form, a spell his father had taught all his children, and he was free to cross the magical line of Esme's sanctuary.

The French doors were open and the scent of vanilla greeted him when he stepped inside. He took a deep, appreciative breath. Several dozen candles were lit around the room and the resulting glow was warm and inviting.

He removed his backpack and dropped it into a chair near the door. On the table next to it was a small pile of crumpled scraps of paper covered with some sort of shorthand known only to her. She'd written ROSE in large, block letters but the E was backward. There were several other notations but most had been crossed out with a heavy hand as if she'd started to write something then changed her mind.

He frowned and picked up a paper and stared hard at it. If he didn't know better he'd almost think Esme was illiterate.

He turned when he heard a soft clatter. Artificial light spilled from a doorway to the right and he heard Esme swear under her breath.

He moved toward the door, anticipation heavy in his gut. He'd done nothing but think of her during the hours they'd been separated. At this point, he knew no more about her reasons for conjuring a man than he did the moment she'd cast the spell. The only thing he did understand was that he was completely, totally and utterly obsessed with her and the past twenty-four hours had only cemented his fascination. Tonight he would claim her as his woman, thus ensuring his total and unarguable claim of her as his bride.

Esme stood near the sink of her spacious bathroom clad in a frothy ivory dress that outlined her full breasts and generous curves. She was arranging her hair in a complicated arrangement of fat, tumbled curls.

Desire unfurled in his gut.

Soon, soon…

He crossed his arms over his chest and leaned against the doorjamb, waiting for her to notice him, and it didn't take long.

She was humming under her breath when she caught sight of him in the mirror. Her eyes widened and she made a startled noise. A soft flush stole over her cheeks and her hands fluttered about until they came to rest at the base of her throat.

"You startled me," she said.

He smiled and shoved off the doorjamb. "I could tell." His hands came down on her shoulders and he pulled her toward him. "Do you have a proper hello for me, Esme?"

Her dark brow arched and her gaze dropped to his mouth. "You've invaded my sanctuary here, Mister. Seems to me you owe me the proper hello." She tilted her head back and gave him a wicked smile that caused his cock to harden. "Or shall I call Shani to come to my rescue?" she teased.

He ran his hands down her arms then back up before his head dipped toward hers. "Ah, but if you did then your spell would become superfluous, wouldn't it? You wouldn't have brought me all this way only to send me off now."

She smiled just seconds before his lips touched hers. This time she opened for him and he groaned with the erotic sensation of sinking into her damp heat. She sighed and he could have sworn he felt the ground shake beneath his feet when she leaned into him.

Desperate for more but knowing he didn't dare indulge himself quite yet, Hawk settled for nipping her lower lip as he slowed and gentled the kiss, amazed at how quickly it went from teasing to scorching hot.

Esme's eyes were dazed and soft, and her smile was slightly lopsided. "Hi yourself."

Staring into the near perfection of her face, his chest felt tight and his breathing was labored. She'd been promised to him as a mere child and now, with the grown woman in his arms, he was about to make his lifelong dream come true. Shaken by the unexpected depths of his feelings, he gave her a quick hug then set her away.

"Are you ready?" he asked.

She leaned against the vanity, a vision in cool ivory. "I am, but what am I getting ready for? I thought we'd just…" She gestured toward the bedroom as a rush of color moved into her cheeks.

"You didn't read my note?"

A look of dismay washed across her face only to be replaced with a forced playfulness that set his senses on alert. What was she hiding from him?

"Well, I am impatient to further the lessons we began last evening." Her voice dropped to a throaty murmur.

He was both pleased and gratified by her eagerness but he wasn't about to rush through anything. "Not so fast, Enchantress. Tonight is a full moon and we're going outside for fresh air and to enjoy the spectacle the Goddess has in store for us."

Her eyes brightened and she gave a delighted clap. "I'd love to go for a walk in the moonlight." She spun around and fluffed her hair in the mirror before rushing past him in a flurry of vanilla-scented air. "I just need to grab a jacket and find some comfy shoes."

"We're in no hurry." He glanced at his watch. They had several hours to complete their joining before the moon would begin to descend. As long as the moon was on the ascent they would be well within the confines of the ritual requirements. "We have time, the moon isn't going anywhere."

Esme chuckled and pulled on a deep red sweater. "We need to hurry as we don't want to waste it." She scurried into the walk-in closet and her voice was muffled. "I know the perfect place we can sit and watch the moonrise. About a half mile from the house, there's a clearing on the side of a hill that overlooks the forest."

He knew the spot of which she spoke. In his animal form, he'd scouted the property before heading for home and he was familiar with every square inch. In his pack he'd stowed a blanket, snacks and a flask of wine. He was looking forward to wooing Esme and finding out more about her...after the deal was sealed, that is.

"Sounds perfect." He moved slowly around the room, his avid gaze devouring her private space. Her altar was immaculate and a wreath of fresh autumn flowers was arranged around a fat white candle in the center.

"It is. We'll have a good view from up there."

"Fine."

The Proctor Book of Shadows sat on a shelf over the altar and Hawk knew better than to touch it. The legendary power contained in the tome dictated that only a Proctor woman could open the book. Still, his fingers itched to see if the stories were true. He longed to examine the contents of the book. He'd only seen Esme perform the simplest of spells from the tome and he wanted to delve into the more complicated spells that were rumored to be kept in there.

Out of the corner of his eye he saw a movement near the terrace. A soft breeze crept in through the door and sent the white object fluttering.

It was Esme's wedding gown.

Without realizing it, Hawk walked toward the display. The garment was fitted on a dressmaker's dummy and tucked into the corner near the door. The icy white material glowed with an almost unearthly light as if it were lit from within. Crystals gleamed on the bodice and sleeves and the voluminous skirt fluttered as if it were a living, breathing creature. On a small table near the dummy were arranged dainty white shoes, sheer stockings and a delicate diamond tiara fit for a princess.

Esme would be breathtaking in the gown. His finger brushed the sleeve, and almost immediately images of the Proctor women who'd worn this gown on their wedding day crowded his mind. Repulsed, he dropped his hand. None of their marriages had ended as they'd envisioned upon the day they donned this dress. Some had lived well enough, though the sense of loneliness was hard to deny. They'd married and had children, but one had left her husband and Esmerelda's mother had died far too young. The material had been imbued with love and joy as well as unhappiness and deceit.

He turned at the same time Esme exited the closet. Deceit appeared to run in their family as the woman he was about to bed had conspired to take another man only two days before their wedding. But who was deceiving whom this time?

"I'm ready!" Esme said. "I found some white tennis shoes at least."

He looked down at her feet shod in sturdy white tennis shoes that were at complete odds with her floating dress and bright red sweater.

"So you have." He held out his hand. "Let's go."

With her soft palm in one hand and his pack in the other, he led her from the room and onto the terrace. They walked down the steps and when they reached the yard he realized he'd have to play dumb.

"What way is it?" he asked, though he knew perfectly well where it was.

"Over this way." She led him toward the north.

The air was redolent with night sounds and the scents of coming autumn. The wonderful loamy aroma of decaying vegetation and the coming evening dew was music to his senses.

"What about your keeper? Doesn't he worry about you wandering alone at night?" He glanced back at the house and all the windows on the north side were dark.

"Not really. He knows I can't get into much trouble here." She shrugged and led him deeper into the forest.

Hawk didn't know about that. The confinement spell would keep humans out, but it did nothing to deter the dangerous animals that were plentiful in this area. It was a miracle that nothing serious had happened to her yet.

Despite the moonlight, he could barely see once they entered the woods, but Esme seemed to know exactly where she was headed. They walked down a narrow path, and with his gaze fixed on her pale clothing he could do little more than follow the soft sway of her hips.

After a short distance the trees thinned and they emerged into a small clearing on the side of a gentle slope. Under the brilliant moonlight the clearing had taken on the look of an enchanted glen. The grass was plush and welcoming and trees hovered along the edges as if eager to create a safe haven for them.

Esme released his hand and took a few running, dancing steps, spinning around and flinging her arms outward. "Isn't it heaven?"

Hawk's throat went dry and he couldn't utter a word. She resembled a faery creature dancing in the moonlight. The ivory dress clung to her lush curves and her wide smile ignited a sense of joy in his blood. He forced himself to nod. "Just beautiful," he murmured.

She headed toward the center of the clearing. "The view is spectacular from here."

He followed and had to concur with her assessment. It was a magnificent view. The hillside sloped down into acres and acres of thick forest and it looked to be completely untouched by man. Nowhere within sight could he detect anything manmade, even the light pollution was nonexistent.

"Great, isn't it? I come up here a lot."

"I can see why." He dropped his pack on the ground then crouched to unload its contents.

"What did you bring?" Esme dropped beside him and pressed close, her perfume and the primal scent of her invading his senses.

"I figured we'd need a blanket." He pulled the item from the bag and handed it to her. "Why don't you spread this out?"

"Sure." She took the blanket.

He removed the flask of wine and two plastic cups, which he set on the blanket along with several compact containers of food and some napkins.

"You're certainly prepared." Esme seized a container and opened it. "Mmm, my favorite cheese." She popped a small chunk of cheddar into her mouth.

He dropped the bag and moved onto the blanket beside her, snagging a piece of cheese as he went. "Quiz time. What else do you love?"

"The color red," she spoke without hesitation. "I always feel good when I wear red, like I'm more confident or something."

"You need confidence?"

She shrugged and offered him another piece of cheese. "Doesn't everyone at some point?"

"Sure." He took another cube. "I'd think with your looks that most men would line up to lay at your feet."

She snorted with laughter. "Hardly. In my family women are secondary citizens."

"Is that so?" That was an interesting position for Edmund to take considering he'd married into the Proctor family. The lineage of the women was long and exalted in the world of the Craft and they were anything but secondary.

"Can I ask you a question?" She put the cheese down and reached for another container.

"Sure." He picked up the flask of wine.

Esme tilted her head. "Do you have a life? I mean, before I called you to my side?"

Tricky question.

"You could say that." He poured some wine into a cup and offered it to her. "I didn't exist in a vacuum before I met you, if that's what you mean."

She frowned. "How could that be? I mean, spells should never be used to alter anyone's life, yet this spell has altered yours."

In more ways than one...

"I don't think of your spell as having 'altered' my life, I think of it as enhancing it." He filled his glass. "You can consider me a rental I guess."

Esme laughed. "You mean Rent-a-Stud?"

Hawk forced a smile though it didn't please him to be reminded that he was the one she'd intended to cuckold with another man. "You could say that." He capped the flask and set it in a safe spot before stretching out beside her.

"What audio books do you like to listen to?" he asked.

"Romances, mostly. I also enjoy fairy tales." She dipped a fat strawberry into her wine. "I love Sleeping Beauty."

His brow arched. "You mean the children's book?"

"Yup." She sucked on the wine-coated tip of the berry and his groin tightened at the unconscious sensuality of her movement. "What woman wouldn't want to be awakened by true love's first kiss?"

It was on the tip of his tongue to ask if that was her fantasy, but he stopped himself. It was obvious that wasn't what she was looking for or she'd have saved herself for her wedding day. Irritation streaked through him again and he grabbed her hand and yanked it toward him to take a bite of her berry.

"Hey, I have more," she laughed when he released her.

He swallowed the tart fruit. "It's sweeter when your mouth has touched it first."

Her dark eyes gleamed with a mixture of arousal and amusement and she reached for another berry. "You do say the sweetest things."

"I aim to please."

"Do you have a family?" She bit the berry in half and offered him the rest.

His lips touched her fingers and he nodded as he chewed. They were definitely moving into dangerous territory. He didn't want to tell her much about his background, as it would be too easy for her to put two and two together.

"Do you have siblings?" He caught the wistful tone in her voice.

"No, I'm an only child." Which was a lie. He had three sisters and three brothers. He was the first of seven.

"I always wanted to have a ton of brothers and sisters. I want to know what it was like growing up in a house with other children. Sharing secrets under the covers at night and always having someone to play with." Her gaze was faraway, dreamy.

Now he was confused. Esme had six sisters and had lived with them until she was moved to Hill House. What had happened to separate her from her sisters? When he'd returned home this morning he'd asked his brother Stuart to look into the whereabouts of the other six Proctor daughters.

"So you were an only child as well?" he asked.

"No, I have sisters…" Her voice trailed off and he couldn't help but notice her sad expression.

"Where are they now?"

She shook herself and forced a smile. "I really don't want to talk about them right now. I have a handsome man at my mercy in the moonlight and I'd be a fool to sit around and talk about my family."

He let the matter slide, for now at least. "Do you think I'm at your mercy? I think you forget our arrangement."

She wrinkled her nose. "Well, a girl can always hope."

He plucked a berry from the dish and held it out to her. "Here we are in the moonlight, alone. We have food, wine and each other. What do you suggest we do now, Enchantress?"

She took the berry from his hand with her mouth and her eyes gleamed with sensual amusement. She chewed and swallowed. "Make love with me, Hawk," she whispered.

He glanced at the moon. It wasn't in quite the right position but that didn't mean he couldn't pleasure her first.

"I do like the way you think," he said.

Chapter Five

One minute she was sitting on the blanket munching berries, and the next she was in his arms. His sudden move managed to knock the wine from her hand, but before she could form a protest his mouth was on hers.

She opened for him and he swept her into a maelstrom of heat and need. He covered her with his big body and their tongues tangled in a carnal kiss of need and promise. Before she realized it, he'd caught her wrists and hauled them over her head.

"My," she whispered against his mouth. She was amazed at his strength as he held her captive with one hand.

"Mmm." He brushed his lips over hers, allowing her no more than the slightest measure of relief. "You taste good."

She smiled. "It's the wine and berries you taste, not me."

"Trust me." He nipped her throat. "I can taste Esme as well. The wine and berries are like icing on the cake, an added bonus but not completely necessary for my enjoyment."

His attention strayed to the buttons on her dress. As he released each one he paused to lavish attention upon the newly exposed skin. His touch was so confident, so sure, that Esme relished the consummation of their mutual desire. Silently she thanked the Goddess that such a wonderful man had been sent to her.

But I can't keep him…

The intrusive thought flew from her mind when he parted her front-clasp bra and her breasts spilled forth. The soft evening air caressed her flesh and he released her hands to nuzzle the plump curve of her breasts. She tangled her fingers in his dark hair as he teased her nipple with his tongue. She groaned and a rush of wicked desire streaked through her body to pool at the apex of her thighs.

His warm tongue licked one nipple then the other. The motion sent spirals of heat through her body despite the night air. The damp friction of his tongue created chills that raced along her nerves. He gave her hardened nub a strong suckle and she pressed her thighs together in an attempt to relieve the growing ache.

His hands seemed to be everywhere at once, stroking and petting her flesh until her dress was opened from neck to hem, leaving her exposed to her lover and the caress of the moonlight.

Her breathing was ragged and she couldn't seem to control the whimpers and sighs that came from her throat as he teased her body into awareness. She clutched at his broad shoulders and knew he was wearing too many clothes for her liking, but she just couldn't bring herself to make him stop long enough to remove them.

He kissed and teased a heated path down her stomach to the waistband of her panties. With her help, he removed them before kissing a trail to the thatch of hair at the apex of her thighs. He urged her to spread her legs, then with his fingers he parted her damp flesh. Her head came up when he touched her clitoris. Hawk was crouched between her spread thighs and his heated gaze was fixed on her face.

"I have to taste you, Esme." His voice was low, dark, and just the sound of it increased her arousal. "I need to feel you come against my mouth."

She shuddered at the powerful image his words evoked and she allowed her head to fall back onto the blanket. She spread her arms and offered herself to him.

"Please, Hawk, put your mouth on me."

Her eyes slid closed when he lowered his head and swirled his tongue over her. She bit her lip to stifle the scream that blossomed in her chest. His big hands held her thighs wide, giving him full access to her body as he teased and seduced her.

His experienced touch brought her closer and closer to the edge, taunting her with release yet not quite allowing her to achieve it. He seemed to sense when she was about to come and he'd back off and shift his attention elsewhere, allowing her time to cool down before moving back to her clit and starting the torment all over again.

Both frustrated and wildly aroused at the same time, her nails dug into his flesh as he forced her to scale the peak again. She tried to concentrate on the pressure of his tongue and the magic touch of his fingers as he stroked her wet flesh. She couldn't take it anymore. If he didn't let her come this time—

"Please, Hawk, please. I can't take anymore."

"I love to hear you beg," he spoke against her flesh. "Say it again, Esme."

"Please…"

He closed his mouth over her tiny bud and sucked hard. Her back arched and she convulsed against his mouth as pleasure rolled through her body in a thick, hot wave. He continued his ruthless assault until she screamed her pleasure out for a second time, this one leaving her limp and breathless when he released her.

Struggling to catch her breath, she blinked as he rose to his feet. Standing over her, he was a vision of masculinity dressed in black from head to toe. He pulled his sweater over his head and dropped it carelessly on the grass. Moonlight cast a silvery sheen over taut muscles and a rippled belly. With his shaggy hair and eyes the color of a coming storm, he resembled a warrior god of old. His hand went to his belt and she struggled to her knees.

"Let me." She reached for him, pleased when his hands dropped to his sides. She opened the button on his jeans then reached for the zipper.

"Careful," he said. "I'm hard for you and it could be tricky."

Esme rubbed her hand over his jeans-covered bulge. "You're really big," she blurted and he laughed.

She gently worked the zipper open to reveal his black silk boxers and the impressive bulge behind them. "Mmm, nice." She slid his jeans down to his ankles and he stepped out of them.

She ran her hands over his silk-covered, hardened mound and felt him leap beneath her touch. Fascinated by this unknown entity, she stroked and caressed his flesh while watching his handsome face for signs of what pleasured him most. Judging from the strained look on his face and the noises he made in the back of his throat, she was doing a good job of arousing him. She ran her fingertips around his wide head, causing his hips to jerk toward her.

"You'll have to stop, Enchantress, or we'll be done before we get started."

"What do you—" She stopped and a wave of heat washed over her cheeks. "You were enjoying that too much."

"Definitely." He removed his boxers then dropped to his knees and removed her sweater and dress before easing her back onto the blanket. "I have too many things I want to do to you before I take my pleasure."

Completely bare and amazingly at ease for a woman who hadn't been seen fully naked since she was a toddler, Esme stretched across the blanket and reached for him, her gaze locked on his impressive erection. "Like what?"

"Like this." He leaned over to kiss her between her eyebrows then sat back and reached for his backpack to retrieve a small jar.

Esme propped herself on her elbows and watched as he opened the jar. "What's that?"

He offered her a roguish grin. "Something with which to worship my Enchantress better. Now lay back and let the worshipping begin."

She grinned and laid back. "I thought you'd already 'worshipped' me."

He settled beside her and dipped his forefinger into the pot. "In some respects I suppose I have, but there's much more to come."

She let her eyes slide shut but she couldn't wipe the smile off her face. Who knew sex could be so much fun?

Hawk rubbed a tiny amount of the salve into the sensitive area between her brows. She sniffed and detected the mingled scents of cinnamon, pine and orange oils.

He moved to her nipples and gently rubbed the unguent into each of them until she was aroused and squirming beneath his hands. Her breathing grew shallow as he painted three lines on her lower abdomen just above her woman's mound. It seemed to her that her skin where Hawk had placed the salve was growing warmer as time passed.

"Now it's your turn."

Her eyes flew open and Hawk held the container out to her. He wasn't going to…no, it didn't look like he was.

Esme scrambled to her knees and with him sitting back on his heels, she dipped her finger into the salve.

"You only need a little bit," he said when she touched the area of his third eye on his forehead.

"Okay."

The salve was heating her skin and her fingertips as she worked her way down his body. His flat male nipples tightened under her touch before she moved to his lower abdomen to draw the three lines as he had on her lower stomach. Her hand brushed his jutting erection and she heard his sharply indrawn breath. When she was done with the three lines, she sat back on her heels.

"Now what?"

"Now we anoint each other." He dipped his fingers into the pot and brought them out well coated with the salve. "Now you." She did the same then he took the pot and set it aside. "Now sit on your backside and part your thighs like this."

He positioned her so that she sat on the blanket facing him, her legs parted and on top of his splayed thighs. The position left her open and vulnerable.

"Now touch me." His voice was low, guttural.

Her hand encircled his hard, steely length with a tentative touch. She'd never touched a naked cock before and she found the sensation quite exhilarating. She ran her salve-covered hand up and down his silk-over-steel length then across his broad head until he was coated as well. While she stroked the sensitive shaft of his cock, a drop of pearly liquid appeared at the narrow slit at the tip. Perspiration broke out on his skin and his breathing grew harsh.

His hand covered hers.

"That's enough," he gasped.

Esme released her newfound toy reluctantly. She'd wanted to—

Her thoughts scattered when his hand covered her mound and parted her nether lips to dip inside. She stretched out on the blanket, allowing him better access, and his fingers zeroed in on her clit to cover her nub with the warm salve before he worked his way across her labia. He slipped his fingers into her vagina and drew out moisture to rub it into her flesh until she was warm, slick and squirming and near to going out of her mind with wanting him.

Desire hummed in her bloodstream and the call to mate was hard and heavy in her abdomen when he finally removed his hand, leaving her empty and swollen with need.

Her lover looked up at the moon then down at her and a strange glint flashed in his eyes.

"It's time, Enchantress."

She could barely breathe by the time he lowered himself between her thighs. The smooth head of his cock probed her virginal opening, and for a split second she felt a rush of unease that was quickly replaced with an answering wave of heat as the unguent worked its magic. His big hand slid between her thighs to stroke her clit before he entered her with his fingers to ignite a bolt of pure pleasure up her spine.

Esme moaned and knew it wasn't nearly enough. She wiggled against his hand, unable to vocalize her suddenly insatiable need. He removed his hand and replaced it with the broad head of his cock. He pushed forward and slid into her slowly, inch by inch, until her maidenhead was breached with barely a whisper of pain.

Overhead, lightning flashed across the heavens and thunder rolled across the sky.

* * * * *

She surrounded him like a damp glove, so tight and hot he almost came with his first thrust. Her hands clutched his hips and her beautiful face was awash in sensual delight. Her eyes had closed to mere slits and her plush pink mouth was parted ever so slightly.

She arched her back as she urged his slow thrusts to increase. Her breasts jiggled with their movements and her rosy nipples begged for his mouth, his tongue. He lowered his head and took one into his mouth, stealing a scream from her when he gave it a sharp tug before settling into a slow, deep suck.

Beneath them he felt the power swell in the earth, a mixture of moon magic and their personal magic. While he wanted to make the most of their first time together, he knew he couldn't last long—not this time.

Allowing the power to fill him, he gave his body to the demands of the universe. His pace increased and he thrust into her as hard as he could, forcing her to accept his dominance, his mastery over her.

Esme moaned and her head thrashed against the blanket. Her eyes were closed and her breathing was harsh, ragged. Their fingers tangled and he clung to her and she to him as his hips thundered into her, his cock disappearing into her luscious cunt as their mutual pleasure mounted.

Their bodies strained in the moonlight. He'd never felt so totally possessed. Never had a woman wrapped herself around him, body and soul. The sweet clasp of her cunt was slowly killing him and he changed his angle to one he was sure would hit her clit dead on.

Her legs wrapped around his hips and with a low, sobbing moan she came apart beneath him. Harsh, powerful spasms gripped her pussy as he rocked in and out in time to his heartbeat. Helpless to stop, to do anything other than follow the lust that held him in a vise, Hawk relished her juicy cunt as it gripped him in its rippling hold.

He groaned and his orgasm exploded with an intensity that drove the breath from his lungs. He roared out his satisfaction, tilting his head back and directing his cries toward the moon.

* * * * *

A few hours later Esme ran her inquisitive fingers over his cock, stroking him until he stood partially erect. She lowered her head and gave the tip a lick and Hawk's head popped up.

His gaze was sexy, sleepy and he looked a little confused. His eyes widened when he saw her crouched between his thighs.

She slid her fingers around the thick base, luxuriating in the silk-over-steel feel of him. His breath hissed through his gritted teeth and his hips jerked as she ran her thumb along the base of his shaft.

"Rise and shine, sleeping beauty," she teased.

He gave a raspy chuckle then cleared his throat. "You've got that right. Sorry I fell asleep."

Her smile was wide, saucy. "I'll do the work this time and you can save your energy for later."

She ran her thumb over the broad tip, experimenting with her touch by taking cues from his changing expressions. With their gazes locked, she lowered her head and took him into her mouth.

He tasted of the sea and warm, potent male and she dragged her tongue over the tip, relishing his unique flavor. His hips involuntarily twitched when she rubbed her thumb along the sensitive underside of his shaft.

His voice was strained. "You have no idea what the sight of you between my knees with my cock buried in your mouth does to me."

Oh, but she did.

A rush of feminine power surged through her body. She wrapped her hand around his thick length and began moving up and down in long, somewhat clumsy strokes as she worked his hardened flesh with her mouth. He caught her head with his hands and showed her how to move, and with each movement, his hips thrust harder and his breathing grew more strained.

"Esme, you're killing me," he gasped.

His fingers tangled in her hair, loosening the soft twist at the back of her head and she closed her eyes, concentrating her entire being on taking more of him into her mouth. He tried to control her movements, but she resisted, wanting to keep him at her mercy.

She swirled her tongue around his sensitive head, tasting the salty-sweetness of him. She increased her movements, her hand stroked his thick root when she took him deep into her throat.

"You have to stop. I'm going to…"

She resisted his attempt to warn her and continued her sensual assault. Within moments, his body tensed and his hips jerked as he climaxed into her mouth with an anguished groan.

Esme continued stroking him for a few moments, feeling him relax before she released him. She let his cock slip from her lips and she rested her cheek against his thigh, her gaze glued on his handsome face. His eyes were closed and his breathing was rough as if he'd just run a marathon. For someone who liked to be in control, he'd certainly lost it willingly enough.

Chapter Six

Their return to the house was leisurely and they held hands as they walked through the woods. Neither spoke, content with their private thoughts and each other's company.

Hawk entered her room first and he dropped his bag on the floor. With their fingers still entwined he pulled her toward the bathroom. She flicked on the light and they both were forced to shield their eyes against the intrusive brilliance. After a few moments, his eyes adjusted and he wasn't forced to squint.

His lover had the look of a woman thoroughly pleasured by her man. Her dress was rumpled and buttoned wrong and her hair was tumbled by his fingers and their unrestrained romp on the blankets. Her lips were crimson and swollen from his kisses and her eyes held the soft afterglow of satisfaction. Just seeing her like that, disheveled and well used, caused his blood to heat.

He released her hands and turned the knobs on the tub, careful to check the temperature of the water, as they needed to chase the chill away from their romp outside. Flicking the lever, the shower came on.

Esme stood against the vanity, peering into the mirror as she pulled out what few hairpins remained. Hawk stepped behind her and placed his hands on her shoulders. Their gazes met in the mirror and she flushed.

"I'm a mess." She looked away and pulled the last pin out.

"You're beautiful." He slid his finger along the neck of her sweater to touch the tender skin underneath. "Let's take a shower."

Her gaze flew up and her mouth rounded. "Together?"

He smiled and turned her toward him. "We've already been naked together." He brushed his mouth over hers. "I've seen every delectable inch of your body." His hands landed on her hips and he pulled her against him until her soft belly cushioned his burgeoning erection. "And soon I'll be seeing it again."

Her hands landed on his chest. "Well, when you put it that way."

He nipped at her lower lip then pulled back to lead her toward the shower. There was a small stereo on a shelf near the vanity and she flicked it on as they passed. The soothing sound of Celtic flutes floated from the speakers.

Esme kicked off her shoes and Hawk eased her sweater from her shoulders to fall on the floor before he unbuttoned her dress. Her hands landed on the bottom of his sweater and she began tugging, forcing him to stop long enough to pull the garment over his head.

She shivered when he slid the dress off her shoulders, taking time to stroke every inch of exposed skin before allowing it to drop.

Her nimble fingers worked at his belt while he removed her bra, baring her beautiful breasts to his gaze. He couldn't prevent himself from teasing her rosy peaks until they were plump and full.

She applied herself to removing his pants and gave him a gentle squeeze. He ground his teeth together at the sensations her touch aroused in him.

Eager now, they removed their undergarments until they stood nude in the harsh light of the steamy bathroom. She was even more exquisite than he'd remembered in candlelight and moonlight. With her lush, womanly curves she resembled the perfect earth mother. The neat thatch of dark hair at the apex of her thighs made her skin seem luminescent.

"Come." He opened the shower door and allowed her to step inside the wide cubicle before he followed, shutting the door behind him.

The water was the perfect temperature and he stood against the wall watching as Esme wet her hair. She stood under the spray and it sluiced over her skin until it was slick and the warmth had chased the chill away. She reached for the shampoo and he intercepted her.

"Allow me," he said.

Pouring some into his hand, he lathered her long hair. He massaged her scalp until she groaned with delight and was leaning against him for support. When he was done he took his time rinsing her hair clean.

Picking up the soap, he lathered his hands then turned his attention to her body. He soaped her breasts, stomach and thighs, taking great care to massage every inch of her. When he reached her feet he sank to his knees so she could brace herself against his shoulder as he attended to one then the other before rinsing them.

When he rose he was met with an Esme who had a devilish glint in her eye. She plucked the soap from his hand.

"My turn," she said.

They switched positions with much unnecessary squirming and touching, and by the time he was fully under the spray he was hard as a pike.

She washed his hair and he was subjected to a knee-weakening scalp massage. Hawk leaned against the shower wall and watched as she lathered her hands and her breasts until a thick layer of soap foam covered her body. She reached for his shoulders and he almost swallowed his tongue when she pressed her slippery, soapy body into his and began to move up and down in an effort to wash his chest.

He bit back a groan and tipped his head to allow the water to pour over his face as she continued to work her earthy magic. His breathing grew labored as she worked her way down his abdomen but he was disappointed when she skipped his cock completely to work her way down his legs.

When she was done, she rose and kissed him on the chin before she slid her soapy hands around his cock.

He went utterly still, not daring to breathe. His gaze burned into hers and her hands began working his flesh with slow, soft strokes. A gentle smile curved her plump mouth and she stroked him from thick root to broad head. Turning him slightly, she pressed him back against the wall so the spray could rinse him off.

His breath caught as she sank to her knees to touch him with her tongue. A tremor shook him at the first touch of her slick flesh. At the sight of her plump lips encircling his cock his head swam.

With her hand now wrapped around the base of his cock, she stroked and teased him with her hot little mouth until he gave a strangled groan. He pushed her away lest he spill himself a second time.

"Hey, I wanted—"

He caught her by the shoulders and pulled her to her feet, stemming the unwanted flow of words with his mouth. Their kiss was hot, torrid, as he pushed her against the opposite wall of the shower. Their tongues mated, and he ground his cock into the swell of her sweet pussy until he was in danger of disgracing himself.

Grasping her thighs, he picked her up and forced his hips between her legs. Sliding his hands beneath her knees, he gripped her ass and forced her legs even wider apart. He entered her with a roar he muffled against her shoulder at the last second. She fit him perfectly, and without missing a beat his hips began hammering into her. Her sweet cunt took him deeper than before and her nails scored his skin.

His heart pounded in his ears as he continued his ruthless assault. She reached release several times before he allowed himself to follow. A tingling started in his balls and shot through his system as he came deep within her. Stars exploded before his eyes and he felt himself sway with the power of their mating.

Slowly they slid to the floor of the shower until they were sprawled in a boneless heap. Never had he found such an amazing connection to a woman. Stunned, he wrapped his arms around her.

There was no doubt in his mind Esme was the one meant for him.

* * * * *

Esme lay in the darkness curled in Hawk's arms, listening to his rhythmic breathing. After their shower romp they'd finally made their way into her bed where he'd fallen asleep almost immediately. With a small fire crackling in the fireplace her room was comfortable, a haven from the world and the approaching sun.

Her lover was stretched on his back and she couldn't help but stare. With his tousled hair and face relaxed in sleep he looked much younger. His chest was well muscled, proving he was no couch potato, and she could barely resist running her fingers over the thick pads of flesh. He was smart, funny and had brought her more pleasure than anyone ever had in her life.

She sighed. If only he were the man she was to marry.

Esme laid her head on his shoulder. Not that it mattered now. Her virginity was gone and her marriage contract was null and void. She dreaded the inevitable showdown with her father, because he'd hit the roof when he learned what she'd done.

And she'd be free for the first time in her life.

She squeezed her eyes shut. Yes, she'd be free and alone, all alone. With no Shani or Ivy to see her through her days. With no money or means to support herself and no clue about how to exist in the outside world.

She had no idea if her sisters would help her or even where they were. She opened her eyes and stared into the fire. She didn't understand why they hadn't tried to contact her. Marnie, her oldest sister, would be thirty-five now. What had happened to her? Where was she?

In truth, Esme was terrified of what the future held. For the first time in her life she'd be on her own and now that she was so much closer to realizing her dream, she was terrified of making a wrong move.

She sighed again and stretched her arm across Hawk's flat stomach. It was too bad she couldn't keep him. She grinned. Maybe they could run away to a pacific paradise and live on fish and coconuts as they lazed their days away on a beach making love and —

He isn't real.

Her grip tightened. Well, he certainly felt real enough, especially when he'd been inside her. She giggled then smashed her lips against his shoulder in an attempt to stifle the noise.

* * * * *

Hawk didn't know what Esme was thinking about. Her expression had been serious until her sudden giggle had her ducking her face against him. He rolled over until she was sprawled beneath him, her face pressed into the pillows.

"Can't you even let a man sleep, woman?" he asked in a mock growl.

She laughed into the pillow. "Well, you *were* asleep."

"Until you decided to start giggling." He settled his big body over her, the crack of her ass cradling his cock. "What's so funny?"

"Nothing." Her voice was muffled.

"Is that so?"

He licked the curve of her shoulder, eliciting a squeal from her. Firelight kissed her exposed skin and he eyed her curves appreciatively. She had the most beautiful bottom he'd ever seen. He ran his hand over her soft globe, stroking and squeezing her flesh with a gentle touch. He moved to kiss the base of her spine then let his tongue follow the curve of one plump cheek.

Seeing her naked and ready for him brought forth a rush of lust so powerful that it threatened to steal his breath. He wanted to take her from behind and feel the soft slap of her bottom against his stomach as he brought her to fulfillment.

"Spread your legs for me, Enchantress."

Her dark head popped out of the pillows and she looked back at him. Then a soft flush moved over her face as she wriggled to do his bidding.

He slid his hand between her thighs, parting her flesh to expose her glistening dusky-pink core with his fingers. She sighed as his finger brushed the nubbin still hidden by soft curls.

"So beautiful," he whispered. "And so wet."

He parted her further, exposing her clitoris. He slid his fingers deep into her damp flesh as his thumb caressed her bundle of nerves. Her hips lifted and she gave a loud moan before pressing her face deeper into the pillows. Her hands knotted the sheets as he continued his sensual assault on her body. Her hips rose with each stroke.

"Hawk?" Her voice was faint, strained.

"Yes?"

"Make me yours."

"I already have, Enchantress. I already have."

He bent his head and applied his tongue to her flesh. Suckling her hot inner core, she cried out as his fingers increased their gentle assault, stroking and teasing. He wanted to make her cry out. No, he wanted her to scream and he would accept nothing less.

"Hawk!"

She reached for his free hand and their fingers twined as she twisted against his mouth. She cried, a long and hoarse sob of release, as she tightened around his fingers.

He stroked the soft skin of her lower back as she slowly quieted and her body went limp, her skin damp with sweat. With their fingers entwined, he stretched over her, nudging her thighs wider with his knees, then slid into her from behind in one smooth movement.

"Mmm…" She arched her back, taking him deeper. "Just lovely."

He raised her arms so that her hands were near her head and he could balance his weight on his elbows. He brushed his lips over her cheek, her hair tickling his skin as he nuzzled her ear. Buried deep within her with her soft buttocks cushioning his belly was the closest a man could get to perfection.

He fought the urge to simply drive himself mindlessly into her body. His movements were slow, sensual, keeping them both aroused, but doing nothing to bring them to release. How long they remained in that drowsy, aroused state he didn't know, but all too soon her insistent wiggling motions and the rhythmic clenching of her flesh around his frayed what little self-control he possessed. He clenched his teeth as he felt her shatter beneath him. Her body bracing his, he drove into her, hard, deep. Once, twice, three times…his head came up and he shouted as he came.

Trembling, he collapsed over her, lacking any desire to move away. He nuzzled her neck and the soft curve of her shoulder. Her curls tickled his nose as he nibbled the back of her neck. Nothing would take this woman from his side. He'd see to it.

* * * * *

Esme was on edge.

She was huddled in a thick quilt in her favorite armchair near the fireplace. A cup of tea sat on the table near her elbow and tendrils of steam rose lazily into the chilly air.

She'd awoken alone in her bed, the scent of her lover still on her sheets and her body, while outside the world experienced its first serious chill of autumn. Her French doors were shut tight, though she'd left the drapes open to capture what little sunshine that might break through the thick layer of clouds.

Esme shivered and gathered the quilt tighter. Underlying the autumn chill was the bite of something ominous, a feeling of foreboding that hung in the air as if the universe were waiting for something to happen.

She closed her eyes, frustrated by her inability to pinpoint the origins of her unease. In twenty-four hours she was due to be married and that was enough to unsettle anyone. One last day before the showdown with her father and her future would be in her own hands.

She rubbed the furrowed skin between her eyes. She didn't think it was the impending discussion that had her tied in knots. Was it Hawk?

She reached into the universe with her mind and came up against a wall of seething darkness filled with anger and the coppery taste of imminent betrayal. Her eyes flew open.

It wasn't Hawk, but she was pretty sure that this new threat was male.

Disturbed, she flung off her quilt and rose from the chair. Shivering slightly, though whether from the chilly air or fear she wasn't sure, Esme stalked to the shelves that housed her crystals. She needed something for safety and protection, and when Hawk returned this evening she'd make him take something as well. When she selected the small turquoise pendant, a knock sounded on her door.

Startled, she turned to see Shani in the doorway with an armload of cardboard boxes. Without asking her permission he stepped into the room and placed the boxes on the bed.

"Your father called, Miss. You're to pack your things today and a car will pick them up this afternoon."

She frowned. "But why today? I'm not to be married until tomorrow." She ran her fingers over the smooth stone and her palm prickled. "I thought I could come back and pack after the ceremony."

He shook his head. "Plans have changed, Miss. A car will pick you up at 6:00 p.m. and you're to be married this evening."

She gaped at him. "Why—"

"I don't know, Miss. I'm merely following orders." He gave her a slight bow and backed out of the room. "I'll bring you some more boxes and Ivy will be up to assist you shortly."

With her heart in her throat, Esme turned toward the French doors. Her wedding dress stood in the corner, pristine and cold as snow, mocking her with its icy perfection.

She couldn't leave today. Hawk would return in a few hours and they would laugh and talk—

He wasn't her destiny. He wasn't hers to keep...

She looked down at the small chunk of turquoise in her hand.

It was too late. The other shoe had already dropped. She let the stone fall from her icy fingertips.

Chapter Seven

"No one knows where the other daughters are. The moment they reached majority, they took a small inheritance from their mother's family and vanished."

Hawk stared at his younger brother, Stuart, in disbelief. "How can six women—Proctor women at that—just vanish off the face of the earth? These women are from one of the most prominent witching families in the world. Someone had to have noticed their disappearance or aided them in their getaway."

Stuart sauntered to the liquor cabinet and helped himself to some brandy. "If someone gave them aid then it's a well-kept secret. I checked all the best gossips and they knew nothing." He shrugged. "They concurred that the Proctor family has always been very eccentric when it comes to their women and they have a long history of being sequestered. Until they marry, it isn't unusual that the daughters aren't seen or heard from."

Hawk shook his head. "By now all of the daughters are well past a marriageable age, yet we've heard nothing of their whereabouts or even plans for their marriages."

"And a Proctor marriage would definitely make the grapevine," Stuart added.

Hawk raked his hand through his hair. "Esmerelda was moved to Hill House when she was fourteen, so her oldest sister would have been well past twenty by then."

Stuart took a sip of his drink. "It is a mystery. I think we need to call in Quinn or Maeve—"

A loud clatter in the hall broke off their conversation when Evie, the youngest Montgomery child, raced into the room. Her knee socks were down around her ankles, her shoes were splattered with mud and she had a dark smear on one cheek that looked suspiciously like chocolate syrup.

"Stu, you have to come now! Greg is cheating at Demon Racer Five again and if he doesn't stop I'll turn him into a toad!" She put her little fists on her skinny hips and stuck her chin out.

His brother chuckled and put his glass down. "We can't have that, you little terror. This family has too many frogs in it already, not to mention the fact that Mom will blister your little bottom if you do such a thing." He took her hand and led her from the room.

Hawk turned toward the desk and looked into the depths of the gazing globe. Esme and another woman, the cook he assumed, were packing her altar items. Neither woman looked at each other, they just kept their heads bent to their tasks as items were wrapped and stowed into cardboard boxes.

One more day…one more day…

"Ethan." His father's voice interrupted his contemplation.

"Yes, Father?"

Kiergan Montgomery was almost the same size as his eldest son. While his hair was sprinkled with gray at the temples and his face sported a few more wrinkles around the eyes, he looked much the same as the man Hawk remembered from childhood. Quick to laugh and fiercely protective of his large family, he was known as a dragon outside his family circle. His children couldn't help but laugh at the outrageous stories that circulated about him.

"I've received disturbing news, son." The elder Montgomery dropped into a wing chair near the desk. "It seems that Proctor is trying to deceive us. He's arranged to marry Esmerelda to another man this evening."

Hawk blinked. "What?"

Kiergan nodded. "He's making arrangements to spirit her off this evening and marry her to the Whiddington heir." He made a big, beefy fist, then released it. "I was right not to trust that bastard."

Anger curled in the pit of Hawk's stomach. He'd known something was up. He'd felt it in the very air when he'd left Esme's bed that morning. He'd been so distracted by their joining and his plans for their next meeting that he'd pushed the uneasy feeling aside. "We can't let this happen."

"Ethan." Kiergan held up his hand. "I signed that contract in the hopes that you and Esmerelda would grow up together and share some of the same life experiences, that you'd come to love and understand one another as your mother and I did. That didn't happen and now the girl is a virtual stranger to you."

Hawk shook his head. "Esme was never a stranger to me. I've loved her since I was sixteen years old and I won't relinquish my claim to her hand in marriage."

His father remained silent and they stared into each other's eyes for a few moments. He rose from the chair. "You're sure about this?"

"Yes."

His father nodded. "I'll send Michael to keep an eye on Hill House and Stuart to keep an eye on Proctor." He grabbed his son's hand and gave it a quick shake. "Don't worry, we'll secure you a bride before nightfall."

Hawk watched his father leave the room with a spring in his step. Kiergan enjoyed nothing more than a good challenge and this one had him fired.

His gaze returned to the globe in time to see Esme pick up one of her crystal globes. Her beautiful heart-shaped face stared into the crystal and for a moment he felt as if she could see him as he saw her. Her beauty kicked him in the gut and knocked the wind from his lungs. He was struck by the sadness in her expression. She picked up some tissue and wrapped the globe, preventing him from watching her further.

Hawk sat at his desk and reached for the phone. He had to meet with Proctor before Esme and her father came face to face. Who knew what his reaction would be when he found out that his daughter had trumped them all?

Chapter Eight

Esmerelda hadn't been in the family chapel since her mother had died.

Complete with arched doorways and stained glass windows, the chapel was a perfect replica of a medieval church. From a distance it looked like a real church, until one inspected the windows and realized they depicted scenes common to pagan beliefs rather than Christian ones.

She stepped through the doorway and walked across the floor, feeling the cold radiating from the stones beneath her feet. She trailed her hand over a mahogany sideboard that had been freshly polished and decorated with a spray of white roses and rich greenery. The scent of beeswax, furniture polish and bayberry hung heavy in the air.

On wooden legs, she drifted toward the sanctuary. To her surprise the room was almost bare save for the massive wrought iron candelabras in every corner, each bearing at least a dozen fat white candles. The benches and chairs that had once populated the sanctuary were gone and the room had an unused feeling, a chill in the air that told her it had been a while since anyone had spent much time here.

Her slippers made little noise as she walked to the circular altar in the center of the room. The altar was placed on a stone dais and it was high enough to allow everyone in the room a good view. Lifting the hem of her wedding gown, she ascended the steps.

The mahogany was polished to a bright gleam and in the center was a towering arrangement of flowers and bayberry candles, their flames dancing in the drafty old building. There were several containers of water, salt, and an arrangement of small apples, a gourd and an evergreen branch. An ancient broom leaned against the table and she knew it was for jumping over once the ceremony was complete.

Not that it would come to that.

She touched the cold wood of the broom handle and a rush of power moved up her arm. It had been her great-grandmother's, and she remembered her mother had used it from time to time. How she wished her mother were here now.

Esme ran her hand over the altar. Her mother's casket had sat on this very wood for two days while the family had gathered to mourn her untimely death. She shivered. So many memories crowded this place and none of them were good.

She heard the front door open and several men's voices. She turned in time to see her father and five strange men enter.

"So you're here." Her father walked toward her with his gaze glued to the pocket watch in his hand. "And on time, too. Excellent." He snapped the gold watch shut and tucked it into his pocket. "We're ready then."

Esme couldn't speak as her gaze traveled over him. She hadn't seen him in several years, though it looked as if he'd aged ten since then. He'd gone almost completely gray, and he'd put at least forty pounds on an already generous form. Had it been that long since last she'd seen him?

She cleared her throat. "Father, I need to speak with you." She shot a pointed look at the other men. "In private."

He shook his head. "There is nothing to discuss." He started up the steps toward her. "We're here to see you married and that's that."

Esme stepped in front of him, preventing him from reaching the top and forcing him to look at her.

"Did you get my message, father?" she whispered.

His lip curled and she was shocked by the expression of dislike that came over his face. "I did."

"And?" she pressed.

"And what?" His tone was sharp.

"Release me from this contract."

"No."

Father and daughter stood eye to eye, neither willing to give an inch on the matter. If he didn't relent, she'd have to reveal her secret even if it would humiliate her father in front of his associates.

One of the others, a tall blond man, stepped forward. "Is there a problem, Edmund?"

Her father's eyes narrowed. "No, no problem at all." He stepped around her to drop a sheaf of papers on the altar and Esme's heart fell. "Gentlemen, if you could give me a few moments alone with my daughter, I'd appreciate it."

The blond man nodded and ushered the others toward the entrance while a shorter man with a somewhat round red head stared at her. She felt as if he were sizing her up like a juicy steak or a dessert that he coveted. Her skin crawled.

Finally, he moved away, and when they were all in the outer chamber, Esme couldn't help but notice they hadn't bothered to close the door all the way.

"What is it, Esmerelda? We're running out of time."

Her father stood beside her and for a moment she felt like a small child again with her father towering over her, disapproval radiating like sunlight.

She shook away the feeling and squared her shoulders. She was a child no longer and quite capable of making her own decisions.

"As I said before, I wish to be released from this contract."

He shook his head and placed his big hands on her arms then jerked away as if just touching her was unpleasant. She caught a glimpse of the distaste on his face before he carefully masked it.

"I'm only looking out for your best interests." His tone was stiff. "You're a special witch and it would behoove me to ensure you're taken care of and your particular talents are preserved…"

She noticed he used the term witch rather than daughter. A father should fight for his daughter's happiness, but it appeared that Edmund Brooks-Proctor believed no such thing.

"You signed the marriage contract because the Montgomery family offered you the most money for my hand in marriage." Her tone was flat, cold. "This has nothing to do with seeing to my welfare."

Anger washed over his bloated features and his eyes narrowed. "You selfish little twerp." He leaned in close and spoke in little more than a hiss. "You're barely marriageable material, you little retard," he spat. "You and I both know that you're dumber than a mule and can't do a tenth of the spells your mother could perform at your age. No respectable witch would marry you knowing this, seventh Proctor daughter or not."

Esme lifted her chin while something inside her shriveled in the face of her father's obvious hatred. "But that didn't stop you from selling me like a whore on the street, did it? That didn't stop you from selling my virginity for a packet of cash—"

Before she could blink, her father struck her across the cheek with the back of his hand. The sound of flesh striking flesh was obscenely loud in the stillness of the chapel. Esme's breath caught at the sudden shock and pain that rocketed through her and she straightened her spine and placed her palm over her stinging skin.

The silence that fell was thick and cloying. The men had abandoned their pretense of giving them privacy and they'd opened the door, blatantly staring at the spectacle being played out before them.

"Your mother was a whore," Edmund snarled. "She turned me from our bed after Margaret was born. We didn't share a bed again as she was determined to stop the line of Proctor women at six. But several years passed, and she took a lover and accidentally became pregnant with you."

Esme's knees began to shake.

"You are the daughter of a whore and a retard at that." Spittle flew from his lips and his cheeks were red with exertion. "That was your mother's sin to bear. I could barely stand to look at you. The moment I could I sent you away so no one would find out your dirty little secret until you were safely married and your dower money was safe in my account."

She turned and allowed her hand to fall away from her face. "You failed, Fath—" She stumbled over the word. She couldn't ever call him that again.

"And how exactly have I failed?" he snapped. "We're going to marry you off. Your bridegroom, the witnesses and the minister are here as well and they've been paid enough to overlook the fact that you're a nervous and somewhat unwilling bride."

Her stomach churned and she lifted her head to meet his victorious gaze. "I've thwarted you, Edmund." She spat his name through icy lips. Her body had gone completely numb. "I'm no longer a virgin and you have nothing to barter with."

Edmund gave a half-hearted laugh as whispers broke out near the door. "You're joking."

She shook her head. "I'm not."

His eyes widened. "Who could it... Shani...it can't be... I cast spells..."

"It was no one you know." She smiled even though her face ached and her heart was sore. "He was a man who surpassed your feeble magical abilities."

And I really wish he were here right now...

Edmund shot a nervous glance at the whispering men before he grabbed her arm and yanked her toward him. "You will marry the man I've chosen," he hissed.

"No, I will not." Esme shook off his touch. "You've lost this time. You will leave Proctor House tonight. Take only your clothes, as that's all you deserve. I wish to rid my mother's family home of your stench before morning."

"You fucking bitch!" He raised his hand to strike her again but she brought up her own hand in a claw-like position. His expression changed from rage to fear, and for the first time in her life she understood the power she held. To her surprise he backed away until she lowered her arm.

"You can't do this to me…betray me like this," he whined.

Her brow arched. "Like you did to me, you mean?"

He reached for the sheaf of papers on the altar and held them high. "Do you know how much these are worth? Marcus Whiddington offered me a lot of money, more than double what Montgomery paid for your hand in marriage. I'll give you half—"

With a flick of her finger, the papers burst into flame and Edmund flung them to the ground. He snarled and shook his hand as if he'd been singed.

"Others have arrived," one of the men in the doorway spoke. "What is going on here, Edmund?

Walking through the throng came several newcomers. The older man in front looked vaguely familiar and when he stepped to the side her heart stopped.

Hawk.

Her gaze darted from the older man then back to her lover's. The resemblance was unmistakable. This had to be his father.

"Proctor, you bastard," the older man thundered. "Come down here and face me like a man, you witless worm."

Edmund stepped behind his daughter. "I think not."

"Who are you?" Esme said to the approaching man.

"I am Kiergan Montgomery, your soon-to-be father-in-law."

Bewildered, her gaze darted to Hawk. If this was Kiergan Montgomery, then which Montgomery was Hawk? Her breath left her in a rush. Her betrothed?

"Who is that young man, Esmerelda?" Edmund snapped.

"My lover," she whispered. She gathered her skirts and started down the dais. She'd taken the first step when she heard a rush of multiple indrawn breaths.

She looked up to see an expression of complete horror on Hawk's face just before a tremendous pressure hit her square in the back. Thrown off balance, her feet tangled in the voluminous skirt and she flew off the dais heading straight for the stone floor.

She felt her wrist give when she hit the cold steps and a blinding pain raced up her arm. She caught a glimpse of Hawk racing toward her and just before her head struck the floor, she heard her father laugh.

Chapter Nine

"Are you feeling better, dear?"

Esme's eyes flew open at the strange voice. In the doorway stood a short woman with a bright blue dress and a tumbled mass of blonde curls that made her look like a misplaced faery. She would have been perfectly at home perched on a mushroom in the midst of a forest. Her smile was wide and she held a tea tray.

"I think so." Her voice was rusty and she tried to clear her throat.

"Good. My name is Emmeline and I'm Ethan's mother." The woman bustled into the room and set the tray on a bedside table. "I must say you are the spitting image of your mother."

Esme blinked. "You knew my mother?"

The other woman gave an energetic nod, then grabbed some pillows from a chair and began tucking them behind Esme. "Oh my yes. I grew up just a few miles from this very house where your mother was born. She was a bit older than me, but I spent many hours in these kitchens begging lemon tarts from Isolde, the cook. Do you remember her?"

Esme frowned and tried to dredge up the few memories she had of living in this house. "Did she wear a red cloth over her hair?"

"Oh yes." The other women quit fussing with the pillows. "She was as bald as a baby's bottom, thanks to your mother." She set the tea tray over Esme's knees.

She wrapped her hands around the mug of tea, grateful for its warmth. "How is that?"

"A misdirected spell, or so I'm told." The woman sat on the edge of the bed. "Your mother was but a child and your granny was teaching her how to light a fire with a flick of her wrist. Unfortunately, Isolde was in the way and her hair went up like a torch." The woman made a tsking sound. "Luckily, she wasn't hurt, but her hair never did grow back. Didn't matter to Isolde one whit as she was so devoted to your mother and her sisters." She chuckled. "I don't know that I'd be so complacent if someone struck me bald."

Esme couldn't help but laugh. "I'd have to agree with you." She took a sip of the hot Darjeeling, pleased to find it sweetened exactly as she liked it. "So where is my f-f-fa—uh, Edmund?"

"Oh, somewhere over Canada by now, I'd imagine." Emmeline chuckled and rose. "How I'd like to see that sight."

She frowned. "What do you mean, Canada?"

"My dear husband got so mad when Edmund pushed you down the steps that he turned him into a goose." Emmeline shrugged. "Seriously, though, Edmund is being guarded in the stables as no one has been able to convince Kiergan to restore the bastard to his usual, nasty self. I personally think he should have been turned into a troll as it would have suited his disposition much better." She gave a wild giggle that set her curls to bouncing. "You should have seen his face! I won't forget that look very soon."

Esme shook her head, feeling oddly bereft yet amused at the same time. "Why a goose?"

"Why not?" The other woman shrugged. "My husband is very angry with Edmund. Not only did he try and deceive our entire family, but the man refused to reveal the whereabouts of your sisters. Kiergan has refused to release Edmund or return him permanently to human form until he tells what he knows."

Esme frowned and rubbed her forehead. "I think I'm confused. How did he try to deceive your family?"

"He found another family to pay double the bride price for your hand in marriage. He'd contacted Ethan about moving the wedding date forward then at the last minute tried to spirit you away and marry you to the Whiddington boy." Emmeline snorted. "As if you could marry that halfwit. My boys chased those worthless Whiddingtons off with their tails between their legs," she chuckled. "Marcus Whiddington won't be fool enough to try and double-cross the Montgomery family again."

Feeling suddenly weary, Esme leaned back and closed her eyes. "Where is Hawk…I mean—"

"Right here."

Her eyes flew open when Hawk came into the room. He was dressed in black from head to toe with his dark hair loose about his shoulders. Esme's tongue felt oddly thick and she suddenly felt like crying for no reason she could discern.

"Ethan's been hanging about your bedroom door all evening," his mother blurted. "I kept telling him not to worry, but I couldn't budge him anyway." She bustled toward the door. "I'll leave you two alone then." She poked her son in the side as she passed. "No roughhousing. I'd imagine she's feeling a little discombobulated right now." She shut the door behind her.

Suddenly uneasy, Esme wasn't sure what to say. So she settled for something simple. "Hi."

He smiled and sat on the edge of the bed then removed the tray from between them. "How are you feeling?"

She shifted. "Sore, but not as bad as I'd have thought."

He picked up her hand and examined her wrist. "My mother is a whiz with broken bones. She had to be with my brothers around."

"I broke my arm?" Even as she said it, she remembered the sharp pain as she'd hit the floor.

"Your wrist, actually." He touched her forehead. "And you hit your head."

"That much I remember." Esme crossed her arms over her chest and studied the man sitting next to her. "So you're my fiancé?"

He nodded. "And you're mine." He reached for her then let his hand drop. "I'm sorry I couldn't get to you—"

She placed her hand over his mouth. "There's no need to be sorry, Hawk. I needed you and you were there. I can't ask for anything more."

He kissed her fingers before gripping them tight. "Like Edmund, I also deceived you."

"That you did." She tilted her head and her eyes narrowed. "I conjured a lover to take my virginity and render the marriage contract null and void. Instead, it was my fiancé that appeared, not that I knew it. Just how did you manage that one?"

An attractive flush moved into his cheeks. "Well, that's kind of a long story. For now, let's just say that I heard you were looking for a man and I knew I couldn't let my woman—"

"Your woman?" Her brow arched and a warm glow ignited in her stomach.

"My woman." His eyes turned darker, heated. "I fell in love with you when you were fifteen years old."

Her eyes widened. "How can that be?"

"One day I snuck into the woods to spy on you and the moment I saw you, you stole my heart." His expression was distant. "You were wearing a white dress and carrying a wounded animal in your arms. I couldn't get you out of my mind."

"B-b-but I didn't even know you."

"It didn't matter because I felt I knew you, even then." He took a deep breath. "Afterwards I sent you those globes on your sixteenth birthday and I've been watching you through them ever since."

Aghast, she stared at him for a few seconds. "You watched me? You could see what I did in the privacy of my home?" Shocked, she pulled her hand away. "How could you do that to me?"

"How could I not? Your father had forbidden us from meeting and your image occupied my every waking thought."

"So you decided to invade my privacy?" she snapped. "Basically you were stalking me."

His eyes widened, then he grinned and ducked his head slightly. "I'm not sure I'd put it quite that way." He caught her hand again. "I've watched you mature into a beautiful, compassionate woman and you stole my breath away when you and I spoke that first night. I'd watched you for years, a shadowy image in a crystal globe, and you'd bewitched me, but it was nothing in comparison to meeting the living, breathing person."

Esme looked away, her throat tight. "I'm confused and not sure how I feel right now," she whispered.

"I can't tell you how to feel about us, but I can tell you how I feel." He stroked her hand in his. "I want to show you so many things, take you to places you've only dreamed of. We can go to Venice and float down the canals, to Egypt to see the pyramids, maybe visit Italy and sample some wines. I have friends who live in Provence, France where the food is beyond compare and the wine flows like water." He brushed his lips across the back of her hand and sent shivers up her arm. He raised his head and his direct gaze burned into hers. "Let me show you the world. Let me teach you, Esmerelda. Marry me."

Startled, she pulled away. She could barely breathe. She couldn't even think about marrying anyone unless they knew the truth about her and her heritage.

She pulled her hand from his and fixed her gaze on the pale pink sheets. "I need to tell you something."

He caught her chin and tipped her head back until their gazes met. "There's nothing you can tell me that will change my mind about my love for you."

She shook her head. "You have to hear me out. I might be the seventh daughter of a seventh daughter, but I'm a worthless witch." She spoke in a rush when she felt her eyes prickle with tears. "I can't even cast the simplest of spells. I turned Ivy into an animal once and I tried to conjure some fruit pies and ended up destroying a kitchen." Her shoulders slumped. "I'm a disgrace to my name."

"You're not a disgrace. Your problem is your reading skills aren't up to par. Do you know why that is, Enchantress?" He ran his thumb over her chin.

"I can't read because I'm stupid," she whispered.

"I suspect that you're dyslexic."

She blinked. "Dyslexic?"

"Yes. It took me a while to come to that conclusion. Through the globe I'd only seen you perform the simplest of spells and some of them you botched and that didn't make much sense to me. It was only when I saw some notes you'd left on the table and noticed that some of your letters were backwards and others were out of order. With dyslexia, the brain confuses letters and rearranges them until you can't tell what you're reading." He gave her hand a squeeze. "We won't know until you're tested, though."

Mute, Esme gave a shaky nod, not quite daring to believe he could be right. She'd spent so many years believing Edmund's cruel, hateful words that she was terrified to believe he might've been mistaken from the beginning.

Hawk moved to sit next to her and lean against her pillows. Sliding his arm around her he pulled her close until her head came to rest on his shoulder. "Dry your eyes, my Enchantress. We need to contemplate what a wonderful life we'll have together."

Joy mixed with tears and her laugh came out as part sob. "That is a wonderful thing to think about," she sniffed.

"Indeed. Think of the things I can show you. Once you learn to read properly there won't be a spell you can't cast, Esme. The world will be yours."

A sob caught in her throat and she buried her head in his chest and inhaled his familiar scent.

"Your future is so bright, you can be anything you wish," he said. "I want to be the one to help you reach your potential, if you will let me. I want to be right by your side every step of the way."

Her heart melted and she gave a noisy sniff. "I guess it's a good thing you gave me those globes. Without them you might not have caught on about my disability."

His arms tightened. "So you forgive me?"

"I'm still thinking about that," she said. "You won't get off that easily, Hawk."

"You're entitled."

She heard the tone of amusement in his voice. She raised her head and scrubbed at her cheeks. "I guess it's also a good thing that I'm a lousy witch."

"Why is that?"

"Because if I'd been competent then my lover spell would have worked and another man would have been in my bed, not you. He wouldn't have cared enough to look deeper and I might have been stuck at Hill House all my life."

He kissed her on the forehead. "I guess everything has worked out as it should."

Esme frowned. "But what about my sisters, Hawk? What happened to them?"

She felt him shake his head. "I don't know. One by one they grew to majority, took what little inheritance your mother left them and walked away from Edmund and Proctor House. Edmund hasn't said a word, though I have a feeling Father will work it out of him sooner or later." He chuckled.

"We have to find them. I can't be content until I know where they are…if they're safe and happy."

His arms tightened around her. "We will, Esme, trust in that. We'll find your sisters."

Also by J.C. Wilder:

About the author:

J.C. Wilder left the world of big business to carry on conversations with the people who live in her mind, fictional characters that is. In her past she has worked as a software tester, traveled with an alternative rock band and currently volunteers for her local police department as a photographer. She lives in Central Ohio with 6,000 books and an impressive collection of dust bunnies.

The award-winning author also writes as Dominique Adair.

J.C. welcomes mail from readers. You can write to her c/o Ellora's Cave Publishing at 1056 Home Avenue, Akron OH 44310-3502.

Half Moon Magick

Chapter One

Black Isolde carefully poured a small amount of oil over the water in her wide bowl of hammered copper. The scents of lavender and mint rose as the water warmed the oils. She inhaled deeply, closing her eyes for a moment, letting the fragrances relax her body and clear her mind. She opened her eyes and stared into the bowl, her gaze unfocused.

The surface of the oil smoothed, the shimmer of the pouring subsiding. The image of the cottage ceiling appeared briefly. In its place came swirls of color, blues and greens, random shapes that gradually resolved into recognizable figures. Tree boughs heavy with summer leaves grew to fill the vision, her perspective falling lower until only the huge trunks loomed around her.

The forest she saw was unknown to her, a quiet place of deep shadows. 'Twas too quiet. Unsettled, she searched the vision for other signs of life, birds in flight or squirrels at play. Nothing moved in the dappled light.

Mist began to rise from the ground, wreathing the trees in first gray and then white as it gathered and thickened. Through the gauzy streamers came a man.

Oh, dear Goddess, what a man!

She'd seen him before, in dreams of prophecy and visions of her future. Now he strode boldly toward her, parting the mist. Behind and around him crowded the denizens of the forest. Flocks of birds and families of animals—deer and wolves, bears and rabbits—soared and romped as the fog dispersed.

Above him, sparrows flew around a hawk, unconcerned, indeed teasing the raptor with close dives. The sly tap of a wingtip sent them tumbling downward in a feathery cascade.

Isolde could almost hear their excited chatter as they recovered and climbed to begin their game anew.

Like the creatures he led, the man wore nothing more than the Goddess had blessed him with.

Had She ever blessed him!

Silken hair poured in golden sheets across his broad shoulders and framed the sharp contours of his face. His clean-shaven chin was strong and hard. Darker brows formed slashes over his rich amber eyes, the deep color startling against his pale complexion.

The hunger in those eyes was for her, as was the desire evident in his rampant cock.

Aye, she'd seen him before, but never like this. Not as the embodiment of the forest, the Green Man come to life.

He stared straight at her, licking his lips. Holding her gaze with his, he reached one hand out to her. The other fell to stroke the length of his cock.

She leaned forward, aware that her body was responding to his blatant invitation. The memory of joining with him, matings she'd experienced in her dreams, enticed her. She knew the texture of his skin, the touch of his lips on her neck, the puff of his breath in her ear. She longed for the length and width of his cock to fill her, and shifted to spread her legs where she sat. She longed to feel him move within her, bringing her joy and completion. Her pulse beat faster. Her nipples hardened into pebbles beneath her soft linen shift. Her cleft wept for his touch.

"What are you doing?" Her apprentice and cousin Kara shattered the vision as she bumped the table and set the bowl to shaking.

Isolde bit her tongue. Hard.

"Oh. Are you scrying?"

Isolde fought an urge to shriek at the child. The dampness on her hot skin quickly cooled, adding discomfort to her frustration. "Aye. Or rather, I was, until you interfered. I have told you again and again, Kara, not to speak or touch anything until you understand what is happening. Sometimes the things we do can have consequences if they are not concluded properly."

"So says our new priest. I keep forgetting."

"He is correct. Try harder to remember your other instruction. You remember well enough the spells you want to use." An apprentice should be appreciated, not dreaded, but of late Isolde could not teach young Kara with the enthusiasm she once had. She stifled a sigh and set aside the bowl. Naught but the rafters showed now in its surface. "I thought you were making cheese. Come, show me what you have done." Pushing away from the table, she rose and motioned Kara ahead of her.

"Oh, aye, 'tis ready." Kara stepped into the sunshine and threw her thick plait over her shoulder, narrowly missing Isolde's nose.

Isolde glanced at the sky, calculating the hour and wondering if she'd lost track of time. Had her vision taken hours instead of minutes? Nay, the sun had yet to reach its zenith. She slowed her stride to match Kara's lazy pace. "Ready? How can that be? You were to stir up the settled paste with the paddle until it all thickens, and then call me. I expected that would take you until noon at least."

Kara shrugged. "I just spelled it, and it thickened in no time."

Isolde stopped and regarded her solemnly. "You cannot be serious." What another might have posed as a question came out as a flat statement.

"Why not?" Kara had the gall to roll her eyes. "The others may spend hours stirring cream if they wish, but I don't like to stand up for that long. If I can cast a spell to speed the curdling of the cream and hasten the cheese, why should I have to wait?"

The girls gathered just inside the dairy door stirred restlessly while Isolde shaped her reply.

Kara was quite serious, further evidence that she had not the temperament to be a mage. Her undeniable talent had moved her father to send her to Isolde for training, but after a year Isolde was at her wits' end. Her cousin argued over the use of what she was learning, chafing under small practice drills and being forced to do things properly instead of what she called "quick enough to serve".

Isolde's handful of other students this season were learning housewifery. They were sent by parents who looked to pair their precious daughters with men in higher stations, men who held manors or castles. Isolde was charged with teaching the young women embroidery and manners, and the brewing of simple potions for household use.

Their interests lay in the management of a small estate, the proper care of fine linens and the production of good food. One could not properly oversee a dairy, a kitchen, or a brewery if one did not know how the tasks should be done. None of the others had much patience for Kara's quibbling or any interest in magick.

Kara showed far too much interest in magick, for all the wrong reasons.

"Expending your talent to rearrange the world to suit yourself, subverting the natural order of things, is arrogance and abuse of the worst kind. Magick is not to be used to serve your laziness. The Goddess gifts a few of us with these abilities so that we may all benefit. Do not speak so to me again, or I will put an end to your apprenticeship and send you home immediately."

To Isolde's surprise, Kara ducked her head and muttered a quick apology as she turned away. She might not fear her teacher, but she certainly feared her father. Cedd was brusque and filled with pride, a petty and self-important man. Isolde could not imagine living under the same roof with him.

Plump, pretty Della, a miller's daughter who was to marry a minor lord in the autumn, giggled nervously. Isolde could not see her cousin's face, but from the way Della blanched and shrank back, Kara had leveled her worst glare on poor Della. The other girls closed ranks around their friend, stepping between the two.

Isolde stifled a sigh and closed her eyes for a moment. *Dear Goddess, may there be peace in the loft for another fortnight, until Kara is safely away, and may You help me find the words to train Kara properly.* In her silent plea, Isolde invested the word "properly" with resolution of all the flaws she saw in her cousin, from laziness to a tendency to show off her magickal talent—along with the patience she herself would need to accomplish that task.

The rest of the day passed in a state of tension. Isolde carefully kept Kara and Della apart, giving them tasks that sent one to the henhouse and the other to the spring. She didn't let her guard down until evening, when Kara dragged a stool close by the fire to polish the runes she was making and the young ladies had settled around the largest table to work on embroidering Della's gowns and linens.

Behind Kara, one of the girls around the table snickered.

'Twas going to be a long fortnight.

* * * * *

Harmon set aside his trencher and wiped the table clean with a pass of his sleeve. The Call came clearly, from somewhere west of here. The tug he'd felt this morn, so strong it penetrated his fever, had set his blood to tingling. It tingled still. 'Twas strong Power, then, to make such a lingering impression over a distance.

The question was, did it come from his quarry or was it evidence of an unexpected complication to his plans? He needed to know the nature of what he faced. No mage went into battle unprepared.

The village lass would arrive in a little while to clear away his meal. Time enough to serve.

Pulling his drinking vessel close, he cupped his hands about it and peered down.

"Bowl of water, still and clear
Show me that which led me here

I sense strong magick from afar
But will it blend or will it bar?
Show me now for I must know
The source of it as friend or foe."

The dark interior of the mug flashed bright white before presenting a pleasant picture. The interior of a neat cottage, filled with women. Not much help there, although he examined them each in turn.

One he immediately recognized as the most annoying person in the village, young Kara. He'd seen and heard that her father was not above harsh discipline but it had apparently had no effect on the wench's behavior. Even her voice grated on his nerves, by turns strident and shrill.

Without intervention, she would soon become a mage of the worst kind — vain, selfish, and unprincipled. The sooner someone took her on in a battle of magickal wills, the easier she would be to defeat. Although he was no longer certain that Kara was the reason he'd been Called to this place at this time, he planned to be the one to change her future.

The other young women were unknown to him. Several gathered around a table, apparently preparing bread. One was quite pretty in a soft way, but they were too young for his taste and didn't hold his interest. He passed over each in turn and discarded them as being the source of the tug he'd felt.

Ah, but the older woman, the one sitting by the door with a lap filled with wool, fairly glowed with magick — and beauty, although her Power drew him more than her sweet face and coal-black hair.

He took a closer look at her and his breath hitched. Her face was familiar to him but her body, concealed by a woolen gown and apron, was more so. He'd explored those soft curves in vivid dreams for years.

Remembered desire had him shifting on the bench to accommodate his growing cock. In his dreams, she'd been an abstract entity, the object of his lust and a source of release during his long celibate years of training. He'd never thought her real, never thought to find her, let alone discover that she was a mage. She had to be a mage, and this must be where Kara had been sent for instruction.

Odd, that none of the other young women appeared to possess Power of any sort. Their garments were too fine for them to be servants. What sort of apprentices were they?

Not for the first time, he regretted that his visions never let him hear what was happening, only see. He would give much to hear the conversation between his woman and Kara. He wished to know the complete nature of what he faced, although their identities were clear.

Both his quarry and a complication.

'Twas not good news, but mayhap he could turn it to his advantage. He'd learned to twist a situation to suit his ends from one of the best practitioners of the dark arts.

Chapter Two

Black Isolde plucked the wool apart in her lap, separating soft tufts from twigs and bits of bracken. Kara sat at her knee just inside the cottage door, etching runic characters on her polished stones and humming a lullaby. Della and the others were busily kneading bread at the long table behind them.

"Oh, look, Cousin Isolde. This cut reveals a flash of color. Is that important? Did I choose the right rune for this stone?"

"Everything is important, Kara. How many times have I told you that? As you work with your runes and the particular stones you have chosen for each sigil, you will learn to listen, and to heed what they tell you."

Isolde took the offered stone. Where the strokes crossed in the center of the sign for Breakthrough, Kara's cut had pierced a crystal in the heart of the tiny stone slab. When she tilted it, the crystal caught the midday sunlight and glittered with a rainbow of colors against the dark surface.

"I think this is an excellent stone for Breakthrough. How often does the solution to a problem or the appropriate next step come to us in a flash of insight?" She handed it back and received a delighted smile in return.

Isolde had purposely kept Kara out of the household activities since the incident in the dairy, giving her other tasks and keeping her close by. 'Twas clear her cousin relished being set apart. Isolde hoped the peace would last a few more hours, until Kara's father came to take her home.

"Kara, tell me about this new priest. You haven't mentioned him before. Where is he from?" She pulled at a strand of kemp embedded in a knot of softer wool. When the thick fiber refused to yield, she reached for a fork and used one of the tines to work it free.

Kara shrugged. "No one knows. He came when we needed him, less than a moon after we buried Young Ned."

"I still have trouble believing that Young Ned has completed the cycle of his life." Isolde shook her head. The pain of losing a friend was still fresh. "He was young, far too young to fall prey to such a trivial illness."

"Who can guess the Goddess's ways?"

Isolde narrowed her eyes. Those words came from someone else's lips, parroted by her cousin. "Does your priest say that often?"

She jerked at the question. "Aye, he does."

Hmmmmm… Isolde pondered the meaning of that. Such platitudes, from what she'd seen, came from those seeking to conceal the truth, to turn aside scrutiny.

Who was this priest, and why had he arrived just when he was most needed?

Should she accept this as indication that the Goddess was indeed watching over them all? Was merely asking that question a betrayal of her faith?

Nay, seeking the truth was never wrong. What was wrong was the failure to recognize truth once it was uncovered. Could she keep an open mind, when she already disliked this priest? How could she dislike him, when she had not yet met him?

"You should meet him."

She gaped at her cousin, who might have read her mind. Kara had shown indications of Power, but none in that direction. So far. Had Isolde underestimated her?

"He really is wise. He is drawing followers from all the villages around ours to his ceremonies. You should come, too."

"Do those villages not have their own priests or priestesses to lead them?"

"They do, but our priest is better. Even their leaders come to our rituals and celebrations. He travels to invite them to worship with us. I'm surprised he hasn't yet been here to see you."

Isolde controlled a flinch. That smacked of pride. "Do you think the Goddess cares by what person we are led in our ceremonies?"

"Why should She not? If I feel better in the care of one priest than another, should I not seek out that priest?"

Isolde frowned. She liked this not at all, this talk of preferring one leader over another. All were equal in the circle raising Power, or should be. The importance in any celebration lay in the deities, the Goddess and the God, not the person handling the tools. What kind of priest would pervert holy worship into his personal following?

Kara was young and clearly smitten with the man. Isolde was older and wiser. To criticize him would entrench her cousin's feelings and widen the gulf stretching between them. Even being as diplomatic as Isolde could be, 'twas likely her days of instructing Kara would soon come to a close.

She framed her reply carefully. "There should be no competition for attendance at ceremonies. The Goddess and the God are present at the ceremony of a single worshiper as much as when an entire village assembles for a ritual."

"I will not argue theology with you, Cousin Isolde. I only know what my heart tells me."

"Then mayhap your heart has been deceived."

A deep voice joined their conversation. "And mayhap you are jealous that Harmon has not sought you out, to invite you to join us." Kara's father Cedd stepped across the threshold.

Isolde considered her snort to be sufficient response.

"Or mayhap you need to find a man, to swive you out of your anger at the world."

"And mayhap you overstay your welcome." Dear Goddess, the conceit of the man! What made him think he could advise her on anything?

"I've piled the goods I owe you for this season on the bench in the shade, with the ram tethered beside. He's already scented your ewes and is eager to mount them, pawing at the ground. You might want to let him at them before he chews through the rope. I don't take kindly to having my best stock running free. Take a lesson from your ewes, and find your own lusty ram." He smirked as he hefted Kara's chest to his shoulder and shepherded his daughter out the door. "May the Goddess bless you with a desirable union before we meet again."

"And may the Goddess bless you," Isolde responded aloud, adding in a mutter, "with a civil tongue and regard for your own affairs. Pompous meddler." She indulged her anger, slapping the fork down upon the table with a sharp crack.

A few deep breaths restored her equanimity.

You give others the power to hurt you. Do not permit them to upset your life.

She liked her life as it was, well-ordered and predictable. Why then did Cedd's words rankle?

Cedd drove off with Kara beside him in the cart. Isolde waited until they were out of sight before she crossed the yard to deal with the goods he'd left. The two fresh hams and a small wheel of herbed cheese filled a shelf in Isolde's larder. Cedd spoke the truth about the ram's eagerness. It took her but a moment to get his prized ram into the pen behind the dairy, where the sturdy beast was even now courting the ewes.

She ran a hand over her face. Uncle Cedd was unpredictable, which is why she hadn't come right out and told him his daughter was a lazy bully unworthy of the abilities the Goddess had given her. He might refuse to believe it, but he was just as likely to beat Kara half to death. Or anything in between.

The village gossips claimed his wife Oda had been helped out of the stable loft, that her fall was no accident. Isolde didn't wish to think ill of anyone without proof, but Cedd made no bones about refusing to share his bed with a cripple. Oda cringed and scuttled to do his bidding, no matter how menial the task, despite the two wenches he'd hired to keep their house.

Isolde lowered her weary body into the armchair by the fire. Three families left to fetch their daughters home, and then she'd be alone through the next full moon. At least the remaining girls got along with one another. No need to watch them like a hawk, ready to intervene or head off an unpleasant confrontation.

Fine. She expected her remaining students to leave on the morrow. What she needed this afternoon was a trip to gather herbs. Having taught all of her charges herbal lore over the last weeks, her stores were low. High summer was the best time to replenish her stock, while the plants were abundant and had not yet gone to seed.

In minutes she had checked the progress of the bread, gathered her scissors and a basket, donned sturdy boots, and taken the path into the woods.

The search for herbs soon permitted the cool, serene forest to work its magick on her. She paused with her task barely begun, taking the time to admire the play of sunlight on the leaves over her head, and how the rich loam gave under her feet.

The blessings of her valley were many. Game abounded here beneath the leafy canopy. The dark soil along the river supported diverse crops. A wide variety of herbs and sweet springs made Isolde's mage work a simple matter, but a few steps from her door, she could gather whatever she desired.

A wren serenaded her from a nearby thicket, while a pair of finches followed her through the woods, swooping low in response to her whistled greeting.

Her basket was half-filled by the time the finches deserted her with raucous warnings. All around her, the woodland creatures disappeared or fell silent. Rustling along the path ahead sounded clearly in the resulting silence. The skin prickled on the back of her neck.

Stepping off the path, she leaned against a tree and wrapped a quick concealment spell about herself. Whoever approached would find their eyes slid aside should they try to look directly at her.

A man's baritone rang through the forest.

"And so he dove into the bay,

Bent on saving his love so gay

With a hey-nonny-ho

And a hey-nonny-hey."

'Twas a pleasant voice but the singer lacked talent. No bandit or thief he, to announce his presence so boldly with song.

Still, instinct kept her in her place, hugging the shadowed bole of the great oak. A woman alone, even a gifted mage, must needs take precautions. The Goddess helps those who help themselves. As she'd drilled into her apprentices, they must ask Her aid, not expect Her to accomplish their tasks for them.

He rounded a curve in the path. Garbed in brown and green hues of leather and wool, he was set for traveling. Several pouches and a long knife depended from his belt. He walked with a staff and carried a pack. A light cloak hung over one broad shoulder. Heavy linen braes covered his legs. Dappled sunlight played across his golden hair and the planes of his face.

Isolde couldn't suppress a gasp.

'Twas the man from her visions.

He stopped in mid-verse and turned to stare directly at her. His bright eyes, alive with good humor, focused on hers.

She felt as if she were falling freely, into his soul. Her head spun. The earth, moments before a solid and stable support, shifted beneath her feet.

His aura flared a brilliant gold, indicating the strength of his desire. Desire for her. His eyes promised her intense delight, should she share his bed.

The visions had not led her astray.

As it had before, her body readied for him, loosening and softening in preparation for his touch. She licked her lips and he followed the motion with his gaze. Without volition, she found herself taking a step toward him, away from the shelter of the oak.

He held out a hand and she took it.

His clasp was strong and sure, an anchor for the maelstrom of her senses.

Desire flooded through her at his touch. Reality proved much more intense than her visions.

Their clasped hands became a portal, through which emotions and sensations poured into her. His was a compelling, vital, male presence, bringing her almost to tears with longing.

Longing for what? She struggled to maintain her identity under the onslaught of feelings that cascaded from him, flowing through the link of their hands.

Desire.

Nay, well beyond desire, 'twas lust he gave off in a glow brighter than sunshine.

He pulled her close, into his embrace, and bent his head. He made a noise that was half-growl, half-purr as their lips touched.

Satisfaction.

She arched into his embrace, seeking greater contact with him, pressing her body against his. Her softness molded around the hard muscles of his chest and arms.

The thrust of his tongue parted the seam of her lips, demanding and receiving entrance. She opened to him fully, and felt the touch of his mind, in much the same way his flesh pressed against hers.

Possession.

Without being summoned, the presence of the earth mother rose up through her feet, swirling across her skin and wrapping around both of them. An answering force emanated from his depths, a wild and turbulent magick the nature of which she didn't recognize. The two forces met in their kiss, in the press of their hands, and in the beating of their hearts.

Power.

Her laces fairly undid themselves and her gown and shift fell to the ground. She didn't know what happened to his cloak, woolen tunic and well-wrought braes. One moment the garments encased his form and the next, his skin was naked and hot against hers.

He moved to lay her down. Soft grass cushioned her back. She wrapped her arms around him, although she could not possibly hold him any closer.

This was too swift an onslaught, too great a gift for her to resist. She didn't protest when he lifted her hips, interrupting the plundering of her mouth, to move lower. The first time he plunged his tongue into her hot, dripping cleft, she cried out and anchored her fingers in his hair.

He growled again, with his mouth pressed firmly against her. The vibration rumbled deep into her womb.

The penetration of his tongue, so much like the memory of his thick, hard cock filling her, was sheer ecstasy. He supported her hips with his large, hot hands, stroking the flat of his tongue across her sensitive folds, only to thrust the tip home again.

Home.

Sweet Goddess, it felt like she was coming home. Or mayhap he was the one coming home, to her, as he continued to lap up her juices and stab at her in an increasing tempo.

Through it all threaded the magick. Their two Powers mated as well, the joining forming something new and exquisite. Each touch, of his tongue or hands, filled her nigh to bursting with a new and unfamiliar Power.

She was dimly aware of him parting her cheeks to stroke her with one fingertip, *there*, where she'd never guessed she could be so sensitive—or enjoy a touch so much. His finger began a circling motion that drove her to buck her hips, she couldn't tell whether to increase the pressure of his mouth or his finger. Each movement only served to winch her tension to new heights.

He began timing the thrust of his tongue with the stroke of his finger, and sensation overwhelmed her. The heady rush of her climax meshed with a crescendo of Power and she fell into darkness.

She opened her eyes to find herself alone, standing as she had been in the shadow of the tree. Only birdsong filled the clearing. The expanse of grass before her waved whole and undisturbed by any passage.

Exhausted and confused, she sank to her knees. She raised a hand and found her lips slightly swollen. What had just happened? Had she experienced a waking vision? Her skin still tingled, all the way to her toes. She was certain her chest was flushed, and knew her nipples were taut and sore. Searching inside herself, she found traces of an unfamiliar power, seething in the recesses of her belly. Had she not known better, she would have said that she had just joined her body with that of a man who wasn't present, who might be many leagues distant.

Dear Goddess, was such a thing possible?

Chapter Three

Harmon fell back against his pallet. The fever that had plagued him for a day and a night had finally broken, and with such a dream! In his experience, fever-dreams were made of terror and sweat, frightening in their intensity, but not this one. Nay, this one was made of lust and sweat, a sweet dream that kept the darkness at bay. The slick heat of it lingered on his skin, cooling rapidly to a damp chill. After tossing and turning for hours in the throes of illness, he lay quietly and at peace.

The woman he'd scried in his mug had come to him in his dream, and the ramifications of that occupied his now-clear thoughts. The task he'd traveled far to accomplish looked to be both easier and more difficult than he'd expected. But what exactly was the task set before him?

In this dream, his Power had meshed with hers, becoming something different, something other than his or hers—mayhap more powerful than his alone? Even now, remnants of that mingled magick lingered within him, lighting the shadowed recesses of his soul. While he reveled in the sensation, he reminded himself not to grow accustomed to it. Darkness would close in again all too soon.

What remained to be seen was whether physical joining made them both stronger, or if it bled off her might, weakening her to feed him. He'd not heard or read of this, but either seemed possible. Would the increase in his Power be limited by their sexual endurance, or by her death?

Was this blending of their magicks only possible through physical joining, or could he avail himself of her Power through touch alone? Mayhap the dream showing him the way had required coupling because of the distance between them.

There was only one way to find out. He grinned, deciding the research would prove enjoyable, more enjoyable than any he'd undertaken so far. This task did not involve musty powders and complicated preparations —unless he wanted to give the Goddess a helping hand.

* * * * *

Black Isolde reveled in the restored quiet of her home. The last three girls had finished their embroidery late in the night, and by noon the sisters Gerda and Inga had accompanied their father on the mounts he led, yawning and rubbing their eyes. Only Della remained, and Della had gone for a leisurely bath to the sheltered pool behind the cottage.

Isolde's solitude was broken only by the presence of the man in her visions and dreams. Although she had tried to set aside the memory of her disturbing waking dream in the woods, she was still aware of him in a way she'd never experienced. At odd moments she would feel as though he watched her, as though he lurked in the shadowed corners of the room or above, in the deserted loft.

Why did she regard him as a potential mate, when she knew nothing of him beyond his presence in her dreams and what she saw in the scrying bowl? Were she to be completely honest, her body's enthusiastic response to him was inexplicable—and disturbed her for that very reason. If there was aught ready to upset the order of her life, it was the arrival of a lover.

Thinking of him merely served to fuel the sexual need she felt whenever she beheld his image. None of her visions gave any indication of a time or a place for his arrival. Did he draw near, even now? Might he arrive in her village soon, mayhap today?

Her concern over her cousin's infatuation with the priest Harmon evaporated in Isolde's need to see again the object of her infatuation. No one now was likely to disturb her. She felt no fatigue, had no need for a nap to find him in a dream. The scrying bowl would serve.

Quickly she gathered her candles, the copper bowl, a pitcher of water, and a beaker of the fragrant oils she preferred to view.

"Show to me oh water clear

The one destined to hold me near

A lover who will share my time

And travels now to become mine

In visions past he hunts for me

From leagues away his face I see

As wild mint doth spread and grow

So he seeks his seed to sow

Dear Goddess, bring my love to me

As I will so mote it be."

With the final words, she poured the oil carefully down one side of the bowl, inhaling the fragrant aromas of mint and rosemary. The oil spread evenly across the water, barely disturbing the surface as it formed a smooth layer.

Leaning in close, she let her breath blow softly across the bowl. The shimmer of the oil fogged for a moment, then cleared, revealing a scene unlike any she'd scried before.

Wordless chanting filled her head, thrumming in her ears, more a vibration than a sound. A large figure in a dark robe swayed back and forth before an altar in a wooded clearing. A circle of robed figures moved in closer to him, slowly stepping in time with their chant.

The altar bore the items she was accustomed to seeing, the familiar chalice, cauldron, wand and candles, but tethered next to it was something unusual.

A young goat?

A chill ran through her. The thought of taking a life, any life, for a ritual honoring the Goddess was anathema.

She had asked to see her lover. Was he here, among those gathered as witnesses to the dark rites?

The vision lasted but a moment, no longer than it took for her to fully comprehend the scene. When she drew in her next breath, the oil fogged again. When the surface cleared, nothing remained but the reflection of the ceiling above her and the dancing light of the candles.

Clearly the Goddess had more important news for her than the location of her lover. Somewhere nearby, there was a practitioner of the dark arts.

The question was, what should she do with this knowledge? She was a mage alone, untrained in battles of magickal wills, unready for such a task. Who could counsel her?

Her mentor had passed on into the Light a year ago. Lyse, the wise woman who aided with births and deaths, was gone for the summer, in the south visiting her sons.

Her own family was out of the question, Cedd being the most sensible of them, and his recent behavior had given no indication that he would be helpful. Insulting him hadn't helped.

On top of that, she had to wonder if Kara was somehow involved with what she'd seen. She'd often worried that without intervention, her cousin was destined to become a dark mage, and had yet to find a way to set Kara's feet firmly on the proper path.

The images in the scrying bowl troubled her all through her household chores. Not even Della's pleasant chatter could lighten her mood. The unsettled feeling in the pit of her stomach remained through the afternoon. Finally, she determined to do something about her nervous state before it ruined her night's sleep as well.

The runes chimed a melodious welcome when she lifted the leather bag from the shelf. The set, carved of bone and colored with a dye worn pale with use, had belonged to her grandmother, and her grandmother before her.

Polishing a place on the table with a wipe of a cloth, Isolde concentrated on clearing her mind as easily. Only her question remained forefront in her mind.

Who was the practitioner of the dark arts?

Since the Goddess had given her this revelation, how might she best discharge her duty? Was she to unmask the mage and let the dark priest's adherents know just what sort of person they followed?

She could not believe that any would gladly choose to follow a path into darkness.

Surely she would not be asked to do more. She never claimed to have much Power, just a firm appreciation for the Goddess's blessings and the way the world—and its people—worked.

So why would the Goddess show her this vision? Was it something that was, something that would be, or something that might be?

Perhaps the runes held the answers she sought.

She picked through the flat scales of bone, reciting their names as she touched each glyph.

Truth.

Health.

Seeking.

The soft click of the stones in her cupped hands was comforting, a connection with her foremothers. Not that she needed that sense of belonging, given that she lived surrounded by items her ancestors had used and cherished. Even the cave in the hillside above her cottage held reminders. Carved figures and worn ledges abounded in its shadowed corners, and the fires she kindled there rested atop layers of ash older than she could imagine.

With a flick of her wrist, she cast the stones across the soft leather pad. They came to rest in a familiar pattern.

Her breath caught in a gasp.

Death.

Danger.

Destruction.

Surrounding her young, irritating cousin.

Dear Goddess, this was more serious than she'd suspected. What part would she play in this drama?

She snatched up the bones and shook them again, concentrating on how she might fit into the scenario revealed by her first roll. Another toss, this one made with her other hand.

Destiny.

Eternity.

Love.

Surrounding herself.

Surviving this trial, passing the test the Goddess had set before her, would result in a love beyond any she could imagine.

Now *that* was worth fighting for.

Isolde swept the stones together. As she poured them back into the pouch, they chimed soft whispers of destiny and fate.

Somehow, her future was entwined with her cousin's.

* * * * *

Isolde saw them both in dreams that night, the beautiful forest man and her cousin. Confusing images swept her along. First she bobbed on calm water alone in a small boat, before she hurtled helplessly through cascading rapids.

Friends and family danced with her former students on the banks, laughing and calling out to her to join them.

Her dream man awaited her, where the water pooled and swirled before rushing headlong over a waterfall. He was dressed for travel, as she had seen him earlier. The current took her to him safely, arrowing the craft to the ledge where he stood.

His band of forest creatures gathered there as well, peering from branches overhead and through bracken around his feet. He took her hands and lifted her effortlessly from the boat to join him.

Their clothing evaporated.

From this close vantage point, she admired his sweeping muscles and bronzed torso. His hand was warm in hers.

His eyes bored into hers. "Black Isolde."

His deep voice sent goose bumps feathering across her skin. His gaze dropped lower, to where her nipples puckered into tight peaks. He licked his lips and she shivered again. He had every appearance of devouring her on the spot.

"I have waited too long for you." His grip tightened and he pulled her close. Heat emanated from his body, warming her.

She fell away from him, out of his grasp, dismayed as her arms thickened and her legs grew shorter. Now he wore a dark hooded cloak and held a tether, attached to the halter on the cow she'd become. He led her through the woods, to a clearing with a stone altar in the center. The altar held only a long, sharp knife.

She awakened with a jolt, covered in sweat, her heart pounding in her chest.

Chapter Four

Isolde set aside her broom and took a moment to stretch her aching back. With all the help she'd had from her students, she'd grown soft and forgotten how much work keeping her house really entailed. However, an aching back was a small price to pay for a respite from her worries over the change in her dreams. Seeking out dirt and dust was cathartic, and it cleared her mind for the decision she had to make. Where was that flash of insight she'd mentioned to Kara? Where was her Breakthrough when she needed it?

Only Della remained. There was little to do before she was ready to leave but pack some of her gowns and linens in chests for travel. She was bound directly to her bridegroom's manor.

Isolde climbed to the loft. No one had troubled to throw open the tiny window in the eaves. She stopped with one foot still on the top rung, staring into the gloom. A faint glow surrounded the neatly folded garments that lay stacked by the chest.

The glow of magick.

She stepped fully into the loft before she sank to the rough planks of the floor. One deep breath and one complete exhalation centered her, and she opened her mage sight.

The gowns and kirtles and belts blazed like beacons in the dimness, the crackling light of a strong spell shining forth. Between them were dark layers of the fine linens, unmarred by magick. The spell affected only the garments, dancing along the lines of the seams and the detailed embroidery, promising disaster to come.

Kara had taken her revenge.

Isolde absently chewed on her thumb while she examined the threads of the spell. In general, the mage who wrought the spell must undo it, but latent spells — not yet in effect — were an exception. This had to be but a simple spell of dispersal, to be triggered at a later time.

The pattern was more sophisticated than she'd expected of Kara's youth and inexperience. Unless, Goddess forbid, this was not the first time Kara had woven spells of destruction. No matter. Something must be done about Kara, but now, before the garments were packed and while no one else learned of it, she had to dismantle this spell.

Reaching out with her mage-awareness, Isolde followed the glittering lines through their dance. Once she lost control of the pattern but soon picked it up again. A few more twists and turns and she saw the whole.

The wicked wench had spun a spell of disintegration, to be triggered by buoyant emotion in the wearer. In her time of greatest happiness, Della's garments, whatever she wore from the skin out, would part at the seams and reveal her in her entirety.

Isolde's anger grew as she untangled the threads of magick, teasing apart the knots until the whole evaporated in a flash of bright light. Tension she hadn't realized she'd built up fled from her back and neck and she slumped against the top of the ladder.

Magick was not meant to be abused in such a fashion.

Kara had some explaining to do, and she would do it in front of her father, before Isolde terminated her apprenticeship. She refused to train a dark mage.

"Mistress?" Della's soft voice floated up from the room below. "Let me take care of that. You have done enough, giving Gerda and Inge a hand with their things. My box is far too large for you. Leave it for Hugo. His back is strong."

Isolde summoned the strength to sit up straight and readied herself to face her favorite student. "We should at least pack the chest for him. I doubt you want anyone else to handle those delicate fabrics and beautiful embroidery."

"Aye, Hugo has a workman's hands, with fingers rough as teasels. I accept your help, and gladly, for you are the reason they are so beautiful." Her shining face came into view as she climbed the ladder.

Isolde glanced back to be sure the garments were no longer broadcasting signs of magick, then chided herself. Down-to-earth, solid Della wouldn't recognize a spell if it jumped up and down in front of her.

Della stepped off the ladder and crouched beside Isolde. "When I first came to you, I had no idea of what could be done with a simple needle and thread. You have made me a bride worthy of a lord. For that, I can never repay you."

"Your father's goods, as agreed upon, will be adequate. Teaching you has been a pleasure, Della." Isolde reached out to stroke her hair. "You have given me several embroidered towels. I will treasure them, and think fondly of you whenever I see them."

"Oh, I will miss you. And the other girls. Even Kara, I must confess, although she would not believe me if she heard me say it. I do consider her a friend, despite her arguments and prickly nature."

"Your willingness to overlook her attitude does you credit. I know you will be a good lady to your lord husband, and care for his people and lands as he wishes. Of all my students, I count you among the best." Isolde smiled and drew the girl—nay, the young woman, for she would be a wife and mayhap a mother by the following year—into a hug. She knew she would never let Della know how close she had come to social ruin, at the hands of her "friend".

* * * * *

Isolde watched the cart disappear around the curve of the hillside. A quick glance at the sun, still well above the horizon, told her she had just enough daylight left to make the trek to

Cedd's holding. Unsure of what her uncle's hospitality would be after she lectured and discharged Kara, she knew she would be welcomed at her friend's home nearby. Lyse was visiting her son, but the couple hired to look after the sheep and chickens would be pleased for the company.

Pausing only long enough to wrap up a chunk of bread and a slice of cheese, she set off. Her path soon took her off the road and through the meadows skirting the forest.

Cedd's holding lay on the banks of the river, well above his village. If she wished to get there before dark, she had to hurry, and the shortest route took her not by the winding road between the two villages but straight across the countryside. Without a mount or a cart to hinder her, she clambered over fences and splashed through streams. Damp feet were a small price to pay for the opportunity to unburden herself of Kara as soon as possible.

She'd misjudged the time. Dusk fell as she reached the meadows beyond the forest. The waxing moon, not much more than a quarter and hanging low in the sky, was of little help. Had she not trodden this path so many times before, she would have quickly lost her way.

Hedgerows and copses gave way to low walls of stone as the path wound around the final hillock above Cedd's village. She paused outside her uncle's gate.

Below her in the village, the folk had gathered in the square. A large fire had been lit in the marketplace between the well and the tavern. A tall man faced them, his back to the flames. Long before she could hear his voice, Isolde knew him, by his confident stride and the way he tilted his head when making a point.

The priest, the man Cedd called Harmon.

Her dream lover.

She knew where to find her uncle, for Cedd would consider no such gathering to be complete without him. The square was hidden by buildings as Isolde wended her way down into the village proper. The glow of the fire lit the sky, almost obscuring the stars.

She hung back among the buildings, hidden in the shadows below the eaves. No matter. Everyone in the village, whether gathered in the square or still in their homes, heard him clearly. He had one of those rich, deep voices that carried like a bell.

"My friends and neighbors, I have recovered from the sickness that took me from you for several days. Many of you brought me food and drink to ease my rest, and tonight I wish to repay you for all of your kindnesses, both past and present. When I arrived here several moons ago, a wandering pilgrim in the service of the Lord and Lady, you offered me a place in your midst. Nowhere else have I found such generosity, for all of you have opened your hearts and your homes to me."

He paused and surveyed the crowd. Isolde felt more than saw his gaze travel over the assemblage, reaching even to where she stood.

"I ask you all to join me in the humble repast that my housekeeper and I have prepared for you. My humble door is always open to you, but tonight you all may visit at once."

A ripple of laughter ran through the gathering. Isolde knew how small Young Ned's cottage was, and surmised Harmon had taken it over. That made sense, for Young Ned was the last of his family.

She followed the shuffling, chattering families as they made their way to Young Ned's — now Harmon's — cottage. The feast was no surprise, for most bore bowls or plates and spoons they'd brought with them. 'Twas good the weather was fine, for there was little room for more than half a dozen people at a time to walk in the front door, pause by the trestle table long enough to load those plates and bowls, and file out the back door into the garden.

From there they dispersed, some remaining in the adjoining yards, others returning to the square, where they perched on benches dragged from the neighboring houses. Those leaving the tiny cottage carried heaping servings of ham, cheese, roast venison, cooked greens, fresh bread, and sweets. The mingled aromas made Isolde aware of her hunger, that she still carried her bread and cheese. She had not eaten since late morning.

The villagers greeted her warmly, for aside from having family there, she was a frequent visitor. Several wives of the more prosperous merchants, as well as the lord's wife and eldest daughter, had spent at least a season studying with her. During Young Ned's final illness, she had often brought poultices and infusions for him.

"Ho, Black Isolde, did word of the feast travel all the way through the woods to you?" Goody Mags called out from the other side of the well. "Where's yer bowl?"

"My niece has no need to bring anything with her, I can supply whatever she needs," Cedd retorted, with a jerk of his head at Oda. Before Isolde could protest, his wife shoved her bowl and spoon into her hands and hobbled off up the hill, retracing Isolde's steps to their holding.

Cedd smiled and nodded at his neighbors as he pushed Isolde ahead of him. He told everyone, "Come now, we must show our neighboring mage the honor due her station." He drew over an older woman Isolde hadn't seen before.

"Isolde, may I present Hurna. You have met Hector, Lord Raymond's steward, have you not? Hector is married to Hurna's sister. She is visiting from the north shore. Hurna, this is my niece, Black Isolde. You may have heard us speak of her. She is training my daughter Kara to master her massive talents."

The way Hurna refused to meet her eyes grated on Isolde. Why did her uncle persist in puffing up her importance? She made an extra effort to put the woman at ease with her response. "'Tis pleasant to have you visit us here, Hurna. Was your journey uneventful?"

"Aye, mistress." More words were clearly beyond her.

"I hope you enjoy your stay. Although my cottage lies outside Lord Raymond's demesne and I have not met him myself, I've heard only good things of his hospitality."

Eyes wide, Hurna kept bobbing up and down in a sort of half-curtsy as she backed away.

Cedd wore a satisfied smirk. He lowered his voice and leaned close. "I did not expect to see you again so soon. Have you come to meet our priest? Look elsewhere for that swiving you need, though. I've chosen him for my Kara."

She edged away and glanced sideways at him. "Uncle, has he agreed? How fortunate for you that the world falls in so neatly with your plans." Isolde swallowed the sharper words that rose to her lips. "Isn't Kara a bit young to be thinking of marriage?"

"Oda," he paused to spit on the ground, "was only a year older when we wed."

"But you were younger as well, were you not?"

He scowled. "You're paid, and paid well, to teach my Kara to use her gifts, not interfere with my affairs. I didn't ask your advice."

"I would not presume to tell you what to do." Isolde inclined her head. She was unwilling to start an argument during a communal celebration. Cedd would be distressed enough when she terminated Kara's apprenticeship. She allowed herself a smile at the thought of his reaction.

"Your village is fortunate to find a replacement for Young Ned so soon after his passing."

"Aye, we are blessed. One cannot know the ways of the Goddess."

Isolde eyed the crowd. Had they all adopted the stock phrases of this Harmon? He must be a very powerful mage, to have cast a spell over them all. If so, she must count herself among those he'd ensorcelled, for her vivid waking dreams of him indicated she had been firmly caught in his snare. She blushed at the thought that she might not be the only one to experience such visions of him. Then again, she was the only mage she knew of in the area. The only other mage, she corrected herself, now that Harmon had come.

The line shuffled closer to his cottage.

"I will be pleased to introduce you. It is fitting, since you are my kin." Cedd took her elbow in a proprietary grip. Isolde felt the urge to pull away but resisted. It cost her little to let him have his moment of pride.

Harmon stood just inside the doorway. As each guest stepped across the threshold, he greeted them with a kind word, bending his head down to better hear those who spoke softly. Isolde liked the way he held their hands while they spoke, looking into their eyes and focusing his whole attention on them as if they were the most important person in the world.

Mayhap she'd been wrong in her negative speculations about him. Mayhap he was simply a man with a good heart, one who appreciated those around him and treated them well.

Cedd pushed her forward, crowding beside her in the doorway. "Master Harmon, this is my niece, Black Isolde. I know you have heard me speak of her. She is the mage in the neighboring valley, the woman who is instructing Kara in the use of her Power."

His hand was warm as it enveloped hers in a firm clasp. The slight tingle she'd felt when he touched her in her dreams feathered across her skin. To her amazement, there was no recognition in his warm gaze. Only courtesy and curiosity.

She wondered if she'd been wrong. Was he fated to be her lover, as the scrying bowl had shown? Or was he the practitioner of the dark arts she'd seen?

Sweet Goddess, he couldn't be both!

Could he?

"Isolde. I have indeed heard much of you."

His voice was the rich baritone she'd heard singing in her forest vision. The memory of his soft whispers in her ear tightened her nipples and brought a soft ache to her belly. How could he not have shared in that vision? How could he touch her without showing any reaction? She couldn't stop the tremble of her hand in his. Never before had she experienced a vision involving another mage without their awareness of it.

He continued to speak, polite interest evident in his smile but nothing more. "Welcome to my humble home, and please help yourself to refreshment. I did not expect you, but one more celebrant is no burden. As you can see, there is plenty for everyone. Your uncle and his neighbors have built a reputation for generosity and hospitality, one I can only hope to uphold." He leaned a little closer. "I will try to find a moment to speak with you privately at some point, for a mage-to-mage discussion, if you will. If not this evening, then mayhap on the morrow? Will I find you at your uncle's home?"

Cedd patted her shoulder. "Oh, aye, she'll find a welcome bed in the loft. 'Tis too late for her to return home tonight."

At another time, Isolde might have bridled under her uncle's management of her affairs, but 'twas a good thing he'd answered for her. She had trouble organizing her thoughts and her dry mouth was incapable of speech.

"Then until we meet again, Mage Isolde." With a squeeze of her hand, Harmon stepped back and gestured for them to enter.

She felt his hand on hers long after he'd released her. The tingle of his Power remained, while she allowed one of the village women to load her plate, and even after Cedd found room for the three of them on a vacant bench.

As those she knew well came to greet her and exchange news with her uncle, for once, she remained quite content to let her uncle provide her responses, nodding and making noncommittal sounds when it seemed appropriate. She duly ate and drank. Although she could see the quality of the meat and the care that had gone into preparing every dish, she could not appreciate the flavors. Her awareness was centered on *him*, for his voice carried clearly and his tall form was readily recognizable in the crowded marketplace.

He moved easily among his guests, making sure each had a sufficient portion and no mug languished empty for long.

Chapter Five

"Aye, Goody Mags, there's still plenty of raisin cake. Go help yourself. Unless you'd like someone to fetch it?" He began to raise his hand, to catch the eye of one of the serving wenches.

Her gnarled hand stayed him. "Nah, she'd like to bring me a short ration. At my age, I take my pleasures where I can."

"Then go, and eat what you will. You might want to get there before Maryam's family." He watched her hobble across the square, waving her empty plate and calling out for the children to respect age and let her go first.

Her path took her in front of Isolde.

Harmon willed his heart to slow and struggled to keep his expression under control. The surge he'd felt when he took Isolde's hand had rocked him a bit. She commanded a greater amount of Power than he'd thought. She was also much more beautiful than he remembered from his dreams.

She sat before his cottage, between that windbag Cedd and a chattering Kara. Her head nodded and she ate, but he could tell her thoughts lay not with her companions or the food.

Goddess, what a woman!

Black Isolde. She was named well, with her coal-black tresses and large dark eyes. Some might consider her too tall and robust, but in her he saw the strength he needed. She looked to be a woman who could bring a caravan across the desert, lead troops to storm a castle, or wrestle a steer into submission.

.By the Green Man's beard, she would be a blessing to bed, and a pleasure to bleed Power from. It cost him a moment of concentration to will his cockstand to relax. He no longer feared draining her completely. She clearly had Power to spare. His mind reeled at what he might accomplish with her assistance.

Tonight was as good a night as any to test his theory.

If she proved able to increase his Power sufficiently, he would arrange for a ritual in a few days. The half-moon would serve, being a time of balance between light and dark. After all, 'twas balance he sought to restore to this part of the world.

Once that task was completed, he would wait and see what turned up for him next. He would be sorry to leave this place. In his welcome speech this eve he'd spoken the truth. Here he'd found an acceptance unrivalled elsewhere.

If only he could be other than he was. Too soon, he would feel the Call and move on. He must, before the darkness that dogged his travels caught up with him. He did not yet feel ready to face it, and he would not endanger these people who had shown him such acceptance and kindness.

He began to cross the square. His steps faltered and turned aside.

It had been years since he'd wooed a woman, well before his training began. He thought back to the youth he'd been so long ago, and how he had approached the object of his desire. Nay, 'twas no comparison between his situation then and now.

What might appeal to a mage, one unmarried and independent? He pondered this while he saw to the entertainment and enjoyment of his guests.

The trestle table in his cottage was nearly empty of food when Dan the miller's son went home and returned with his lute. Big Frieda fumbled in her voluminous skirts, found her pouch and drew out her pipes.

Soon the marketplace rang with a lively tune and the square filled with dancers. Harmon found himself close to his doorway, where Isolde still sat, bracketed by her uncle and cousin. She looked bored and less than pleased.

A guest, unhappy at his feast? Intolerable!

He strode over, took her hand and pulled her into the frolicking couples. She hung back for a moment before catching the beat and measuring her steps to his.

Aye, he'd been right. She matched him perfectly.

Surely there could be no other who looked him boldly in the eye, who reached out to grasp his hand with assurance whenever the simple dance called for it, who was always there and ready when the steps separated and brought them together again?

The lilting tune seduced her. He had little to do with it, merely watching as a gleam came into her eyes and her steps lightened. No need for a magickal nudge here or a slight mental push there. Before the first dance ended, she was bending to him like a flower to the sun. Her laughter enchanted him.

The dance was well on its way to seducing him as well.

That realization had a sobering effect. He couldn't afford entanglements, no matter how lovely or appealing. Nay, he needed to retain his distance. She was a tool to him, nothing more. He went where he was moved to go, where he was needed. A lone mage.

A lonely mage.

The thought sprang unbidden and he hastily shoved it aside. All great callings required sacrifice. Early on, he had gladly—nay, eagerly—surrendered any hope of the companionship and legacy of a family. The shadows he'd taken on had merely reinforced that decision. He no longer had a choice.

Kara spun by, giggling in the arms of the steward's son. He recalled his task and set about charming Black Isolde.

When the second dance ended with them both breathless and laughing, he tucked her under his arm. She fit snugly there, the perfect height to hold against him. He discovered by chance that, should he wish, it would take only a slight dip of his head to kiss her.

He did wish. Two swift steps moved them into the shadows between his cottage and the next.

Her lips were soft beneath his, that much was clear to him before the surge of Power intruded. It felt much as before, in his vision, but 'twas much more compelling in the flesh. He shifted her into a complete embrace, cradling her to him while he explored the depths of her silken mouth. She was open wet heat, welcoming him with a whimper of pleasure.

He thrust his hands into her hair. His fingers wove into and around her locks, massaging her scalp to the beat of the pulse in his loins. She pressed closer, raising the heat as her hips thrust against his thigh.

"Do you feel it, Black Isolde?"

His mouth moved over hers in a fevered rush. He tasted her mouth, redolent of roasted meat and mulled cider. The scents mingled with her exquisite female essence, intoxicating him and causing his head to spin. He struggled to retain control — and failed.

Surrendering with a moan, he swung her into his arms and kicked open the door to the village stable, the only place they would be unlikely to find interruption. His experiment could not wait. He had to know. His cock demanded satisfaction as much as his curiosity did.

* * * * *

"Do you feel my Power?" He trailed kisses down her cheek and around her ear. His hand pushed back her hair. His breath tickled, teasing her skin with tingles of his Power mingled with delight. Oh, aye, she felt it, as well as she felt the scratch of the rough woolen blanket he'd tossed down onto the straw.

His teeth caught her earlobe in a quick nip, a sudden flash of pain, over almost before it began. And all the more potent for it. The pounding of her heart increased.

"I feel your Power, sweetling. It Calls to me, as it has Called to me every night of my life." She felt the words more than heard them. Wonder filled her, that he might have dreamt of her as she had of him. Another thought niggled at her, but she couldn't quite grasp it.

He paused to caress the skin just below her ear and the thought fled completely out of reach. Another place she'd never suspected of such sensitivity. She shuddered as his tongue lapped up her neck, sending waves of desire through her to bloom in her belly and urge her legs apart.

Just the very tip of his tongue, hot against her, traced the fine whorls of her ear. She shuddered again and moaned. "Aye, I feel it."

His hungry eyes were level with hers, his mouth returning to brush her lips. His hand anchored in her hair held her in place once more, this time forcing her to meet his eyes. All of her growing lust and stirring desire shone out at him, she was certain, for what she felt was mirrored in his devouring gaze.

He stared more deeply into her than he had in her vision. And the heat she felt now was more intense as well. She shifted her legs and found her nether lips slick with arousal.

She made a small sound. His cock swelled and pulsed, hot against her thigh. She'd known when he carried her up the short ladder into the loft, but when had they lost their clothing? "I do not understand what is happening between us."

'We are going to celebrate the best of all gifts. We are going to make love." His voice was muffled by her hair. His fingers moving over her skin sent shivers of delight through her, blurring her thoughts and making it hard to concentrate. Something was important, but she couldn't find it in her disordered thoughts. What did she have to remember?

He touched the underside of her breast and she gave up trying to figure out what she'd been worried about. Instead she pondered, how did a man know to seek out the sensitive places, as he did? She focused and wondered, are the same places as sensitive on him?

As he caressed her, she became bolder, returning each touch with one of her own. Her reward was the quickening of his pulse and the hitch in his breath when she found a sensitive spot.

His hot and eager mouth claimed the hard peak of one nipple, sucking and stroking across the tender, puckered flesh. She gasped as he nipped with his teeth, once again the pain fleeting and yet more arousing than she would have ever imagined. She gave up exploring his body when he pinched her other nipple with his fingers, wringing more cries from her throat. Shudders racked her when he reached down to stroke her labia, sliding her juices over sensitive skin and tracing the swollen folds. He found the tight nubbin there, and timed his strokes with gentle tugs on her nipples. Her womb contracted and her head thrashed back and forth.

As tension built within her, her magick rose as well. Although separated from the source of her wellspring, the earth, her Power found her, snaking up the walls, to twine about her limbs. The walls after all were made of wood, which has long conducted the earth's Power aloft to join with that of the sky. Just as her Power joined with Harmon's.

The air of the loft around them began to glow. She marveled, for she had never heard of such a thing. Kara's strong spell had gleamed in the darkness of the loft, but faintly and only right where the spell was centered. There was no spell at work here. A familiar tingling began in her toes, sweeping in a sweet rush through her, percolating out to her skin, where it met and meshed with his Power.

He lifted his head and waited to speak until she calmed enough to meet his eyes. "You are the embodiment of the Goddess in this moment, the giver of life, all that is beautiful in woman."

Holding her gaze, he slowly thrust two fingers up into her. She spread her legs to ease his way, trying not to force him by pushing her hips up to meet his slow penetration.

Progress stopped. His eyes widened. "You are intact?"

She pulled back, ducking her head and trying to close her legs. "Aye."

His other hand came up and pulled her chin up. "Do not hide. There is nothing shameful. I just don't understand. You are a woman grown, a desirable beauty who responds to me as no other has, yet…"

Shoving aside her instinct to conceal her virginal state, she boldly met his gaze. "My mentor required celibacy during my early training. By the time I was ready, the man I'd fancied in my youth had wed. Since then, I have not found anyone I wanted as much as the lover in my dreams. As much as I want you."

"Ah, sweet Isolde, you are truly precious. Intact, filled with Power—and mine." His lips covered hers in a devouring kiss. He invaded her mouth with the velvet heat of his tongue. "'Tis difficult to keep you to myself, not to parade you in the square right now and claim you before them all. What we share, they can never know."

Once more, his tongue caressed hers. He moved against her, sparking arrows of heat from her breasts to her womb. She felt branded by his passion.

Once more, his fingers moved inside her, while his thumb found and circled her nub.

Once more, the blending of their magicks pushed her higher. She rode the tide that heightened her emotion, heightened her sensitivity to his touch. He stroked the very walls of her womb. Every touch, every kiss, every movement of his hands and mouth, drove her higher and higher, into a thickening cloud of desire.

When the explosion of her climax struck, she fairly flew aloft, to float in a shining place redolent of bliss and light and Power.

The strength of the magick sweeping over them came near to overwhelming her senses. She cried out, whirling in a funnel of glittering light, held tight by Harmon's embrace and presence.

When she began to recover, it was to find he still held her in his arms. Their blended magicks still skirled through her, still sizzled along her skin. She opened her eyes and gazed at him in wonder.

"Aye, now I feel *our* Power." He smiled down at her. "We are connected. I know not how, I only know we are and have been."

She licked her lips, his eyes locked on the motion. His cock jumped against her thigh, sparking an answering contraction within her womb. She worked to focus her thoughts.

"And will we now make love? I want to feel you deep inside me. I want to know fulfillment as a woman."

"Your maidenhead is too precious to squander here, in a stable loft. You deserve better." His eyes glowed. "I will devise a ritual, and we shall offer our love to the Goddess."

What could a woman say to a mage claiming her virginity was worth so much? Disappointment rode the lingering swell of arousal, but she had no argument to challenge his plan. Indeed, why should she? No other had ever indicated she was such a prize. None but her dream lover.

She relaxed against him. His body was firm, hard where she was soft. They fit together as though made for each other. "How long have you had dreams of me?"

"They began with my training, but I've had them more often since I started the last leg of my journey to this village. I was drawn here, mayhap by you."

"How can that be?"

"There are bigger things at work here than we are aware of. I have a destiny, one I've been working toward all my life. You are part of that. I long thought you a vision, nothing more than imagined perfection." He cradled her closer. "Do not seek a cot at Cedd's. I would have you in my bed. 'Tis more comfortable than this pile of straw, and we can see just how far our magick will take us. I want to explore the many ways we can enjoy ourselves without piercing your barrier."

She began to laugh. "Cedd warned me that he plans to have you for Kara."

"That simple wench?" He shuddered. "I'd sooner wed a viper. Not that I shall ever wed."

"You sound serious. Why shall you not take a wife?"

"My destiny precludes it. I have long known such was not for me."

She stilled for a moment and something inside her went cold. But then, she'd asked the Goddess to bring her a lover, not a husband.

Be careful what you ask for.

Chapter Six

"You spent the night with *him*, with the man I specifically told you I had selected for Kara!" Cedd raged and ranted and stomped around his yard, until Isolde feared, nay, hoped, he would have a fit, fall senseless and not recover until long after she was safe at home. "Do you think so little of your obligations to family? What kind of example do you set for your cousin?"

Kara had fled back inside when Cedd first opened his mouth but was certainly listening at the door, if not watching through a window as well. Along with most of the village. Aye, her coupling with Harmon would be the topic of gossip for days, and her uncle's reaction for far longer than that.

Isolde spoke softly to get his attention, so softly he had to cease his tirade to hear her. She repeated, "Cedd, I did not come here for you to scream at me."

"I am not screaming!" His protest ended on a high note that some might term a shriek rather than a scream.

"Is aught awry here?" Harmon entered the yard, shutting the gate behind him with a decisive thud. "May I be of assistance?"

Cedd swallowed his rage as best he could, turning an interesting shade of purple. Isolde watched him carefully for signs of an impending fit. She had never liked him, but she didn't wish him lasting ill. With a final shake of his shoulders, he managed to restore calm to his countenance if not his heart.

"I do not think so. You have done enough." Cedd spat in the dirt at the mage's feet.

Harmon raised a brow.

Isolde did not want the details of where she'd spent the night and what she'd done recounted for the villagers' eyes and ears, so she hastened to speak. "I fear my uncle has taken exception to the dismissal of his daughter as my apprentice."

Both Cedd and Harmon gaped at her.

"She has shown an unpleasant and unacceptable tendency to use her gifts not only selfishly but to the detriment of those around her. She is argumentative and does not heed my instruction. I will not train an arrogant girl to become an even more arrogant mage, for that is where she is headed. Half-trained arrogance can only endanger all around her."

Her words fell into silence. She sensed tendrils of magick seeping out from the house, angry ribbons headed in her direction. She muttered a spell of protection, aware that beside her Harmon did the same.

Together they stepped forward, weaving together their magicks and forming a protective shield around the three of them. Without any need to communicate, they worked in tandem, partners who pushed the shield out, curving the edges to become a bowl, concentrating and reflecting the magickal attack back to its source.

The dark streamers curled back upon themselves and the loops disappeared into the house. Kara shrieked, a mingling of frustration and pain.

Isolde lowered her hands and turned to her uncle. His skin had paled and his eyes were wide with fright. "You see, Cedd, your daughter is a danger, to herself and to others. You have declared that you do not want me telling you what to do, so I'm afraid you will have to ask for my advice should you want it. After you apologize for the way you have treated me this morn."

Cedd looked in appeal to Harmon.

The village mage crossed his arms and widened his stance. "You shall have no aid from me, either, until you make a suitable apology to your niece."

Cedd's gaze swiveled helplessly from one to the other. His mouth moved silently a few times before he swallowed and managed to utter, "I am sorry I, er, screamed at you. I was, ah, mistaken."

Isolde barely had time to acknowledge this with a gracious nod before her uncle rushed on, "Now, please help me! I will never sleep soundly with the monster my daughter has become lying in the next room! Must I kill her?"

"No!" Harmon spoke sharply. "I will train her. Kara must learn that she is blessed and has an obligation to the Goddess for her gift. All Power carries a price. Humility is the coin with which she must pay for hers."

A deflated and contrite Cedd babbled his thanks as Harmon laid out the terms of Kara's new apprenticeship. One of those was that Cedd work with Harmon to find a husband for Kara. Someone with a strong will. Someone other than Harmon.

Walking away with him after the arrangements had been settled, Isolde said, "I wish you well. Curbing her will not be an easy task."

"This is not the first such for me, and surely not the last. Accomplishing difficult tasks is my payment for my gifts." He paused and raised a hand to stroke her hair. "In the morning light, your hair glows like a raven's wing."

She smiled at him. "And yours is pure spun gold."

His eyes heated. In a low voice, he told her, "I cannot wait to possess you completely. The full moon is too far away. I will craft a celebration around the half-moon. Return to me in four days' time and you will become fully mine. Come for dinner. Stay for me. I promise it will be even better than last night."

The rampant desire in his voice made her womb clench in impatience. Sweet Goddess, would she survive such bliss?

* * * * *

The half-moon hung above the clearing as Harmon lit a fire and prepared the altar. A warm breeze soughed through the trees. An occasional flying squirrel floated from tree to tree above, a pale blur against the dark sky, lit by the fire.

A fine night for a sacrifice.

Isolde waited in the shadows, where he'd left her beneath an oak tree. The others were also concealed throughout the woods, waiting to perform their task of witnessing this event.

How fortuitous that the moon was halfway through its cycle. A time of balance between light and dark. A time of giving and taking. A time to share Power, and a time to see just what this complete joining of theirs might bring. Isolde's pure, sweet magick was the perfect balance to the darkness that hovered always at the edge of his Power.

Would their combined might be sufficient for his purposes? Surely enough to deal with Kara, but would there be anything left over? Would he set out again on the road just as he had arrived, or would he have gained in strength, be better able to meet the greater challenge that lay ahead?

With difficulty, he cleared his mind of the turmoil that thoughts of the future now brought him, and began his own preparation for the evening.

Isolde was well-prepared, both by the herbs in their food and by his attentions. He had taken every opportunity to tease her with touches and caresses during their meal, stealing a kiss when the serving wench's back was turned or boldly brushing a taut nipple through her garments. Once he'd delved beneath her skirt to enter her wet cleft with one finger. He'd learned the thrill of possible discovery increased her arousal, a good sign for this night's work.

Her arousal had increased his. Mingled with the aromas of meat and bread came her rich scent, that of his woman, ready and willing. The meal stretched longer and longer as anticipation pushed his own excitement to fever pitch. He'd fought to control his unruly lust to avoid tossing her on the table and taking her in haste, impending ceremony be damned.

When he stripped to don his cloak for the start of the ceremony, his cock had sprung from his confining braes like a tree limb. Even thinking about how Isolde would react to having the villagers present, as witnesses to her first true coupling, made him stretch and throb with anticipation.

He moved through the purification rituals he had performed so many times in preparation of leading a ceremony. This time, he let each motion and action take him over, seeping into his soul. Never before had he felt so much one with what he was doing and a vital part of the world around him.

Soon he would be one with Isolde. Everything he'd done in the past four days had been leading up to this night. Nay, this night was the culmination of everything he'd done for his entire life. He knew that now. The rightness of each motion he made, the depth of conviction he felt with each utterance, all reinforced his commitment to Isolde as his mate and partner. Even the urgency he'd continually felt within him to move on, to seek new challenges, had stilled with the prospect of joining with Isolde.

The villagers knew what to do, what to chant, when to stop, and when to use the staves he'd handed around. Cedd had initially balked but soon came around to see the need for the part he'd play.

With one final glance to gauge the position of the moon, he sought out Isolde where she waited beneath the oak tree. In the darkness, he found her easily. She exuded her particular scent, drawing him like a moth to a flame. "Do you come to me freely?"

Within the shadows of her hooded cloak, he watched her lick her lips. "Aye."

"Do you trust me?"

"Aye."

He held out his hand. "Then come. Join with me."

She was totally in thrall to him and her desire for him. Her eyes were slightly glazed, with both wine and lust. He reached into the folds of fabric and found her soft skin. Running his hands up to her shoulders, he drew her to him for a quick embrace. She arched into him, pressing the fullness of her breasts to his chest. His cock jerked against her belly in eagerness and she whispered a soft moan. Exerting his iron control, he skimmed his hand down to take hers and lead her to the circle.

As he eased off her robe and laid her in front of the altar, she pulled him down for a scorching kiss. She took the lead, exploring his mouth with her tongue. His hips thrust in response, his body ready to claim her. Her hand encircled his cock with a light grip, holding him in place while she explored his mouth with her lips and tongue. His toes began to curl at the upwelling of Power that coursed through him.

That Power brought with it an intense awareness of her as she lay spread before him, a feast for his senses. He knew without looking the long lean line of her legs and how they would enfold around him, drawing his cock ever deeper, until his balls nestled against the cheeks of her ass. He knew the soft fullness of her breasts and how they would engorge with passion to fill his hands and tremble beneath his lips as he nipped and teased their hard peaks.

Sweet Goddess, she was made for him, and he for her. His cock jerked again and he almost spent himself there, right before the altar.

Too soon. He pulled away and rose to begin his part in the ritual. Shoving aside thoughts of driving his cock into her tight channel and pumping her full of his seed, he marshaled his control. Time enough later to enjoy her, and his response to her, fully. Tonight was for the Goddess, not to indulge his pleasure. Aye, the two would coincide, for the Goddess's gift to her people was the gift of love in all its expressions, but he could be selfish later.

He picked up the wand and signaled for the villagers to start. They came from among the trees with measured steps, pounding the ground with the heavy staves in unison as they walked. Once they were where he wanted them, he cast the circle, crossing from the altar to the four directions as he needed.

He closed the circle, with all of them inside. The chant began and the beat escalated, filling the clearing, vibrating up through his bare feet and into his heart as he stood before the altar. Illuminated by the fire, pale against the rich grass, Isolde's graceful, naked body was the epitome of womanhood at its best. He took a moment to enjoy the sight of her. Her breasts were high and firm. Her limbs stretched out to him in invitation. Her eyes grew wider as she watched the robed villagers. Each beat and syllable of the chant sent a tremor through her.

By the Green Man's beard, she was impressive. And she was his.

Desire thrummed ever stronger in his veins, for he, too, had partaken of the herbs and wine. He hoped he could hold out long enough to build the Power he needed. Getting a firm grip on his desire, he began to beguile Isolde.

With touches and strokes, he enticed her. By now he knew her most sensitive places, and he sought them with his hands and mouth. He caressed her with his lips and tongue, laving the sweat from her neck and the salt from her skin. She craned her head and offered him greater access.

When she would have returned the caresses, he pushed her hands away and whispered, "'Tis my turn. Simply enjoy." She whimpered before she dropped her hands to the grass at her side. He claimed her lips once more and she opened for him, surrendering to his attentions. Her taste was heady, but not enough to satisfy him. He wanted to taste all of her. She parted her legs and released the scent of her arousal. Her nether lips beckoned him to share his kisses.

He paused on his way to nibble and tease her nipples, moving from one to another. She arched her back in a silent demand for more. He complied, tonguing her erect buds into harder points. Her breath went from soft moans to hard pants. The rhythm of her cries became the rhythm of the pounding staves. The vibration reached deep into him and squeezed his balls, urging him to satisfy his lust. Lest he climax too soon, he moved on.

While plucking at her nipples and massaging the soft globes of her breasts, he bent to taste the soft flesh of her belly, and lower, until he suckled at the font of her womb. Her swollen pink lips glowed red in the firelight. Her pulse had taken on the rhythm of the staves, throbbing in time with his heart.

Tempted to drink his fill, he tamped down the urge and paid attention to the rising magick within him. To test her, he thrust deeply into her tight, wet channel with his tongue, until he met the fragile barrier of her maidenhead. The rich taste of her flooded his mouth and filled his head.

Sweet Lady, she was succulent. And ready. His Isolde. He rose to his knees and gazed into her eyes.

She cast a glance at the surrounding folk before she met his stare boldly. Her lips curved into a wanton and welcoming smile.

He grasped her hips, pulled her to him and paused, the head of his cock just touching her lips. A slight arching of his back moved his cock forward to part her labia. Poised there, on the brink, he felt more Power than he'd known could be raised, hovering just beyond his reach.

Now. Please. She mouthed the words.

He threw his head back, flinging the first words of the spell aloft.

"Sweet Goddess from whom all gifts flow

Bear witness as our passion grows.

To You who taught us love to make

I offer up her virgin state."

He entered her with a single thrust, breaking through her maidenhead and wringing a cry from her, of pain or pleasure or both, he couldn't tell.

Goddess, she was snug around him, squeezing like a tight fist, resisting his efforts to move. But move he did, aided by her wetness and her weight as he pulled out before thrusting home once more.

Home. Aye, he was home.

The pounding staves urged him onward, to thrust and withdraw, to thrust and withdraw. Four, five, six thrusts and his head spun as immense Power rose within him.

One more thrust and the ecstasy and their combined magick exploded from where they were joined to blossom in his chest. He roared as Isolde spasmed beneath him, the tight grip of her swift climax clenching ever tighter around him, wrenching him over the precipice with her.

When he could open his eyes, Isolde glowed beneath him with an unearthly radiance. Indeed, the whole clearing was brighter than noon, the firelight overwhelmed by their blazing combined Power.

The villagers' feet had stilled, although their staves kept up the beat. He wasn't sure if the pounding in his ears was his pulse, Isolde's heartbeat, or the staves on the earth. At his nod, Cedd brought a gagged and bound Kara forward, dropping her on the other side of the altar.

Harmon linked his fingers through Isolde's and closed his eyes. Isolde was a calm presence at his side, supporting and enhancing him. The way she was effortlessly in tune with him filled him with a sense of awe.

Power flowed around and through them, now as much hers as it was his, a thick pillow of it coalescing above the altar. Working together they shaped it with their wills. The resulting blanket drifted over to settle on the sputtering and thrashing form of Kara. At its touch, she stilled.

He struggled to order his thoughts and force the last part of the spell through his parched lips, ever aware of Isolde's silent and unwavering support.

"In moonlight here we set things right
Restore balance to your plan of Light
May the heartfelt will of these two mages

Put an end to Kara's selfish rages.
Gracious Lady hear our plea,
As we will, so mote it be."

He collapsed atop Isolde, heaving and spent as though he'd run a race. Her arms rose to surround him and hold him close.

For the first time in his life, the shadows he carried did not crowd in on him when he relaxed. He felt complete, no longer in danger, no longer walking the knife-edge of darkness.

* * * * *

Isolde shivered as Harmon rose and cold air washed over her. His skin also puckered in the chill breeze. On the inside, she was a husk, an empty shell, bereft of his possession of her and the heady rush of their combined might.

The sex hadn't been anything to scorn, either.

He wrapped the robe about her shoulders. "Here, sweetling. Warm up. 'Tis time to seek our bed."

"Ah, I like the sound of that." She rested her head on his shoulder. "A bed with a mattress, not straw or grass."

"Well, the mattress is filled with straw, but the ticking is tight enough to keep the poking bits in their place." Humor filled his voice.

She smiled. "Then you must join me in my bed soon. I sleep on feathers, not straw."

"Thank you, both of you." Cedd's voice held genuine gratitude. His expression only bordered on self-satisfied as they watched Oda cut the bonds and help her daughter to her feet.

Harmon shook his head. "You may be a bit premature, you know, for 'twill be some time before we see if she has indeed changed."

"Wait." Isolde stayed him with a raised hand. "Bring her here."

As Kara approached, eyeing them warily, she examined the girl, using her mage sight. Kara should have—would once have—glowed like the sun. She sucked in a breath of amazement. In the weak light of the remaining fire, Kara gave no indication of Power. None at all.

The Goddess is good. She had granted their plea, and more. She had taken back Kara's gift.

She nudged Harmon. "Look," she whispered. "Look at her as a mage."

His eyes narrowed, then widened. His mouth curved into a grin.

Isolde squeezed his hand. "How? I have never heard of such a thing."

"Nor have I, but who can guess the ways of the Goddess?" He raised his voice to its normal volume. "Cedd, we have been truly blessed. We sought to change Kara's tendency to arrogance, but the Goddess has done far more. Your daughter will never be a mage."

"What?" Kara shrieked with indignation. Shaking off her mother's support, she stood up straight and threw her shoulders back. Her eyes blazed with anger. Her hands moved and she muttered spell after spell. To no avail. No magick streamed from her extended fingers, nothing dire happened. She crumpled in sobs against her mother's shoulder.

Harmon pulled her father aside. Isolde watched as the realization sank in that Cedd could no longer boast of his powerful daughter. "I expect you will have your hands full with her for a bit, but you need fear her no longer." Relief warred briefly with disappointment. Isolde thought she detected Harmon giving him a slight mental push before relief won out. She'd never noticed that sort of thing before. Mayhap their link had been strengthened by the ritual?

"Thank you, Master Harmon, and you too, Mistress Isolde." Cedd hurried off after his family.

Isolde looked after him with delight. "That is the first time he's acknowledged my status. Is it possible he's truly changed?"

"After what I have seen, felt, and shared tonight, I believe anything is possible." Harmon pulled her close. "Now, whither were we bound?"

Chapter Seven

Isolde tongued Harmon's fingers as he studied her. She ran her tongue over and around them in a long caress. When she began a slow, pulsing suction, he groaned.

Much more of this and he'd explode, even before he was inside her. The very thought brought him closer to the edge.

In the days since his complete possession of her, they had done little but eat and sleep, and make love more times than he could count. She had the Power to bring him to an aching cockstand with little more than a look and a touch.

For years, he had believed her to be nothing more than a fantasy.

Fantasy had never tasted this good. Had he known she existed, was true flesh and blood, his perfect mate, would he have made the same choices?

Aye, he had to admit that he would have. His life's work had resulted in much less suffering than there would be had he pursued other studies. His small sufferings paled in comparison to what those dark mages he'd dispatched would have wreaked on the world at large.

To fight them effectively, he'd been forced to take on some of their shadows. For him to be the man he was, he could have made no other choices. Had he chosen to walk different paths, Isolde would not be his perfect mate.

But would she join him fully, join his life's work?

Isolde was a woman who could hold her own with him in every respect. A worthy companion and ally in the war he waged, a war they would fight side by side, and win battle after battle.

He opened his mind to her and felt every touch, both as he gave it and as she received it. He laved and nipped at the sensitive places he'd discovered, on her neck, behind her ears, below her shoulders. All of them became even more sensitive under his ministrations, almost pulsing with need. Each place fairly cried out for more attention as soon as he moved on to another area.

Their link was so intense he could even feel the ache within her womb, her eager desire to experience his attentions there. He wasn't ready to fulfill that desire, not yet. First, he would savor every drop of honey he could feel gathering in her cleft.

Suiting action to the thought, he slid down her curves until her fragrance surrounded him, making his mouth water. He would lave her soft lips and suckle that hot little nub until she screamed his name. He would drink in her juices and flavor as she came. There was a thirst in him that only she could quench.

His breath came fast and hot. He breathed in her smell even as she breathed in his. The dual sensations increased his ardor, drove his need to possess her in every way.

Through it all wove the dance of their Powers. He relished the shining purity of hers as it grew within and filled her, spilling over into him. His magick, heavy with shadows, swelled to meet it.

He bent his head and pressed his mouth to her cleft. She spread her legs, granting him greater access. He took every advantage, as was his nature, probing and tasting until she fisted her hands in his hair and cried out his name. When he'd finally slaked his immediate thirst at her fountain, he reared up on his knees.

She lay sprawled across his bed, the epitome of satiation.

"I used to be a little afraid of you." Her voice was drowsy.

"Truly?" He settled beside her, his hard cock nestled against her hip. The early sunlight brought out the sheen in her hair. He gathered up a handful and toyed with the raven locks. She shifted closer to him. Her little sigh of contentment made him smile. His Isolde was a wildcat in battle, but a kitten in his arms.

Her eyes remained closed. "I had a dream where I found you and I became a cow. You led me to an altar. I woke up before you sacrificed me."

"An interesting dream, and true."

Her eyes snapped open and her jaw dropped. "So it is! I never realized that. So you are not the dark mage I saw in the runes, either. Kara was."

He sobered. This was a conversation he'd been dreading. His revelations would create a rift he could not cross, any more than he could change his nature. But Blessed Lord and Lady, he would if he could. For the first time in his life, he began to regret the choices he had made.

"Don't be too sure of that, sweetling. I have my black moments. Never doubt your foretellings. You are more talented than you know." He trailed a finger down her throat.

She shivered under his touch. "But you say you will not marry and the runes promised me a lifelong love."

His heart skipped a beat. "What else did they show you?"

"The destruction of Kara's Power." She closed her eyes again. "Mmmm. That feels wonderful. In my dreams of late I see you as the Green Man. Families of many different animals surrounding you...sparrows and the hawk."

Her voice drifted off.

He settled down beside her. Kara was no more a danger. He had some time to indulge his fantasies, to conduct his experiments, before he went to meet his greatest challenge. For now, he would pillow his head on her breast and dream of a future that was beyond his grasp.

Time enough for regrets later, when his time here was over.

* * * * *

Harmon awakened with his lungs heaving and a sheen of sweat covering his skin. Lingering panic made him sit up and take stock of his situation.

Isolde remained asleep beside him, one leg thrown over his. The weak light of the coming day illuminated the tree just outside the window. The shutters were as he'd left them, thrown open to whatever breezes the warm night might bring.

He explored outward with his mage's senses, seeking anything unusual.

There.

A familiar shadow loomed large to the north. It grew while he watched.

He had thought he had more time, that he would travel to meet this challenge, that when it came, it would be on his terms. He should have known better. The shadows always found him.

His time with Isolde had been wasted, for he had not begun to explore the possibilities or limits of their combined magicks. There were too many unknowns.

He couldn't risk her life.

"It is not your decision." Her declaration startled him. She sat beside him, regarding him with solemn eyes. He had not heard her awaken or felt the bed move as she rose.

Had he spoken aloud, or was she hearing his thoughts? How much more than Power were they sharing? He met her gaze with a level look of his own. "I cannot risk you. I thought I could, but I cannot."

"You once said you have a destiny. Is defeating this dark mage what you meant?"

He nodded.

"Then you must use every weapon available to you. Our magicks together are more than either of us alone, even more powerful than both of us when we work together, as we first did with Kara at her father's house." She laced her fingers through his. "What is the risk if you are defeated?"

"Disaster of a magnitude I cannot imagine."

She mulled that over. "Who is this dark mage?"

"My mentor."

Compassion shone in her eyes. She reached out to him. "I am so sorry. I cannot imagine what I would do if the woman who trained me had turned to the dark path."

"You misunderstand." He drew back. Her compassion was too appealing. He couldn't stand it if she rejected him. "I chose him because he was a dark mage. I concealed my true Calling from him, while I learned everything I could about my enemy. I was forced to kill one of his other apprentices, who showed promise of being an even greater evil than our master. When my master discovered what I had done, he vowed to destroy me.

"The price I paid for my years of study with him was to take on some of my mentor's evil. My path lies always in the shadows. I walk between the darkness and the light. At times, I must step fully into the dark to accomplish the tasks I have taken on. Because of that change in my nature, and my mentor's vow, I became a danger to those around me. I dare not linger in one place and so I travel. I seek out those like Kara who need to be...helped, if you will." He rose and turned his back on her. "Now leave me, please. I refuse to endanger you."

These were the hardest words he'd ever said, more difficult than all the lies he'd told and all the truths he'd uttered. His soul cried out for her to stay, but he knew she had to leave. To stay was to risk her life—and that of their child.

He had risen in the night and scried her future. He'd seen her paring an apple for a sturdy child, a boy with his golden hair and amber eyes. His son. Surely the boy had been conceived in their last few days together.

The ropes creaked behind him as she climbed out of the bed. He closed his eyes against the tears that threatened to spill over.

No regrets. Ever.

Her arms came around him and with them a comforting warmth. He sighed, a relaxation seeping deep into his soul.

He was no longer alone.

She rested her cheek on his back. Her voice was low and steady. "From the beginning, I suspected that shadows stalked you, that somehow you were involved with a dark mage, mayhap even had become one yourself. Once I saw how you cared for the villagers, I knew you were not lost to darkness. 'Twas then I gave my heart to you willingly. I can do no less with my Power. Without you, I am lost. Come, let us take on this dark mage together. With our Lady's help, we shall ensure he never snares another in his web."

Her words reached deep inside him, the truth of them cutting like an arrow to his heart. He could not defeat his master on his own. Such a battle required him to be whole, and he now knew he was not whole and never would be without Isolde to complete him.

To do this, aye, even to live from now on, he needed his fair Isolde. She of the black hair and pure heart, a balance to his golden visage and dark soul.

He turned to embrace her fully. Gathering her to him, he once more marveled at how well they fit together. Sweet Goddess, there was no other like her. She had been made for him, and he for her.

"Aye, let us do battle together."

She looked into his eyes and smiled.

* * * * *

They met him in the forest, in the glade where she'd had her waking vision, when Harmon's fever broke. Traces of their mingled Power from that encounter lingered in the glade, and they'd gathered it up to aid their defenses. Harmon had shown her how to use her runes in a new way, to focus and anchor her Power.

Garbed in their dark ceremonial robes, joined by their clasped hands, they stood behind the protection of the shield they had erected. Together they stepped into the sunlight as he strode into view.

The feared mage stood a head shorter than her uncle Cedd, a plump jolly-looking fellow that she'd never have considered a threat had she met him in the marketplace or tavern. He wore traveling clothes of good leather and wool, much as she had seen Harmon wear in her dreams and visions. His garments were in shades of red and black. He was fire and smoke to Harmon's forest green and brown.

"Well met by sunlight, Master Rutger. You will do well to return to your estate."

Harmon took a half-step forward and gave a half-bow. She supposed it was an insult to his mentor, for Master Rutger bristled as he responded.

"Not without my satisfaction, lad. I was drawn here by the scent of a new apprentice, one whose magick rivals your own. The chance to dispose of you is a fitting bonus. You've robbed me of my best apprentice, nay my two best, for you are the second most talented I've taught. You deceived me. You have used my lessons to make weapons to turn against me and my kind."

Rutger took a half-step forward. Harmon and Isolde matched it.

Harmon inclined his head. A small smile played around his mouth but didn't reach his hard eyes. "Then you should have followed a different path. You chose your own fate when you set your feet on the path into darkness."

"Nay, I think my fate lies in the future. We all will die and so shall I, but not today." He indicated Isolde with a dismissive jerk of his head. "Yon whore cannot help you avoid your destiny, lad. You still belong to me. I have not released you from your apprenticeship, and under those terms you are mine to do with as I will, even unto death." His face was jolly no longer.

The malice she saw there urged her to flee. With an effort, she resisted. This was her love, her Harmon the dark mage threatened.

Harmon laughed and shook his head. "Nay, Rutger, I left your service when you cast me out. With that, you relinquished your hold on me."

"Never! You are mine!" The mage roared and threw a magickal charge at them, a malignant ball of dull, dark Power that soared across the clearing. It struck the shield around Harmon and Isolde, shattering into dark slivers that writhed and smoked as they dissipated.

The shield held, glowing faintly in the sunlight. Harmon squeezed her hand and tipped his head a bit. Isolde glanced up to see the moon visible just over the trees behind their foe. She corrected herself. The shield glowed in the combined light of the sun and the moon.

This had to be a good omen. The Goddess stood watch over them.

Harmon spoke in a no-nonsense tone. "By the way, Rutger, the young woman you seek as your new apprentice has lost her abilities completely. You should have noticed a change in the scent you follow. Two days ago, we worked to blunt her dark tendencies but in her goodness the Goddess went one step further and neutralized the threat the girl posed. You will find her of no use to you now."

"You could never have done that on your own." Rutger staggered back, staring at Isolde with loathing. "She has done this! She has bewitched you, seduced you to do her will!"

"Nay, she's a powerful mage but she is also much more than that." The pride in his voice warmed her heart. She had chosen wisely. Harmon was worth her support—and her love. She placed her free hand protectively across her belly.

Whatever happened here today, she would reserve enough strength to protect their child. Although the child was barely there, she could sense the boy's strong presence. He would be much like his father.

"She is my perfect complement. Can you not see it? Just as her dark appearance balances my fairness, the purity and clarity of her Power balances the shadows of mine. Shadows you gave me, Rutger. Shadows that recede as the moon waxes. As it does now. You chose a poor time to move against me. My Lady's moon is with me."

"Bah! Your Lady's moon is naught but rot and myth. Power comes from within us all, and depends upon our will for its strength and direction, not on external factors." He paused and made a quick gesture. The air around him thickened and grew darker. "Mayhap on what we eat, for poor digestion does interfere with some spells. But you intend to distract me! It won't help save you."

Rutger took a step backward and muttered as he sketched complicated patterns in the air.

As he began, Harmon whispered to Isolde, "We must move now, before he is ready." At her questioning look, he assured her, "There are no rules, no question of fair play or compassion. We must kill or be killed."

She fed him Power through their linked hands. Her will reinforced his. Her strength poured into him along with her magick, melding with his and becoming so much more than either of them alone. Relief flooded through her along with her love for Harmon. They'd discussed his concern that this contact would be insufficient, that they needed a more intimate joining to facilitate combining their magicks.

Helping him, shaping their joined might, she called on the Goddess for aid in a silent plea. There was no time to craft a suitable spell. Some of Rutger's claim was correct, for the spell was merely a focus for the will of the mage. Rutger was dead wrong about the source of Power, though, and about the value of external forces. The waxing moon, now well on its way to full, tipped the balance in Isolde's favor. Their combined Power held not a trace of Harmon's shadows.

In the shining purity of their onslaught, Rutger would find no handhold to grasp in his efforts to deflect the attack.

As Rutger drew breath and straightened to cast his spell, Harmon formed the Power he'd gathered into a lance and threw it. Using her mage sight, Isolde watched the glittering magick stream across the space between them. She'd thought he had launched a missile but found the lance had no end, only a beginning, a sharp point that struck Rutger full in the chest. As the dark mage faltered, Power continued to pour forth from Harmon's outstretched hand, battering their foe to his knees.

Rutger began to glow, coruscations of light and dark warring for supremacy. Still the Power streamed into him, driving the darkness into submission.

Two apprentices came from the trees and joined Rutger, adding their strength of will to his. The glow of Harmon and Isolde's combined magicks never weakened. It slowly expanded to encompass them as well, until a ball of brilliant light obscured the trio.

Still Isolde drew on her resources, feeding them to Harmon as he had need. She envisioned her hand in his as the tap on an inexhaustible keg, never faltering in its offering. She fed him all she had, holding back only enough to ensure that the babe would not be harmed. She would recover. All she would need was to spend some time curled up in the Goddess's embrace, time to draw on the earth's energy and replenish her life's force.

She gave Harmon the last of the Power she could spare. Darkness came over her and she fell to the ground, gratefully sinking into contact with the source of her Power.

* * * * *

With a clap of thunder and a blinding flash, the ball of magick exploded. The remaining Power that had not been absorbed in the attack slammed back into Harmon in a blow that knocked him flat. He lost his grip on Isolde.

Shaking his head to clear his vision, he slowly got to his feet. Staggering across the clearing, he found three charred areas in the grass, where Rutger and his apprentices had stood together and died together.

"We did it, Isolde! We did it!" He stumbled back to where she lay. "Wake up, sweetling, the danger has passed."

His heart raced and his middle turned to ice. She didn't respond. He bent his head to her chest and found a fluttering heartbeat. Dear Goddess, there *was* a limit to her Power and he had drained her beyond her endurance!

"Nay!" He cried out in anguish. Not her and his child! He would not let it happen.

Clasping her limp body in his arms, he concentrated on the faint pulse that beat in the hollow of her throat. Gathering his remaining magick, he poured his will into her, giving her his strength, pushing his Power into her, feeding every faint spark of life he found within his body. The last thing he heard was the resumption of a steady beat under his ear.

Chapter Eight

Isolde roused herself from a stupor. She must have been terribly sick for a long time, to be so weak.

The sky stretched clear summer blue above her. Nay, she wasn't ill. She was outdoors.

Memory returned in a rush. Harmon's mentor, the dark mage, had engaged them in battle. She'd fed all her might, everything she had to spare, to Harmon.

Harmon. That comforting weight on her chest must be him. She managed to pull herself upright. Harmon flopped off her, into a heap in the grass.

A swift glance across the clearing showed her wisps of smoke rising from the scorched evidence of their victory. Sweet Goddess, what had the battle cost him?

She laid a hand on his neck and found a thready pulse. There was no time to lose. She wrapped her arms about his inert form and lay beside him. Quelling her panic, she steadied her breathing and reached for her center. Lying on the earth, the source of her magick, indeed, the source of all life, she spread out her awareness and opened herself up to the earth mother's unlimited Power.

"Harmon has long worked his will
Defeating those who would do ill
Refuse now his life in pay
Grant that he not die today
He's gladly offered up his years
Embracing what he truly fears
Let him finally justice see
As I will so mote it be."

Her weakness fled as the trickle of Power welling up from the earth grew stronger, beginning to replenish her strength. She pushed it outward, into Harmon where she touched him. She relaxed against him and drifted into sleep. Beneath them, the earth continued to restore her, and through her, him.

* * * * *

"Master Harmon, wake up!"

He opened his eyes to find someone leaning over him, blocking out the warmth of the sun. He knew that form, recognized that voice.

"Kara?"

"Aye, 'tis me." Kara leaned down to help him sit.

"And where is—" Weakness assailed him. His head spun with the effort of bringing order to his thoughts. He thought he might retch.

"Mistress Isolde is fine. She's right here, and she's in better shape than you are." Kara's brow knitted in concern. Not a trace remained of the self-centered expression she'd habitually worn.

He slumped back against the soft grass with a groan. "Thank the Goddess!" For so many things.

"What did you do? What happened? There was an explosion, it sounded like a mountain had fallen. We searched and searched, but found nothing until we got here."

"Who is 'we'?" If he kept her talking, he could recover his strength before she demanded he provide answers to all of her questions. He expected the impatience that got her into trouble so often had not been erased. Her basic nature would not have changed.

"Dan and me, and we met Mother and Big Frieda on the road. The steward joined us once we'd left the fields. He feared the charcoal kiln had blown up."

The nausea threatened again but he fought it. Never had his battles drained him like this. He felt steady enough to sit up and look around, although he risked no sudden movements.

The women she listed were clustered around Isolde, who moved as carefully as he did. To his relief, she was pale but smiling. The steward Hector and Dan squatted on their heels a respectful distance from the scorched remains of Rutger and his apprentices. No need to caution them not to touch the ashes. He'd have to dispose of those properly, in a few days. When he had the strength.

Had Isolde truly lain near death? Had he not poured the last of his strength into her, to give his son a chance at life and a mother to raise him?

How had *he* survived?

Harmon looked over to where Oda and Big Frieda were helping a shaky Isolde to her feet. He had some questions for his perfect mate to answer, as well.

He tested his limbs and found everything in working order. With Kara's assistance, he managed to stand. His knees trembled and threatened to buckle. His legs held as long as he moved with care.

Isolde ran to his embrace. "I thought you were dying, Harmon!"

"I found *you* near death, sweetling." He held her close, breathing in her familiar and precious scent. Dear Goddess, they were both alive. "I thought I gave you my life."

"I asked for it back and the Goddess granted my request." She kissed his hand. "You have sacrificed yourself and your comfort for years. Your life should not be forfeit, too."

"Master Harmon, tell me what happened here." Hector, Lord Raymond's steward, rose from his examination of Rutger's remains and approached.

Harmon was about to ask for a day's grace to recover, but 'twas clear the steward did not wish any delay. Lord Raymond was not known for his patience. No matter, he would tell the man enough for now. Details could wait.

"The short story is that my old mentor long ago vowed to destroy me. He found me here, and we waged a magickal battle of wills. I won." Harmon gestured to the scorch marks. "There lie the remains of the dark mage Rutger and two of his apprentices. When I am back to full strength, I will dispose of the ashes properly. In the meantime, they present a danger to you all. Do not permit anyone to touch or disturb them."

Hector's jaw worked a few times while he considered this tale. Finally, he said, "You have given me sufficient explanation. I will set a guard here until you return. My lord will understand that there is nothing more to concern him, and no damage to his property." He grinned. "'Twill be a relief that the charcoal kiln is still intact."

"If his lordship is pleased, so am I." Harmon sketched a bow. "I am also bone-weary. Isolde, your cottage lies closer than mine. Are you able to offer me hospitality? I believe I will rest better on feathers today."

"Aye, making the world a safer place is hard work. Come." Isolde held out her hand. "I too will rest better on a soft mattress."

They left the others open-mouthed, staring after them. Leaning on one another for support, they slowly made their way through the forest to Isolde's neat holding. Her small cottage was perfect for them. Barely a dozen steps from anything they might want, together they prepared a quick meal to restore their bodies.

A quick joining would restore their souls. The plates had barely been scraped out the back door for the chickens and the old hound before Isolde dragged him to her bed.

With haste born of impatience, he buried his hand into her thick, black hair and pulled her down with him to the feather mattress. Aye, feathers were indeed softer than straw, but she was softer yet. Her eyes shone with an eagerness that matched his own. Her beauty, the soft texture of her creamy skin, overwhelmed him.

She struggled to reach him, bent on conducting her own explorations. He gathered her wrists and drew her arms above her head, holding them there with one hand, while his free hand roamed over her, testing textures and her responses, finally coming to cup one breast. The nipple immediately hardened between his fingers. She breathed his name in a soft moan, one of the most arousing sounds he'd ever heard.

He bent his head and sucked the nearest hard peak into his mouth, scraping the tip with his teeth until she moaned in ecstasy. His need increased as her thrashing eased and little whimpers escaped her throat.

His hand massaged her breast while his mouth moved back to hers. She panted into his kiss, their breath mingling. Her taste was pure ambrosia, a feast for a starving man.

Through it all wound their magick, his shadows yielding to her light, melding into a brilliant colored pattern that nearly blinded him, even without his mage sight, the one time he glanced up.

She moaned and thrashed her hips against him as the tide of magick swirled back and forth between them, ever growing and increasing, becoming more than they both were.

How had he lived all these years without her? How had he survived, let alone accomplished all he had, without the added strength of her Power mingling with his?

Dizziness came in a rush, as if he'd just feasted on the most potent wine there was. How close they had each come to death, and how willing Isolde had been to plead for his life, to offer her life's force to spare him the fate he had thought to spare her.

Lightheaded, Harmon focused on where his thick cock probed her cleft, barely inside, and the way the partial penetration sent a jolt of desire straight to his heart. Nay, 'twas love he felt, an emotion as foreign as it was welcome. With the realization, his heart lifted. He had never believed himself worthy of love—until this moment. The flickers of fear faded, and he rejoiced. He swallowed the lump that threatened to choke him. How close he'd come to losing her!

He couldn't breathe. He couldn't move or take his hands out of her hair or tear his mouth away from hers. His heart pounded out the message that he was home, that he was whole, when he was with her.

Once would not be enough this night, even after all they'd endured. He wasn't done with her yet. He wouldn't be, not for a long time.

Harmon had never known a woman like this before. Certainly not one this strong and independent, a mage powerful in her own right, who welcomed him with open arms. She loved him, shadows and all. She'd trusted him with her life and asked that his be spared.

He wondered how he had ever lived without knowing this kind of unconditional acceptance. Even more unthinkable was the prospect of leaving her, of never again knowing how it felt. Of being suddenly rendered helpless by her absence.

That prospect sent him easing into her slowly, as if burying his cock into her depths would bind the two of them together forever.

Forever.

That had a sweet sound. He smiled down at her as she twitched her hips, trying to hurry him along. No shadows lurked in his soul now. His Power flowed clear and pure, untainted by any lingering darkness.

He lowered his head to her breast. With one touch of his tongue, he brought her nipple to an even tighter peak. With one swift movement, he entered her fully and her head fell back as the satisfaction of being filled by him flowed over her and spilled into him.

She exploded beneath him. As she writhed and cried out in ecstasy, he suckled her—and opened his mind to hers. He felt the scrape of his tongue from both sides, the firm bud caught firmly between his teeth and the slide of his tongue across the sensitive tip.

The repeated clenching of her tight channel around his shaft milked him headlong into his release. As he pumped her full of his seed, he wondered if she had conceived yet, or if his vision of her with his son—nay, with their son—was far in the future.

He hoped the boy would not be their only child.

Panting, he collapsed beside his love and took her in his arms. And uttered the phrase he'd never thought would pass his lips.

"I love you."

The glow in her eyes warmed him. "And I love you."

"Will you join me? Aid me in my work? Together we are far stronger than any dark mage. I cannot do it without you."

Once he might have choked on the admission, but today he could do something that had been unthinkable before. He could stand naked and flawed before Isolde—and trust her not to hurt him.

"Aye, where do we go from here?" She sat up as if to rise and begin packing for their departure.

He pulled her back against him, nuzzling her neck and fondling the curve of her waist. "You are willing to give up your home and take to the road with me? Without any discussion or planning?"

As they fell back into the feathers, he searched his soul. For the first time, he found no shadows. With wonder, he cast out with his mage sense and felt no pull, no Calling to another task. His heart raced a little faster.

Was it possible that in fighting dark mages, he'd been fighting the lingering darkness in his own soul? Could he now have no reason to fight against his own nature?

"Aye. My heart goes with you. How can I do other than follow?"

He laced his fingers through hers and kissed her knuckle. "Do not follow. Walk beside me."

"Aye, I can think of nothing I'd like better."

"I can. Several somethings. Beginning with a repeat of that last joining."

She smiled and he wondered how anyone could ever call her Black Isolde. His heart lifted and swelled with love for her.

"You are pure light, sweetling, my perfect mate and my perfect complement. You have chased away the shadows and left me whole, restored. I may never feel the Call again, never feel the challenge of another dark mage. Will you stay here with me as willingly as you would travel to far places?"

"Aye, I have said that whither you go, so go I."

"I do not deserve you. How can I repay you?"

"You can love me senseless." She smiled and her hand went to her belly. She gave it a little pat. "And mayhap stay to be a father to our son. If he has the stubbornness of my family, he will need your guidance."

He gaped at her. "You know you already bear my child? I thought you wouldn't be able to tell for days, if not weeks."

"Not know what is happening in my own body?" She rolled her eyes, looking much like her cousin Kara. "Please tell me a lie that I have even a small chance of believing!"

He clasped her to his chest and they rocked from side to side, laughing.

"Sweetling, I will give you as many children as you wish, and I will stay to be a father, if you'll marry me."

"Oh, aye, and I plan to hold you to that."

"As long as I can hold you whenever I want."

Also by Liddy Midnight:

About the author:

Liddy Midnight lives, loves, works and writes in the woods of eastern Pennsylvania, surrounded by lush greenery and wildlife. Although raccoons, possums, skunks and the occasional fox eat the cat food on her back porch, she's no more than half an hour from some of the finest shopping in the country. Situated in this best of all possible worlds, how could she write anything other than romance?

Liddy welcomes mail from readers. You can write to her c/o Ellora's Cave Publishing at 1056 Home Avenue, Akron OH 44310-3502.

Wishful Thinking

.

Chapter One

Clara leaned against the gazebo railing, gazing out at the lake in the distance. The cool late summer wind whipped her graying hair in front of her eyes and stirred the tawny sand on the shore. The waning moon lit the world around her with a soft glow, reflecting off the gently rippling lake in bands of bluish white.

The beauty around her didn't interest her on this night. Her mind was focused elsewhere—on the fistful of fragrant powder she held above the grassy yard. Right now, she couldn't afford to concentrate on anything else. When the time was right, she released the powder into the wind, silently visualizing her wish as she imagined the powder hitting the earth and scattering into all corners of the yard and beyond. With a last request that her wish be answered—sooner rather than later—she brushed her hands down the front of her robe and grabbed her crutches to head back to the house before someone noticed she was missing.

"What do you think you're doing out here? It's the middle of the night."

Clara nearly jumped out of her skin at the sound of the feminine voice coming through the darkness. She tightened her grip on her crutches to steady herself so she didn't fall. Breaking the other leg wasn't high on her list of midnight activities.

"Who's there?"

"Relax. It's just me."

Once her niece, Mia, stepped into view, Clara let out a sigh of relief—quickly followed by a groan of frustration. This was not what she needed right now, not as she was so close to finally getting her way. "Go back to bed, dear. I'm just enjoying the night air. It's so warm for this time of year. I will be inside in a little while."

"Uh-huh. Sure you are." Mia walked up the gazebo steps and leaned her hip on the railing, her arms crossed over her chest, and a disbelieving look on her face. "I thought that after you slipped and broke your leg last month, Uncle Lou and the doctor told you to stop wandering around in the middle of the night."

They were all crazy if they expected she'd listen. Foolish men, always thinking they knew what was best for everyone. Clara brushed a lock of hair from her eyes and tucked it behind her ear, pretending she didn't hear the reprimand. "Look at the lake tonight. Isn't it peaceful?"

Mia, not one to be distracted easily, frowned and ignored the question. "What were you doing, Aunt Clara? Since you're out here at midnight, this is more than just simply enjoying the view. You've lived here all your life. You don't get excited about the scenery like your guests do."

"It helps me relax so I can sleep better. And on that thought, what are *you* doing out of bed this late?"

A smile tugged at Mia's lips, despite the fact that Clara knew she tried to hold it back. "Couldn't sleep, either. I noticed the back door open, and I figured you had to be out here. No one else is nuts enough to go running around in the dark yard at this time of night…er, morning. What I still don't understand is why. What crazy scheme have you come up with this time, Aunt Clara?"

Clara sighed. The young. They never understood anything. "Many spells are performed at night, Mia. You, of all people, should know that."

"Oh, believe me, I understand. What I don't get is all the secrecy. You only sneak around behind everyone's back if you've got some idea cooked up, or if there's something seriously wrong." Mia frowned, her expression darkening.

"Please tell me there isn't something seriously wrong with you or Uncle Lou."

"Oh for Goddess' sake, I'm fine. I was making a wish. That's all."

"A wish." Mia repeated, not looking at all sure that she believed it.

Clara nodded as she picked up her crutches and made her way to the gazebo steps. "It seems to be the only way I'm going to get what I want." She ignored Mia's silent offer of help and hobbled down the steps, leaning on the metal crutches for support. She was halfway across the yard before Mia followed her.

"Slow down before you fall and do some more damage to yourself," she said, stopping on the stone path in front of her so Clara had to come to a halt or knock her niece over.

"I'm sixty-four, not a hundred and four. I'm perfectly aware of what my limitations are," Clara told her, ignoring Mia's pointed gaze at the cast on her leg. "You need to worry about yourself and stop trying to mother everyone else. Especially those of us who are older than you."

Mia wasn't deterred that easily, no matter how much Clara had hoped she'd be.

"What is it that you could possibly want? You've got everything you need right here." Mia sighed heavily and shook her head. Clara felt the annoyance radiating from her niece and felt guilty for causing it. But, in the end, it would be worth it.

"It's nothing you need to worry about, Mia. Honestly, you're much too serious for someone so young. Live a little."

She just wanted Mia to be happy. The girl had been alone for too long. She deserved a home and a father for Frances. She had such a nurturing, caring manner, and Clara hated to see it wasted on an aging couple and a tiny bed and breakfast when she could put it to much better use.

Mia *said* she was happy here, but Clara wondered. There had to be some small part of her itching to leave, to live her life the way she was meant to. The girl was only twenty-eight. If her life kept going along its current path, she'd stay single and alone, and never leave Bennett Island.

Mia argued that she had Frances, and yes, Clara understood that the child took a lot of her time. But Frances was happy and healthy, if not a little bit mischievous, and everyone doted on her for the summers they spent on the Island. Mia had no one to make her feel special. Everyone needed someone like that in their lives, and Mia had been without for too long—three years last month. Her grieving was over, and it was time for her to move on. But, for some reason, the girl seemed insistent on moving in permanently and hiding away from the rest of the world.

Clara wasn't about to sit back and let *that* happen. Mia needed a gentle nudge—which Clara was all too happy to provide. She gave her niece a big smile and gestured to the waning moon above. "There will be a new moon soon."

"I'm aware of that," Mia answered, her tone laced with suspicion.

"That's the perfect time for self-improvement."

Mia laughed at that, which Clara took as a good sign. "Are you planning to get a makeover?"

"No, dear. But it would be a good time for *you* to embark on something new—like a relationship."

Mia let out groan and turned away, hurrying the final few steps to the back door. "I'll be inside if you need me. Please be careful out here."

"Goodnight, Mia." Clara laughed to herself as she watched Mia walk away. The girl was nothing if not predictable. Just the mention of new relationships had her running in the other direction. She didn't understand, despite all that had happened in her young life, that she couldn't fight her destiny. And Clara knew Mia's destiny did *not* lie on this little island—at least not in the way she thought it did.

That was how Clara had come to this—her last resort, a wish spell in the middle of the night. With any luck, the spell would take quickly and bring some happiness for Mia to the island soon. The tourist season was winding to a close, winter was fast approaching, and in a little less than a month Clara's Bed and Breakfast would shut its doors until spring. This might be Clara's last chance for several months to help Mia find some true happiness. Clara chuckled to herself.

Sometimes fate needed a little push.

Chapter Two

"Where the hell is Brian?" Jack barked into his cell phone as he tried to navigate his car down the unfamiliar twisting dirt roads of Bennett Island. "He's supposed to be covering for me, right? So why can't I get a hold of him?"

He let out a huge sigh of frustration as he heard his secretary's answer. "This is bullshit. The guy takes vacations all the time, and I cover for him. This is the first one I've taken in six years. You think he could at least pick up his goddamned phone. Just because he's my brother doesn't mean I'm going to let him get away with this crap."

He turned his car down another dusty dirt road, wincing when his car hit a big rock jutting up from the ground. "You have him call me as soon as he gets in. I don't care how busy he is. This is important. *Vital.* I'm not going to cut my vacation short just so he can run around with one of his airhead girlfriends and miss client appointments."

Something large and brown ran out in front of his car, he swerved to avoid hitting it. He slammed on his breaks just as the thing—*a deer?*—dodged his front fender and sped into the woods. His heart pounded hard against the wall of his chest and he leaned back in the seat to catch his breath. The last thing he needed now was to crack up his brand new convertible. "Nancy, I'm going to have to call you back when I get settled in my room. Some kind of wild animal just jumped out in front of me. I don't need to total my car and end up in the hospital."

He disconnected the call, ignoring his secretary's burst of laughter and insistence that he needed to pay more attention to the world around him, and tossed the phone onto the passenger seat. This was *not* the way he'd planned to start his vacation. The traffic on the ride up from Boston had been a nightmare, turning what should have been a three hour car ride into five and a half. By the time he'd driven onto the ferry that would take him across the lake to Bennett Island, his mood had been foul. Getting lost within five minutes on the island's winding roads hadn't helped matters. He'd just managed to get on track again when Nancy called with an important message from a client. Brian, who was supposed to be taking care of Jack's clients until he got back, apparently wasn't answering his telephone.

Almost on cue, the cell phone on the seat next to him rang. Jack snatched it up off the seat and flipped it open. "Jack Cullen."

"Hey, bro."

He narrowed his eyes and tightened his grip on the wheel at the sound of Brian's voice. "Where the hell have you been?"

"Busy. I had meetings all day."

Right. No one had ever accused Brian of being the responsible brother. "Yeah, well, you've got to make time for my clients, too, since you agreed to cover for me for a little while. If I'd known you were going to pull this, I would have asked Dad to help me instead."

"Stop worrying so much. Aren't you supposed to be on vacation? Nancy gave me the messages and I'll take care of all that stuff this evening. Have a great time, meet a nice woman, and get yourself some before you explode. You work too hard. For once in your life, let go and have a little fun. Bye." Brian hung up before Jack could protest—which was probably for the best. He would have hated admitting aloud that his brother was right.

This was *not* a working vacation. He needed the time off—doctor's orders—and he was damned well going to take it. Jack pulled his car back on the road and headed toward the bed and breakfast where he had a room booked for the next two weeks. At least he *hoped* he was headed in the right direction. With all the trees and dirt roads—minus street signs—he couldn't be too sure.

When he saw the white and green sign up ahead that read Clara's Bed and Breakfast, he let out a sigh of relief. *Finally.* He pulled his car into the parking lot and climbed out, grabbing his bags from the trunk before he turned to face the enormous log cabin in front of him. Two stories high with a wrap-around porch and red shutters, the place reminded him of the summer camp his parents had sent him to as a kid. Trees surrounded the house, but he caught glimpses of the lake through the branches when the leaves blew in the wind. This seemed like the perfect place for him to hide away from the real world for a while, and with any luck, help in curing his insomnia.

He walked up the porch steps and through the front door into a huge expansive foyer. The gray flagstone floor would have seemed cold on its own, but the warm beige on the walls and the filmy curtains softened the look. An older style wooden desk stood on one side of the room, an old-fashioned blotter on top.

A small woman with gray streaked brown hair and crutches hobbled through a door on the left side of the room, her leg wrapped in a bright pink cast. "Checking in?"

"Yes."

"Mr. Cullen." It was a statement rather than a question, and it had him blinking at her. Her smile widened and took on a sly look as her gaze traveled over him slowly. He had a feeling she was sizing him up.

"We don't get single people here very often," she told him. "Usually the customers we get are looking for a romantic, private getaway. It's been almost exclusively couples all season. You *are* single, though, aren't you?"

He hesitated, not sure whether he should lie or tell her the truth, but the woman continued before he had a chance to come up with an answer. "Sorry. That was too personal. I didn't mean to pry, I was just wondering what on earth a good-looking man like you would be doing taking a vacation all alone."

"Excuse me?" He'd signed up for a quiet vacation, not a singles' cruise.

The woman shook her head and laughed. "Sorry again. I'm nosy, I know. My niece tells me that all the time. I'm sure she'd advise you to ignore me." She pulled a black, spiral-bound book out of one of the desk drawers and leafed through the pages.

"You're in room 12. It's up the stairs, to the right, at the end of the hall." She handed him an old-fashioned brass key on an ornate key chain from a rack behind the desk. "I'm Clara. If you need anything, don't be afraid to ask. Breakfast is served from six to eight, lunch from noon to two, and everyone sits down for dinner together at six p.m. sharp. The dining room is just off the living room, to the left. You can't miss it. There's a path to the private beach through the backyard. My husband organizes activities like card games and such on some of the nights, but don't feel like you have to participate. Can I get you anything now?"

"I'm all set, thanks," he told her, trying to remember everything she'd said. Activities of any kind didn't interest him. All he wanted to do was head up to his room, take a shower, and unwind.

Clara smiled at him and made a shooing gesture with her hands, not unlike what he'd seen his mother do on countless occasions. "Then go on upstairs. You look like you could use a good long nap. Just remember to be down here at six for dinner, or else you might not get fed until morning. My daughter, Jessica, is the cook and she can get cranky when she gets too many special requests. I wouldn't want to see you go hungry."

Shades of his mother, yet again. When he'd asked Nancy to recommend a nice, quiet, out-of-the-way place to unwind, he'd been thinking more along the lines of a tropical beach than this. If he'd wanted meddling, he could have just gone to Arizona to see his mom. "I wouldn't miss dinner for the world."

She raised an eyebrow at his sarcasm, but didn't comment on it. "Good. I can't wait for you to meet everyone else. My husband and my daughter and my niece and great-niece...and all the other guests. We're like a big happy family around here." She shut the book and slid it back into the drawer. "For now, though, get some rest before you drop. You look like you could sleep for days. Go through the door to the left into the living room. You'll see the stairs from there."

He wasn't sure if he liked the sound of the big, happy family. Very much a private person, he didn't relish getting to know a bunch of people he'd never see again once he went back home. If he ended up feeling like he was stuck in some warped version of the Brady Bunch, he'd have to think of a very *nice* thank you gift for Nancy.

* * * * *

Mia stood in the hallway between the kitchen and the foyer, listening to Aunt Clara check in yet another guest. They had a full house this weekend—not a vacant room in the whole place. But the man with Clara had caught Mia's attention. First, she heard Clara say he was alone. That in itself caused her to wonder. In her limited experience in the tourism business, men didn't take vacations like this without a wife or girlfriend. The brochure billed the inn as a romantic getaway—strange that he'd come by himself for the romance.

And that voice...it was enough to curl her toes. That deep, sexy, molten honey voice curled *everything*. She wanted to sneak a glimpse at him, to see if he was as good-looking as his voice had her hoping, but she didn't dare peek around the corner. If Clara saw her watching, she'd try to play matchmaker yet again. *Whatever* he looked like, she didn't need her aunt setting her up on dates—especially with guests.

Still, she could definitely stand right there and listen to that guy talk all day. He could tell her about the theory of relativity for all she cared, or the entire history of the world. She just wanted to hear him speak.

She snorted and rolled her eyes at her childishness. What would Frances say if she saw her mooning over some stranger like this? She hadn't acted that gaga over a man since she'd met Steven ten years before.

Back in high school.

She wasn't in high school anymore, and she needed to pull herself together before she did something stupid. She didn't even know what the man looked like—he could be a green-skinned mutant for all she knew.

The kitchen door opened and shut, and her cousin Jess came up beside her. "What are you doing hiding back here?" Not having the same reservations as Mia, she stepped into the hall to take a look. When she came back, she had a big smile on her face. "Okay, I get the hiding thing now. You don't want the hunk to know you're watching."

Hunk? "I'm not hiding." No. She'd been admiring his voice. From afar. *Huge* difference.

"He's cute, huh?" Jess asked. "In a stuffy sort of way, I guess, with that suit and tie and all, but cute none the less."

Mia shrugged, wanting to have a look for herself but wanting more to make sure Clara stayed out of her business. "I can't see him from here."

Jess's eyebrows shot up. "Then what are you doing slinking around in the shadows? What are you waiting for? Get out there and have a look."

"I'm not interested in looking. I'm just curious as to what's taking Clara so long with the guy. She never talks to anyone for *that* long, and we've got a week's worth of menus to plan."

With a casual shrug that was really anything but casual, she turned and walked back into the kitchen with Jess right behind her. Mia tried to busy herself with the leftover lunch dishes in the sink, but Jess wouldn't let the subject go. "It's been a long time since she's met a young, single man in here, and she thinks you need one, Mia. She's probably trying to think of ways to introduce the two of you even as we speak."

Mia dropped the sponge into the sink, sending soap bubbles floating into the air around her. "That's what I'm afraid of."

Jess propped her hip against the counter and frowned at Mia. "Would it really be so bad to have a life?"

"I have a life. I have Frances."

"Yeah, and she's a great kid. But you spend all your free time with her. What about *you*? What's going to happen when she goes to kindergarten in a year? You'll be all alone."

"I'm happy with things the way they are," Mia huffed. "Besides, Clara needs help. She's having so much trouble getting around on that broken leg."

Jess laughed at that comment. "Honey, she hasn't had trouble in *weeks*. She's doing just fine. Stop making excuses and get out there and live a little."

"Maybe later," Mia mumbled, returning her concentration to the dishes. "I don't have time for a life now, at least not a social life. I have a job to do, and a daughter to raise. Unlike some people around here, I know what's important."

Jess's laughter just increased Mia's frustration. What was it with people around here? It was bad enough dealing with Aunt Clara's constant meddling and badgering. Why did her cousin have to start in as well? Next thing she knew, Frances would be badgering her to start dating again.

"You don't understand," she told Jess, trying to rein in her temper. "Dating is hard. Most men would turn around and run when they found out about Frances. Could you even imagine trying to explain to them that I'm a witch? Face it, Jessica, I'm a social pariah."

"Don't be such a fatalist. I'm not trying to give you a hard time, Mia," Jess said softly, her expression apologetic. "I just want what's best for you. That's all my mom wants, too."

"Yeah, I know. But only I know what's best for me. One of these days, you two are going to realize I can take care of myself.

Watch out for Clara, though, because she's going to start bugging you next."

Clara walked into the room before Jess could respond, stopping all further conversation. "What's with the two of you today? I've never known you to be unsocial before. Neither one of you has come out to greet a single guest."

"I've been busy. There's a lot of work to do around here with you *supposed to* be staying off your feet," Mia told her. Jess nodded in agreement before she picked up a dish towel and started drying the dishes as Mia set them on the sideboard.

"What a nice man he is," Clara said, lowering herself into a chair at the kitchen table. "Young, polite, handsome. He's a lawyer, you know, Mia."

Mia rolled her eyes. Just what she needed. "That's nice, Aunt Clara."

"We don't get enough like him around here." Clara sighed and brushed her hair out of her eyes. "You'll have to meet him later, Mia."

Jess threw Mia an I-told-you-so look, clearly suppressing laugher.

"Don't get any ideas, Aunt Clara," Mia warned. "I'm perfectly capable of finding a man on my own."

Clara's silence wasn't a good sign. Not at all.

Chapter Three

Mia moved the vacuum over the carpet absently, playing Clara's words over and over again in her mind. Ever since their midnight conversation in the gazebo, she hadn't been able to get them out of her head. This *was* the perfect time to make a change in her life. *If* she really wanted to.

Did she?

She let out a frustrated sigh. Maybe she did. She wasn't bored here, exactly, but her life wasn't filled with excitement, either. She'd come to stay with Clara and Lou after the fire that had taken Steven—and everything she owned—from her three years ago. She and Frances had been lucky to get away with their lives. Frances had been little more than a baby at the time, just a year old, and Mia hadn't had anywhere else to go. Clara and Lou, her mother's sister and brother-in-law, had taken care of her when she needed them. Now Clara needed Mia, whether she believed it or not. She couldn't walk away from that, not when she owed them so much.

And she had her work. She'd always wanted to heal, ever since she was a little girl. Clara had told her she had the gift—a gift she'd passed down to Frances. When most girls had been playing with dolls, Mia had started a toy hospital and pretended to heal her playthings of all kinds of illnesses. Being a healer was an integral part of herself that she'd never give up, not for anyone or anything. On Bennett Island, and the mainland when the island closed for the winter season, the residents appreciated her talents and sought her out when they needed help with medical problems.

Call it a character flaw, but she *liked* being needed.

It gave her life purpose. Did she really want to risk everything she had just for a little personal happiness?

She took a step back and ran into something solid. With a startled gasp, she shut the vacuum off with her foot and turned.

There was a man standing behind her, looking nearly as startled as she felt. Her face went a thousand shades of red.

"I am so sorry."

His lips curved into a friendly smile. "No problem. Nobody's hurt."

As soon as he spoke, she realized it was the man she'd heard Clara talking to the day before. She swallowed hard at the sight of the face that matched the voice. Jess had been right to call him a hunk. He had sandy brown hair and eyes that reminded her of melted dark chocolate. He looked toned and tanned and better than any man she'd seen here all summer.

Jess had also been right about the "stuffy" part.

He wore neatly pressed khakis and a navy blue collared shirt, despite the fact that he was supposed to be on vacation. His clothes looked so tidy she wondered if he'd brought a travel iron.

"You're not hurt, are you?" he continued.

She shook her head mutely, still sizing him up in her mind. Not a hair was out of place on his head. Even his shoes were perfectly scuffless. He might be nice to look at, but a man like that wasn't her type. She could just imagine what his house looked like—neat, uncluttered. What would he think if he saw her suite, with her dried herbs hanging from the walls and the shelves of potions and spell bottles that lined the small kitchenette?

She shook her head. He'd probably laugh and tell her to hire a maid.

She took a step back and embarrassed herself further by tripping over the vacuum hose. He grabbed her shoulders to steady her, pulling her upright with almost no effort at all. The instant he touched her, she felt a shock of electricity travel from his hands to her shoulders. By the look on his face—and the fact that he didn't let go once he had her steadied—she guessed he'd felt it, too.

No. She had to be mistaken. The shock was from the carpet, and the look on his face purely a figment of her imagination. It *couldn't* be anything else. Things like that only happened in the sappy romance books Clara and Jess loved to read. In real life, attraction built slowly over time, it didn't hit like a smack in the face.

Maybe Clara was right—she'd been alone too long. A change in her life was beginning to sound better and better.

"I, um...I'm not usually this clumsy," she told him, backing out of his grasp. Once she broke contact, she expected the funny feeling in the pit of her stomach to go away. It annoyed her by hanging around, playing on her nerves. *Ridiculous, Mia. You've been celibate for so long that the first guy who shows you any sort of attention has you tied in knots.* "I've got to get back to vacuuming. You missed breakfast, but Clara's daughter Jess is in the kitchen. She'll make you something if you hurry."

He didn't answer, he just stared at her. Or rather, at her lips. She shivered, thinking...well, thinking things she had no business thinking of a complete stranger who'd be leaving in a few weeks' time. "I've really got to get this finished now."

His lips curled into another smile, but this one wasn't as friendly as the first. This one was hot, sensual, and totally unlike the image of the cool, collected man she'd formed in her mind. Suddenly the look in his eyes had her wondering what he'd look like out of those preppy clothes, his hair wild and mussed.

Why did her imagination have to choose that moment to go haywire?

She bit back a whimper as he spoke in a slow, sensual voice. "I'm sorry. I didn't mean to interrupt."

"You didn't. I bumped into you, remember? But I do have to earn my keep around here. Aunt Clara will have my head if I don't get this done."

"Aunt Clara?" he repeated. "You're her niece?"

She nodded. "I am."

"I didn't meet you at dinner last night."

She smiled weakly. "I was busy. I took dinner in my room. I do that often." Frances didn't always enjoy sitting around the table with a bunch of loud guests. It made her a little…hyper, and most of the guests didn't appreciate that, so Mia opted to take a tray to their suite most nights.

An electrically charged silence followed. Something about the guy got to her—not that she'd ever admit it to him, or anyone else. She didn't know the guy. It wasn't really any of his business anyway, since she didn't make a habit of getting involved with Clara and Lou's guests.

As he spoke to her, his sensual smile never wavered. "I'll let you get back to work. It was nice meeting you." Between the voice and the grin, she was a little too close to embarrassing herself.

"We haven't actually met." She could have kicked herself the second the words were out of her mouth. She didn't want to stand there talking to him all morning, and she didn't want to give him the wrong idea. Well, maybe she did, but she couldn't think like that. She had *work* to do. People counting on her. Sitting around chatting with the guests was Clara's job, especially since she'd be stuck in that cast for another couple of weeks.

"So we haven't." He held out his hand in a deceptively formal gesture. "Where are my manners? I'm Jack."

"Mia," she said automatically, taking his hand. As soon as they touched, she yanked her hand back. There was that feeling again, the one she wanted to go away. Only this time, bare skin against bare skin, it was much stronger. It figured that the one man her body would respond to was the one who'd be all wrong for her. They were complete opposites.

At least Frances was helping Uncle Lou with some yard work. She wouldn't have to see her mother acting like some immature imbecile.

"It's nice to meet you, Mia." Jack spoke in a tone that went straight to her stomach and fluttered around like a thousand butterflies. "I'll see you around, I hope."

"Probably, since I'm here all the time."

He gave her one final hot glance before he walked out of the room. The man might not be her type, but he really had a great rear end—stuffy dress pants and all.

Once she was alone again she threw herself back into cleaning the living room—this time with a lot more ambition than earlier. She had to do *something* to get her mind off Jack and the voice that made her panties damp just hearing it.

* * * * *

That had been unexpected.

Jack walked into the kitchen as Mia had suggested, his mind still a little dazed. The second he'd touched her, an unfamiliar sensation clenched in his gut. Why had he never noticed anything like that before? Because work had stopped him from taking notice of the little things, like Nancy always warned?

Probably. He couldn't think of any other way to explain it. He'd dated plenty of women, and none of them had ever affected him the way Mia had within seconds of meeting her. But why her? She wasn't his type at all. She was cute, in a rumpled sort of way, but nothing like the polished women he usually dated. Her dark hair had been pulled back into a kind of a loose twist, with some of the curly strands hanging wildly around her face. Her skin was clean, devoid of any makeup, and her clothes a plain blue shorts set. Nothing spectacular there. In fact, she looked way too young for him—like a kid right out of high school.

So why did he react so strongly?

Maybe it had something to do with the air around here, so far north. It messed with his head. Or maybe it was because last night, for the first time in months, he'd gotten a full night's sleep.

He was still trying to shake off the feeling when a woman came out of the walk-in refrigerator set into the far wall. "Hi. Missed breakfast, huh?"

"Yeah. Mia sent me in to find Jess."

"You found her."

For some reason, he'd expected an older woman, maybe in her forties. But this one looked like she couldn't be much older than Mia. They had the same color hair and the same green eyes, but there the similarities ended. Jess was tall and painfully thin, where Mia was shorter and a lot curvier. He smiled to himself. He'd take curvy over bony any day.

"You don't happen to have any coffee hanging around?" he asked. "Leftover is fine. I just need my daily caffeine fix."

"There's some in the pot on the counter. I just turned it off a few minutes ago. It should still be warm." She walked back into the refrigerator, but poked her head back out a second later. "Want me to cook you something?"

"No, thanks. I hardly ever eat breakfast."

She frowned. "You sure? I don't mind."

"Nah." He took a mug from the counter and filled it with coffee. "I'm fine with this."

"Suit yourself. But you might want to start showing up for breakfast. The air and the lake can make a person really hungry." Jess shrugged and disappeared back into the fridge.

After downing the bitter, lukewarm coffee in a few gulps, he made a mental note to get up earlier the next morning. Something told him that breakfast around here would be very interesting.

Chapter Four

On the third day of his visit, Jack sat outside the log cabin, rocking slowly back and forth in one of the large wooden swings that hung from the porch roof. The weather was unseasonably warm for mid-September, and he'd dug a pair of shorts out of the bottom of his bag to wear. He'd even thought about going down to the lake later on for a swim—*if* he'd remembered to bring his swim trunks.

Strange, how settled he felt here. And unsettled at the same time. When he went to bed last night, when everything was so dark and quiet that he couldn't fall asleep right away, he'd thought about his strange meeting with Clara's niece the day before.

Mia.

Why she still stuck in his mind when he hadn't seen her since yesterday morning, he hadn't a clue. But he couldn't banish her, no matter how hard he tried. At home, he'd been too busy to notice anything but his job. For years, pleasing his father and making partner in the family firm had been all that had mattered. Since he'd gotten to the bed and breakfast, his cell phone hadn't rung once, and he'd kept himself from calling the office to check in. With nothing to do that resembled work, he'd developed a new outlook on life. Things had to change once he got back home.

He should slow down. Stop working so hard. The problem was, he'd been alone for too long, and he didn't have anyone to tell him to relax. Nancy had once told him he was going to work himself into an early grave. After visiting the doctor for his insomnia and headaches, he could honestly say he believed her. For him, settling down and taking it easy had never been an option, not even on the weekends. He'd wanted it all—the big house, the fancy cars, the expensive clothes and electronics. Now he had it. But what had it gotten him?

Severe migraines, endless nights of tossing and turning in bed, and an empty apartment to come home to every night.

He supposed he should be happy, never having to want for anything or rely on anyone to support him. He'd fooled himself into thinking he *was* happy. Until this vacation. Now he just had to decide what to do about it.

"Hello," he heard a soft voice call. He looked up to see a tiny, dark-haired child blinking at him unsurely from the bottom of the porch steps.

An uncertain smile broke over his face. "Hi there."

The little girl walked up the steps and took a seat next to him, patting his knee lightly with the palm of her hand. "You look very nice."

"Oh, really?" Nice? He couldn't remember the last time someone had called him nice. Usually they just referred to him as a cold bastard. He sighed at the thought. To be fair, he supposed he'd earned the nickname.

The girl nodded solemnly, her huge green eyes wide. "My momma says that you can tell a lot about a person by the way he looks."

"Didn't your momma tell you not to talk to strangers?"

She nodded again, her little pink tongue darting out to wet her rosy lips. "Yes. But you're not a stranger. You're Jack."

He frowned, taken aback. "How did you know that?"

"Auntie Clara told me." She sighed, and he had a feeling there was more to it than she let on. Strange. She couldn't be more than four or five, but she seemed to be an old soul. "My name is Frances."

Auntie Clara? Could this little girl be Mia's daughter? He stuck out his hand. "Nice to meet you, Frances."

She accepted his hand and held on, a tiny frown marring her delicate features. "Why do you hurt so?" she asked in a quiet voice.

"I-I don't." How would she know anything of what he felt inside? He pulled his hand away from hers, shaken at the power of her gaze. "Maybe you should go find your momma."

She shook her head, her mass of dark curls shaking around her shoulders. "Momma's right inside. She sent me out to the garden for basil." She reached into the pocket of her white dress and pulled out a handful of green leaves. "It cures headaches, you know."

"Is that so?"

Frances nodded, those huge eyes boring holes right through him. She stood and wiped her palms down the front of her dress, leaving dirt streaks on the fabric. "I have to bring these to my momma now. She's making a tea. When you need something to help your headaches, just ask my momma. She'll fix you up."

With that she took off, leaving him wondering how such a little thing knew about his headaches. He shook his head against the thought. She hadn't known, she'd just been guessing. Some of the things she said made him think she'd just been repeating what she'd heard from the adults around her. "Basil curing headaches? What small child would know that?"

"You'd be surprised at what Frances knows."

He jumped at the sound of another voice, this one coming from the front door. Clara hobbled out onto the porch and over to the swing.

"Do you mind if I sit down? My leg is starting to get a little tired."

"Not at all." He moved over to share the swing.

"I take it you met my great-niece." Clara said softly, gazing out at the yard.

"Frances," he muttered, still shaken by her predictions — and those eyes.

"Don't let her get to you. She's young, doesn't understand yet that she needs to keep her gift quiet."

"Her gift?"

Clara nodded. "She's going to make quite a healer someday, gifted just like her mom. I've never met a pair with more natural ability in my life. They know things the rest of us could only wish to know." She sighed. "Of course, the air up here tends to have strange effects on people."

What in the world was she talking about? "Yeah, I can imagine."

Clara shook her head. "There are things here you'd never imagine. This place is very powerful."

"Um, sure."

The silence around them threatened to choke him with weirdness. Did Nancy know the people who ran this little place were all nuts? He was about to excuse himself when Clara spoke again.

"What is it that you want out of life?" she asked, taking him by surprise.

Jack raised his eyebrow at Clara's strange question. "I have everything I want."

"I don't think you do." She looked at him then, her gaze locking with his. What was it about this family? Were they all so strange, or just the ones who lived up here?

"I'm sorry, but you couldn't possibly know that. We just met the day before yesterday."

"And I see it. In your eyes." She clicked her tongue. "You can pretend you're happy all you want, but your eyes don't lie."

Ha. He'd made a living out of bending, if not downright breaking, the truth. Being a divorce attorney, it was a part of his job. That's how his clients got the big settlements, and how he got the big paychecks. Still, one look in Clara's knowing eyes and he knew he couldn't fool her.

"I don't know why I'm telling you this. My life is a little screwed up right now."

"Because of a woman?"

"A woman?" He barked a laugh at the absurdity of it. "I don't have time for women. It's a lot more complicated than that."

"Work, then?" She just laughed. "You can turn it around, you know. It's not too late."

"What are you talking about?"

"You still have time to make some happiness for yourself. Find yourself a nice woman to settle down with. Have a family, a life other than the one at your office."

He sighed. "I'm not looking. Really." He'd have to introduce this woman to his mother. They'd get along famously.

"You should be. You aren't getting any younger, you know."

He scoffed at the idea. "And that's exactly why I'm not planning to waste any more time on a lost cause. I don't do well with commitment."

"You aren't a lost cause, dear." Clara smiled. "Don't write love off just yet. I have a feeling things may be turning around for you."

"Are you some kind of psychic?" Like he even believed in that kind of thing.

She shook her head, seemingly oblivious to his sarcasm. "No. I just pay more attention to the world around me than most people do. Try it sometime. Listen to nature, to the world. You'll know what's right if you go with your instinct, instead of all that fancy training you must have."

She took something out of her pocket and handed it to him. It was a small, red cloth bag, about three inches square. He'd found a similar one in his bedroom—blue instead of red—and had learned that when you picked one of them up and sniffed it, you got a lungful of some pretty pungent spices.

"What is this for? I already have one of these things."

"Not this one, you don't. All of my guests get blue charm bags in their rooms, for harmony during their stay. But you, I think you need a little something extra."

"Charm bags, huh?" Had he slipped into *The Twilight Zone* when he wasn't looking? "What are they for?"

"Oh, lots of things. Different combinations of ingredients produce different results."

A sinking feeling started in the pit of his stomach. "So what does red stand for?" He was afraid he already knew the answer.

She smiled a Cheshire cat smile. "Love, of course."

Love. *Wonderful.* "Listen, I —"

"Hold on a second, Jack. This is important."

So was his sanity. "I don't think I —"

She shushed him with a wave of her hand. "You mustn't think of anyone in particular when you concentrate on the bag. Just the qualities you look for in a woman. If you use it correctly, it will help you find your ideal mate."

He laughed at the idea. What *did* he look for in a woman? Someone who wasn't after his money, for a start. Someone who wouldn't question him when he came home late at night or forgot to call. Someone who understood his need to network, to keep up his business contacts. "Okay. Um, thanks."

He got up to leave, fed up with the weird turn in the conversation, but her small, cool hand on his arm stopped him. "Trust what I say, Jack. You'll be much happier if you follow my advice."

"Sure." And when he woke up in the morning he'd find out that there was a heat wave at the North Pole.

"You should consider taking a swim this evening. The lake water can heal any hurt."

He shook his head as he left the porch and went back to his room. The old woman was crazy. There wasn't any other explanation. They'd just met. How would she think he was there to heal? There was nothing to heal from. He'd never let anyone close enough to hurt him—yet another trick he'd learned from his father.

With a shuddering sigh, he came to a realization. He'd failed at every attempted romantic relationship he'd ever entered into.

Jack Cullen didn't fail.

He never failed at anything. If he didn't think he could do it, and do it well, he didn't bother to try. So what had happened to mess it all up? He'd been so sure. He'd followed his plan to the letter. He'd gone to law school, established his career, went to work for his father and uncle like he'd been expected to. The only thing he hadn't been able to do—and it wasn't for lack of trying, no matter what his mother said—was find a woman to share everything he had. He was too dedicated to his career to give a relationship his all. And if he couldn't manage it one hundred percent, he gave up.

Without even realizing it, he'd given up on something he should have made a top priority. His happiness.

He sat on the edge of the bed, making a fist around the bag in his hand, and thought about what he wanted in a woman. He might not be looking, but it didn't hurt to play along. Hey, if it would make an old woman happy, why not. It was all just for fun anyway.

What *did* he want? She'd be attractive—he was a guy, after all. Tall, model-thin, with a perfect face, long, light blonde hair, and ice blue eyes. She'd have pale skin—no tan, because that would cause sun damage and premature wrinkles—manicured, long red nails, and she wouldn't mind wandering around nude all the time.

He laughed as he tossed the bag on the nightstand next to the bed. Lies. All of it. He didn't want any of that, no matter how much he tried to pretend. He'd described the type of women he usually dated, someone who would look good on his arm at a business dinner and even better in his bed at night. But what about what he *really* wanted, deep down inside?

He hadn't a clue.

He shook his head as he stood up. He didn't care for using some bogus charm, but the swim Clara had suggested did sound fun. But not right away. Later, when the other guests had returned to their rooms and he'd have the beach to himself.

Chapter Five

Jack made his way down to the beach at a little before seven that night. Twilight painted the sky in oranges and pinks, reflecting off the surface of the water. He set his towel down by a small cluster of rocks in the far corner of the beach and toed off his shoes. The evening was silent save for the birds chirping in the trees and the water gently lapping the shoreline. The rest of the guests, mostly honeymooners or folks celebrating anniversaries, were nowhere to be found. That was fine with him—he hadn't realized, when he'd booked the room on his secretary's recommendation, that he'd be surrounded by all the lovey-dovey cooing he usually found annoying at best. Maybe that had been Nancy's plan—to get him away from everything so he could finally slow down and see what he was missing.

He saw, all right. Her plan worked too well. For the first time in his life, he realized how alone he really was.

The sun faded into the sky, leaving him alone in the darkness of the waning moon with just his thoughts to keep him company. He sat for what must have been a half hour before finally deciding to go for a swim.

And that was when he saw her.

Mia was walking down the path toward the beach. He thought about waving to her, but then decided against it. He'd rather watch, unseen, for at least a little while. As far as he could tell, she hadn't spotted him sitting half-hidden by the rocks.

Her robe dropped to the pale sand, leaving her wearing what he first thought was nothing—but upon closer inspection he noticed it was actually a flesh-colored bathing suit.

One piece.

Damn.

This whole aloneness thing was starting to get old.

She stepped into the water and waded in to her waist before she dove under the surface. When she came back up for air, she pushed her soaked curls out of her eyes with both hands and shook her head vigorously, sending a spray of water droplets into the air, shining in the moonlight. She rolled her shoulders a few times and turned.

And then she saw him.

He froze, waiting for her to get out of the water and leave — or tell him to give her some privacy. But she didn't. She raised her hand in the air, and crooked her finger. He was hard instantly, and he didn't even consider not fulfilling her request.

He stood up and stripped off his shirt before joining her in the water.

* * * * *

Mia stood still in the water as she watched Jack's approach. She hadn't expected to see him down at the beach so late, but she wasn't disappointed that he was there. She'd wanted to talk to him, anyway, and this seemed like the perfect opportunity.

All day she'd thought about him, to the point where she couldn't manage to get one iota of work done. Why couldn't she get him out of her head? She couldn't even make a simple tea without wondering what he was doing, where he was, or if he was lonely.

She had people counting on her, residents she'd been healing for several years. If she couldn't do her job, she'd lose their trust, and she didn't want to let anyone down. So she needed to learn more about Jack. She was sure that, considering his job and social status, the more she learned about him the less she'd find to like.

She'd come down for a swim after Jess had offered to read Frances her story and put her to bed. She'd been hoping for some quiet thinking time in the place she loved most, but this was even better. This was a unique opportunity for her to solve a problem that had been plaguing her since Jack had checked into the bed and breakfast. She needed to prove to herself that he couldn't possibly be as attractive — as *sexy* — as her mind seemed to believe.

"Hey," he said as he stopped next to her. It was all she could do not to reach out and touch those toned chest muscles. *Physical attraction isn't everything.*

"Hi." Her response sounded weaker than she'd hoped for, but at least she hadn't swooned at his feet. Yet. The night was still young.

"So, come here often?"

She rolled her eyes at his joke. "As often as I can." No. This wasn't helping. She even found his lame lines cute.

She was in serious trouble.

She turned away from him to get her bearings, and her gaze fell on the sliver of moon high in the sky. Almost there. Almost the new moon. Time for changes, Clara had said, time to bring in the new — new self, new job, new relationships. New awareness.

Sexual awareness?

She smiled at the thought. Clara had always told her that you can't fight your own destiny. The pull she felt with Jack didn't want to go away, no matter how much she ignored it. Destiny? Or something else? Well, there was only one way to be certain.

She spun around and wrapped her arms around his neck, pulling him down for a kiss.

If she thought he'd push her away, she'd been wrong. With his arms around her back, he molded their bodies together and returned her kiss with enthusiasm. She clung to him, taking as much as she gave and not regretting it for an instant. His hand squeezed her hip, pressing her stomach harder against his erection. She moaned into his mouth and wiggled against him. Her pussy was drenched — and not entirely from the lake — and her nipples pebbled. The feel of her wet swimsuit brushing against her skin created a delicious friction she couldn't help but revel in.

When Jack broke the kiss and stepped away, they were both panting.

"What was that for?" he asked, his tone aroused and annoyed at the same time. "You could have given me a little warning."

She shrugged, trying for casual but achieving, at best, anxious. "I felt like it."

"Do you always follow your impulses?"

No. Never. "When they're strong, I do." She splashed him a little before she turned and ran. Or, at least, tried to. He'd grabbed her before she got two feet away and hauled her back against him, her back pressed tightly to his front.

She felt his whisper against her ear. "You've got me tied in knots, Mia. I don't know you. I don't understand any of this. But I want to touch you."

She felt the same. She whimpered as his hands slid slowly down her sides and back up again, stopping to cup her breasts in his warm palms. She couldn't hold back a shudder as his thumbs flicked across her beaded nipples, rolling them gently under his touch. She rocked back against him and delighted in the feel of his rock-hard cock pressed into the center of her back. She wanted to feel him between her legs, thrusting that cock into her waiting pussy.

It had been so long—three years—since she'd felt a man's cock inside her, and Jack made her hormones rage for something she hadn't realized she'd been missing.

With Steven, sex had been good. With Jack, she imagined it would be explosive. Everything inside her told her to stop—that she shouldn't be letting him touch her in such an intimate way. He was a stranger, really, though he didn't feel like one. But she'd put this into motion, and she wasn't ready to stop just yet.

He let one hand slip lower, down her belly, lower still, until he cupped her mound in his palm. Through the thin fabric of her swimsuit, she felt like his heat would scorch her. She moved her hips as she felt her pussy drench with anticipation.

"This is crazy," he told her, his voice no more than a whisper against her neck. "We shouldn't be doing this. I should leave."

"You're right. We should stop." Even as she said the words, she knew she'd do nothing to stop him, just as she knew he wouldn't really walk away.

He leaned in and kissed her neck, small tingling kisses that had her squirming in seconds. His hand slipped under the elastic leg band of her swimsuit and moved it away. The feeling of the cool water against her naked skin was amazing—and arousing. He slid his fingers over her sensitive skin, teasing her folds before he found her clit and stroked in earnest. She bucked against him, the sensation almost too much to bear. He slid his fingers into her throbbing pussy as his tongue and lips teased and tormented the tender skin where her neck met her shoulder.

Her orgasm took her completely by surprise—no slow and steady building like she'd known before. It hit her all at once, the sensation exploding inside her and her inner muscles pulsing. She writhed in the water so much that she wriggled out of his grasp and slid under. Jack pulled her up, laughing. "Are you okay?"

"I think so." At that point, she couldn't be too sure.

She swiped the water out of her eyes and turned to face Jack on shaky legs. The look in his eyes mirrored what she felt inside—unsure, nervous, and very turned on. She bit her lip, not sure of what to say after such an intimate encounter. She felt the inane urge to apologize, yet at the same time her body cried out for so much more.

She reached out and ran a finger down his chest, delighting in his shiver. He caught her hand in his and brought it to his lips, brushing a kiss over her knuckles. He leaned in and kissed her cheek—and then turned and walked out of the water.

Not sure if he expected her to follow, she didn't. Instead, she went to where she'd left her towel and picked it up off the sand.

* * * * *

When Jack turned and Mia wasn't behind him, he felt a sharp pang of disappointment. But what had he expected? He'd touched her in a way he shouldn't have, not for a woman he barely knew. She probably thought he did this kind of thing all the time.

He didn't.

In fact, his actions tonight surprised him almost as much as her kiss had. What had he been thinking? He was many things, but impulsive didn't even make the list. He glanced at her across the sand. She stood looking out into the water, her towel clutched to her chest like a shield. Had he made a terrible mistake? There was only one way to find out. He crossed the sand to where she stood and took the towel from her hands.

"Need some help?" he asked, not waiting for a response before running the towel over her damp back.

"Thanks." Her voice sounded tight, nervous—and aroused.

"Are you okay?" he asked her for the second time that night, fully expecting her to say she was.

She surprised him again. "I-I really don't know. I'm…" Her voice trailed off and she turned to face him. "What happened out there…it was really nice, Jack."

"Nice?" He fought back a laugh. Her actions had told him so much more than her words.

She smiled. "Okay, better than nice. But it can't happen again."

He'd been afraid of that. "Sorry if I rushed things. I'd really like a chance to get to know you better."

"I wish that was possible." She glanced up toward the stone steps that led back to the inn, a frown marring her features. "I have responsibilities. I'm very attracted to you—so much that it scares me since I hardly know you. But I can't do this."

Without another word, she picked up her robe and slipped it on, heading back in the direction of the house.

"Where are you going?" He didn't want to let her go just yet, not when he still needed answers. Why had she kissed him? Why had she let him touch her so intimately?

Why would she admit she was attracted to him, but didn't want anything to do with him, in the same sentence?

She stopped and glanced over her shoulder. "I'm going to bed."

He almost asked if she wanted some company, but he bit it back in time. He needed time to think—and so did Mia. The strong pull he felt toward her unnerved him. But he had to admit to himself that it couldn't be anything more than sexual chemistry. He didn't believe in anything as foolish as love at first sight, no matter how much his mind tried to convince him differently.

He shook his head as she turned away and walked across the sand. His body gave an involuntary shudder at the sight of her hips swaying gently against the billowy fabric of her robe. Yeah, it was lust all right, plain and simple. He'd gone far too long without a woman, and now that he found himself faced with a semi-willing one, his body kicked into overdrive. He needed to get laid—something his brother told him incessantly—but the island wasn't exactly brimming with choices. So it looked like he'd be waiting until he got back home, unless he could convince Mia that they'd be damned good together.

He let out a frustrated groan and waded back into the lake. The cool water lapped against his legs and he dove under, not coming back to the surface until he needed to breathe. His head ached, his gut ached, and his cock ached—he needed some kind of relief. Soon.

He slipped his swim trunks down past his hips and took his painfully stiff cock in his hand and stroking up and down a few times. He was close — *too* close. It wouldn't take more than a few seconds for him to come. Mia did that to him — she'd made him so hot he could barely think straight. He wanted to bury himself in her slick pussy, feel her clench around him as her orgasm took her. He'd been so close. If she hadn't doused herself in the water, he would have been inside her right now, sliding in and out of her hot, wet flesh.

He *needed* that. He needed *her*.

His gut clenched with his impending orgasm as he imagined his cock filling Mia's pussy, slamming into her while she begged for more. He threw his head back and came with a strangled groan. *Jesus.* How was he going to survive the rest of the vacation without falling apart?

* * * * *

Mia watched Jack from a secluded spot on the path, her gaze riveted to the movement of his hand on his cock. She caught her lower lip between her teeth and sighed, unable to look away from the arousing sight. She'd planned on going back to the house and going back to bed, she really had, but when she'd heard him splashing in the water, she hadn't been able to resist a peek. Now she was glad she had stayed. He was so amazing, every inch of him.

She felt her pussy grow damp all over again as she watched him pleasure himself. Part of her wanted to go back there and join him. She'd been here in seclusion for so long she'd forgotten what a real man looked like. Or what he smelled like. Or tasted like.

She leaned against a nearby tree and slid her fingers under the leg band of her swimsuit. When they slipped along her folds, she realized just how wet watching Jack touch himself made her. She thrust two fingers inside her pussy, imagining it was Jack's cock filling her. She found her clit with her thumb and pressed down hard, moving it in slow circles that sent ripples of pleasure through her. Her orgasm rippled through her at the same time as she saw Jack throw his head back and yell out into the night. She slumped against the tree, unable to move for a few minutes. When Jack got out of the water and picked up his things, presumably to head back to the inn, it goaded her into action and she made her way back up the rest of the rocky path to the house.

Where she found Clara sitting on a couch in the living room.

"What have you been doing? Causing trouble again?" Clara asked her, looking her over entirely too closely in the dim light from the wall sconces that stayed on all night.

"I haven't caused trouble in years," Mia answered, brushing a lock of damp hair behind her ear. She didn't need this now, not after what had happened with Jack. And after.

"Uh-huh." Clara laughed. "How's Mr. Cullen?"

"Who?"

Clara gave Mia a knowing look. "I might be aging, but there's nothing wrong with my eyesight. I see the way he looks at you, *and* the way you look at him."

"I don't look at him any differently than I do any of your other guests."

Clara clicked her tongue. "You might as was well accept it, dear."

"Accept what?"

"Destiny."

Destiny? Try serious lust and nothing more. "Whatever." She should have expected this. Aunt Clara never failed. Good thing she'd already formulated her own plan. "I don't want anything to do with the man."

"Sure you don't."

With that, Clara went to bed, leaving Mia alone to think about her words.

* * * * *

Mia woke up the next morning to Frances bouncing on the end of her bed. After her tryst with Jack in the lake, she'd slept soundly for the entire night. Amazing, how just a little activity could relax her so much. She glanced at the clock. *Nine fifteen*? She'd missed breakfast.

"Morning, Momma," Frances said cheerily.

"Stop jumping before you break the springs." She got out of bed and stretched her arms over her head. "Why didn't you wake me up when you got up like you usually do?"

"Auntie Clara told me to let you sleep. She said you needed a break, for once."

Mia frowned. That made it sound like she needed time away from caring for her own child. Nothing could be further from the truth. She loved her time with Frances, and wouldn't trade it for anything in the world. She had her priorities straight—or at least she would from now on.

"Go and brush your teeth, then meet me downstairs. We'll work in the garden today."

Frances groaned. "Oh, Momma, do we have to work today? I want to *play*!" She stomped her feet up and down on the mattress, banging the headboard into the wall.

"Stop it, Frances. Work first, play after. You said you wanted to learn about herbs and healing, remember?"

"But Momma, I—"

Mia held her hand in the air. "Hush."

"Okay." She moped as she walked out of the room. Mia laughed. It would be a matter of minutes before Frances stood in the garden, plucking fat weeds from the beds as she listened in rapt silence to everything Mia taught her.

This was how her life should be. Simple, yet important. Her work did wonders for those around her, and she had the ability to pass the gift on to her daughter.

Jack, unfortunately, had thrown the proverbial wrench into her plans. She was too attracted to him. That could be a problem. She didn't want to rely on anyone—which was why she'd avoided dating since Steven had passed. She had more important things to do, didn't have time to waste with temporary flings.

Until Jack.

He unnerved her, made her sweat, made her want to run in the other direction. She'd been raised to rely on herself, and around him she felt like she could easily lose herself. But she didn't want that to happen. Her life just didn't work that way, not anymore. She had people relying on her—she didn't need to become dependent on anyone, especially a man.

She liked taking care of others. That was what she did. She always had, all her life. Her mother had taught her the ways of witchcraft and healing, the uses for herbs and aromatherapy. She used those teachings every day of her life and in recent years had begun to pass them down to her own daughter. Her inner instinct dictated that she take care of people.

But did that include Jack?

The answer was exactly what she'd expected. *Yes.* When someone needed help, she couldn't turn them away. He'd come here for a reason. He'd probably be averse to calling it fate, but she had begun to believe that it was what brought him to Bennett Island—but not for the purpose Clara seemed to think. Jack came to heal, like many other people over the years.

He needed a change in his life, more so than she did. If he didn't stop working himself so hard, he was going to work himself into an early grave. She'd seen him sitting on the porch, his laptop settled on his lap or his cell phone in his hand. Even when on vacation, the man couldn't let go, even if he didn't use them. She worried about him, just as she'd worry about anyone who couldn't see that there was more to life than a paycheck.

Was that her purpose here? Was she to show him how to make the changes he so desperately needed? He needed to relax, yet she could see how difficult it was for him. Clara had tried, in her usual interfering sort of way, to talk him into taking the much needed time off, but Mia doubted it would have much effect. Men like him usually had to have a heart attack or a similar scare to get them to see how bad for them that type of lifestyle really was. Jack didn't even look forty yet, but she'd seen much younger men suffer from disorders associated with stress.

Why she felt it was her business, she had no idea. She just hated to see suffering of any kind, and she had a feeling he was suffering.

Even if he didn't know it.

She threw on an old pair of jeans, a t-shirt, and a pair of sandals and met Frances downstairs. The weather had taken another warm turn, and Frances stood at the bottom of the stairs bouncing on her toes. Her eyes had taken on the mischievous sparkle Mia knew so well, and she knew there wouldn't be much teaching today. The child obviously had other ideas.

Frances drew a deep, noisy breath before she started her pitch. "Uncle Lou says he'll take me out on his boat today. Auntie Jess and him are taking some of the guests in the lake, and he said I can help him. He said I know how to talk lots and can tell everyone about the island while he drives. Can I please, *please* go, Momma?"

"He's got that right. You sure do know how to talk." Mia ruffled her daughter's hair, unable to say no to her request when she sounded so excited. There would be plenty of time for learning later, but Frances had to take time to be a child. "Make sure you wear your lifejacket, and listen to what Uncle Lou and Jess say, okay?"

Frances clapped her hands and jumped up and down. "Thank you! Love you, Momma. See you at lunch time." She gave Mia a quick hug and bounded off to find Lou.

Mia sighed and went out to the garden to get started, wondering if she'd run into Jack sometime today. And if she did, would she have the courage to face him after what had happened the night before?

Chapter Six

She didn't have to wait long to find out. Jack came around the back of the house toward her gardens as Mia was watering her rosemary and basil. He'd apparently been running, which she'd noticed him do a few times during his stay, and his gray t-shirt was soaked with sweat. Her breath caught in her throat and she tried to ward off the excited yet uneasy feeling just seeing him caused in her. What should she say? Should she ignore him and pretend last night had never happened?

She shook her head and went back to her watering. She'd take her cues from him.

"Hey," he said as he slowed and approached the garden.

"Hi." She smiled at him, but it faded fast at the intimate look in his eyes. She couldn't do this. She couldn't pretend she wasn't attracted when every cell in her body was calling for a repeat of the night before. If she didn't walk away, she was going to forget all her convictions and do something she'd later regret — when Jack had left the island for good and she was once again left all alone. She started to walk past him to go back into the house, but his voice stopped her.

"Don't rush away on my account. I've got to take a shower anyway," he told her, but didn't move. He stayed right where he was, staring at her and making her weak in the knees, and the longer he stood there the more uncomfortable the silence became. Finally, she couldn't take it anymore.

"Jack?"

"Yeah?" His voice held a husky quality that echoed somewhere deep inside her.

"Didn't you say you had to take a shower?"

"Yeah." But still he didn't budge. His gaze locked with hers and she couldn't make herself walk away. She crossed her arms over her chest and tried to put a professional expression on her face to get him to move along.

"Do you want something?" she asked.

He smiled as he lifted his hand to her face, tracing the line of her jaw with his finger. She shivered, but didn't even think about pushing him away. "Funny. Your aunt asked me a similar question yesterday."

Her breath caught in her throat as she spoke. "Did she?"

"She did." Jack moved his finger down her throat to where her shoulder met her neck, making concentration almost impossible. "She asked me what I want out of life."

"What-what was your answer?" Did she really want to know?

"I want what everyone else does, I guess." He dropped his hand to her waist and pulled her closer. "To be happy."

Yeah. She wanted that, too. But she had a feeling that, like Jack, she really didn't know what would make her happy. She thought she'd known once—she'd held that complete and total happiness in the palm of her hand, but when it disappeared in the smoke and ashes of the fire, she'd realized it took a lot more than living someone else's life to make her happy. She'd moved across the country for Steven's job. She left her family and friends to start over with the man she'd loved. She wouldn't trade what she'd had with Steven for the world, but she wouldn't repeat it again, either.

"Why would she think I need to change my life?" Jack asked, his tone serious. She needed to do something to lighten the moment before she started fooling herself into thinking she could really come to care about him. The less she knew about the real Jack, the man he was when he wasn't vacationing, the better for her heart.

"Because you're boring?" she asked, tightening the grip on the hose she held to her side.

He laughed at that. "You don't really think I'm boring, do you?"

Was he kidding? She'd never met anyone like him. She *should* find him boring—the self-confessed workaholic lawyer he was—but for some reason she didn't. "Actually, no."

"That's a good thing."

She pulled away from his grip and stepped back, training the stream of water from the hose on her thyme plants. "*You're* not boring. But I'll bet you think I am."

He barked a laugh and followed her as she walked through the herb patches. "Hardly. I can't figure you out."

"That's probably a good thing. You don't need to waste your time on me when you can go back to Boston and flirt with the big city girls."

He circled his fingers around her arm to stop her forward motion. "Will you stop moving for a few seconds and listen to me? I want to get to know you, to understand you. I want to spend time with you. What do you find wrong with that?"

The fact that he planned to leave, for starters. She couldn't—*wouldn't*—talk about this with him. Not now. Maybe not ever. In an attempt to lighten the mood and distract him from his prying questions—or at least that's what she told herself—she lifted the hose and flipped the nozzle to high.

"Since you don't seem to be in any rush to take a shower, let me help you a little," she told him as she sprayed cold water in his direction. He let out a surprised grunt, but recovered quickly. In seconds, he'd wrested the hose out of her hand and turned it on her, drenching her with the freezing water. She turned to run, but he grabbed her around the waist and hauled her back against him. With her wet chest pressed to his, she could feel the heat radiating off him.

"Jack?"

He didn't answer. Instead, he leaned down and kissed her.

From the second his lips touched hers, she knew it was right. His lips teased and played with hers and she wound her arms around his neck. If she tried to pretend there was nothing between them, she'd be fighting a losing battle. She and Jack had chemistry stronger than she'd ever experienced, and it had taken her by surprise. It made her legs weak and her head spin—which she wasn't sure was entirely a bad thing.

When Jack broke the kiss and stepped away, she let her mind drift slowly back to reality. "We really should talk about last night."

He gave her a slow, sensual smile that had her stomach doing flip-flops. "I want my mouth on you. My tongue inside you."

"What?" She suddenly had a hard time hearing over the rushing of blood in her ears. The thought of Jack, between her legs, his mouth and tongue…oh, boy. She needed to sit down.

She sank down on one of the white wicker benches that sat at the edge of the garden. "You want to…"

"Oh, yeah." His tone was husky, his voice impossibly deep. She could barely control her response. She was soaked from the water hose. Not only that, her panties were so wet—just from a kiss and a few well-chosen words—that she'd have to change everything when she went inside.

"What do you say? You want to go find a quiet place and spend a few hours getting to know each other?"

Yes, she did. But she stopped herself, thinking it was the middle of the day and anyone could be watching. She'd been irresponsible to let him kiss her. Now she needed to get control of the situation before anything else happened. She patted the bench seat next to her. "We can talk just fine right here."

He didn't look happy about it—in fact, he looked like he might be in pain, but she couldn't help it. Clara, no matter how much she wanted to play matchmaker, wouldn't condone fooling around in the public garden. And she had Frances to think about.

Frances.

She had yet to tell Jack about her daughter. That ought to be an interesting conversation.

Jack sat next to her, so close that his bare, damp thigh pressed against her leg. A chill ran through her nerves.

"I have a question for you," he said, his expression dark and sensual, yet probing at the same time.

"What do want to know?" She expected him to ask about her home life, her family — anything but the subject he chose.

"What is it with those little bags Clara's handing out?"

Her breath caught in her throat. No. This was *not* a good conversation to have. Not now. What had Clara done this time? "What did she give you?"

"Some little red felt bag she called a charm bag. Some kind of love thing."

Mia let out a heavy breath. *What are you trying to pull, Clara?* "She's trying to see to your happiness, apparently, in any way she can. When did she give you that?"

"Yesterday afternoon."

Well, at least it hadn't been after their…incident. "Good."

"Why? What's up with all of this natural healing stuff, anyway?"

"Natural healing? It's a little more complicated than that."

He sat back on the bench, his back against the stone wall behind them. "Tell me about it."

Here it comes. The kiss of death to any spark of interest he might have felt. Still, she might as well tell him now and get it over with. No sense prolonging this until it was too late. "Clara's a witch."

"A witch?" He laughed. "Like cauldrons and broomsticks and magic wands?"

She shook her head. "No. Not like the Halloween type of witches you're probably used to. She practices traditional witchcraft."

Jack's gaze shot to hers. "What about you? I see you working in these gardens all the time."

"Yes, I practice witchcraft as well."

His expression was a healthy mix of intrigue and confusion. "So…you're a witch?"

"Yes, I am. I'm a healer." She stared at him, waiting for him to laugh, to walk away, anything to show he thought she was crazy. But he just sat there looking pensive and a little annoyed. She let out a frustrated breath, not wanting to prolong the inevitable. When she'd first told Steven, he'd laughed in her face. It had taken a long time to convince him that she was serious. "Why do you not look surprised?"

He sighed. "I honestly don't know. I guess I knew something was different here. I just couldn't pinpoint what."

"So you believe in it?" She waited tensely for his answer.

He shrugged. "Well, I suppose I do. It's just like any other religion, right?"

"I suppose," she said, a little disappointed at his reaction. She'd been so hoping that he'd be different, that he wouldn't judge her on her beliefs, but that didn't seem to be the case. She watched the interest fade from his eyes as he stood up.

"I've got to get inside and take a shower. I'll see you around, okay?" he told her.

"Yeah. Great. See you around."

He ran toward the house, not stopping until he'd disappeared through the back door.

Mia went back to working in her gardens, but her heart wasn't in the task anymore. For just a minute, she'd held on to the hope that Jack would understand, and that he'd want to get to know her despite what she believed in. But he'd run as if scared without even listening. She tried to tell herself that a man like that wasn't worth her time, but she couldn't help the ball of disappointment that welled up inside her.

* * * * *

Jack stood in the shower, the water as cold as he could get it and still stand under the spray. He was still heated from his run, and the steamy kiss with Mia hadn't helped. The woman, even after her confession, remained a complete mystery to him. She didn't give anything away easily. That was part of what had initially attracted him to her. But this afternoon, everything had changed. The more he got to know her, the more he realized he didn't *know* her at all.

A witch.

He never would have guessed. Not in a million years. Yeah, there was something different about her, but he figured it had something to do with living on the island, being apart from the bustle of the big cities. But, a *witch*?

He'd always laughed at his mother when she'd said he'd know it when he met the one woman meant for him. But the second he'd seen Mia—or, the second she'd backed into him while vacuuming—he'd known. He hadn't wanted to admit it to himself—that would be too impulsive—but he couldn't deny it now. There was something strong between them, and it had nothing to do with sexual chemistry.

But Mia...it *couldn't* be her. They had no chance of making a serious relationship work. They were too different. Yet, the first time they'd made eye contact had hit him like a kick in the gut. The sparks had been instant, for both of them, but she'd thrown a serious cramp into any ideas he'd gotten with her confession.

He could just imagine introducing her at office holiday parties. "This is my wife, Mia. Did I happen to mention that she's a witch? And don't laugh, or she might put a curse on you."

Did witches really do that? Or was it just something in fairy tales? He didn't know. This was all too much. He'd finally found a woman who made him forget about his endless pursuit of all things material, and they were completely incompatible.

Were they really?

He heard his mother's voice inside his head, berating him for acting like a first-class jerk. And the more he thought about it, the more he realized it was true. He felt a connection with Mia. Couldn't that be enough? Was there some way he could convince her that they owed it to themselves to at least give it a try?

He didn't know. He might have screwed everything up by running away from her. The only thing he could do was find her, and really listen to what she had to say. But first, he wanted to find Clara and see if she could give him a little more insight into Mia's world.

* * * * *

Mia worked out in her garden for the rest of the morning, until Frances came back from her trip with Uncle Lou and Jess. The little girl came bustling into the yard, carrying a huge sack of candy. "Look at what Uncle Lou bought for me at the store at the marina!"

"Wonderful." Mia would have to speak to Lou about it later. "Just what you need. Ten pounds of chocolate and sugar."

"It's only five pounds, Momma." Frances sighed as she plopped down on the grass. "Can I help you pull weeds?"

"Not in that dress." She gestured to one of Clara's creations—frilly, but not practical in the least. "If you want to work, you need to go change first."

Frances looked down at her dress and rolled her eyes. "Maybe later." She didn't particularly care for dressing like a wedding cake, Mia knew, but she tolerated it for the summers they spent on the island. Once she got back to the mainland and her preschool she'd be back to dressing in jeans and little t-shirts like the other girls.

"Hi, Jack," Frances said, her voice light and bubbly.

Mia froze. How did Frances know *Jack*?

She looked up, and sure enough, she saw Jack walking toward them, carrying one of Clara's old-fashioned wicker picnic hampers. He sat down on the grass next to Frances. "Hey, kiddo. What are you up to?"

"Watching my momma do the garden. I want to help her, but she said no dresses in the garden."

He glanced at Mia, his gaze questioning. Maybe she should have mentioned Frances a little sooner.

"That's my momma," Frances continued as Mia's heart lodged in her throat.

"I kind of guessed that," he spoke to Frances, but looked at Mia. "You look almost exactly alike."

Mia looked down at her garden. She expected Jack to walk away, but he didn't. He kept talking to Frances. "I was hoping you and your mom would like to take a picnic with me."

Mia shot her gaze up to his. "What are you talking about?"

"I seem to have missed lunch again, but Clara was kind enough to pack me a basket. She said she packed a bit extra, enough for three if anyone wants to share." He glanced at Frances and then to Mia.

Frances's eyes lit up. "Please, Momma? Can we go?"

Mia bit the inside of her cheek. She didn't want Frances getting attached to Jack since he'd be leaving soon, but she didn't want the girl to feel isolated for the entire season, either. And Jack seemed to be making an effort. Maybe he'd accepted her confession better than it had appeared. At any rate, she could at least spend the afternoon with him and get away from the gardens for a little while. "Okay, we'll go."

Frances let out a whoop of delight and followed as Jack led them up a path through the woods that would lead to a small clearing—Clara had obviously given him directions, since he didn't even hesitate along the path. Mia shook her head. She was going to kill Clara later. No matter how many times she insisted, Clara couldn't understand that she wasn't looking for a man—she wouldn't be until Frances was much older.

Especially a man who didn't really understand what she was, and that she wasn't going to change. She'd found that once, with Steven, and she wasn't sure she'd ever find it again.

* * * * *

Jack sat on the blanket next to Mia, watching her watch her daughter play. Clara had shocked him with the announcement that Frances was Mia's daughter, but only mildly. Since he'd met Frances he'd suspected she might belong to Mia, but Mia hadn't mentioned her so he'd put the thought to the back of his mind. He didn't care that she had a child, though it probably would have bothered him a few weeks ago. Since he'd embarked on this vacation, everything had changed.

"You're not married, are you?" he asked, even though he already knew the answer. Clara had told him a bit about Mia and her past while he'd helped her pack the lunch. She'd been through a lot so young, and his heart went out to her. Hearing her story made him feel like even more of a jerk for deserting her earlier.

"No." She shook her head, her expression saddening. "I was. But Steven died." She let out a soft sigh and brushed a windswept curl from her eyes. "There was a fire in our house, in the middle of the night. Three years ago. Frances and I made it out. He didn't."

"I'm sorry," he said earnestly. He couldn't even imagine what she'd been through. Compared to her loss, his father's workaholic behavior and sometimes emotional abuse didn't seem like such a bad thing.

She turned to him then and smiled, and something in the region of his heart—if he had one, since that had yet to be determined—tightened. This wasn't a business deal, or related to money in any way, but for some reason it gave him the same kind of rush. It wasn't just sex either, though he wanted that with Mia, it was something more. Something that scared him and exhilarated him at the same time, like he couldn't get enough. When Clara asked him what he wanted out of life, he hadn't had an answer. He did now. He wanted that feeling to continue. Forever.

With Mia.

Shocked at the direction of his thoughts, he coughed and opened the picnic hamper. When she'd said there'd be enough food for three, she hadn't been kidding. He could feed a football team with what she'd packed. He pulled a couple of sandwiches and a bag of chips from the bag when Mia spoke.

"Tell me something about you. You've been hurt before, haven't you?"

It was more of a statement than a question, and it made him pause. "What do you mean?"

"Tell me who made you afraid to care."

He drew a deep breath, nervous that she could read his feelings so closely. Intuitive, Clara had said, both Mia and Frances. To him, it seemed like so much more. "No one. I'm just too busy to bother with emotions."

She shook her head, apparently not willing to take that as an answer. "Don't lie to me, Jack. I want to be able to trust you, but I can't if you refuse to respect me enough to tell me the truth. I've told you some pretty big truths about myself, and I would appreciate it if you'd respond in kind."

Her questions were too personal, hit too close to home. She tapped into a place deep inside, where no one had ever bothered to touch before. "Where do you want me to start?"

"Tell me about your family."

"My dad and my uncle started the law firm where I work, way back when my brother and I were toddlers. That's all he ever really cared about. He spent all his free time there, leaving before six in the morning and coming home after eight at night. And when he was home, he yelled all the time. Nothing my mother ever did was good enough. Brian and I, well, we weren't worth his time if we didn't plan on going to law school and joining the family firm."

"That's terrible."

"Hey, I survived. There are worse things in life than having an absentee father." He ran a hand through his hair and shifted on the blanket. "My mom eventually divorced him and got remarried. She lives in Arizona now with my stepdad. My dad still works too much, but I can't really criticize him for that."

She laughed softly at what must have been a pained expression on his face. "Was talking about that really so bad?"

He shrugged, unaccustomed to this closeness. "I don't really make a point of sharing my life story with others."

Just like that, she cupped his face in her hands and kissed him. His hand threaded through her hair to hold her close as he pushed his tongue into her mouth. He could easily live the rest of his life just holding her and touching her.

"Momma, can I have a sandwich? Eww! Gross! Kissing." Frances's outburst caused him to break the kiss. Mia's face reddened—an adorable look for her—and she swiped a hand across her mouth.

"Sure, honey," she answered, patting the blanket next to her. Frances flopped down and crossed her legs, accepting the sandwich from Mia.

"My Daddy died," she told him matter-of-factly.

"Your mom told me. I'm sorry."

"I don't remember him cause I was a baby then." She paused to take a bite of her sandwich, continuing around a mouthful of peanut butter and jelly. "I wish I did. Momma said he was a nice man."

"I'm sure he was."

Frances picked up a small bottle of juice from the basket and held it out to Jack. "Can you open this for me?"

"Sure." He twisted off the top and handed it back to her.

"Thanks. Are you going to be my new Daddy?"

He nearly choked on the bite of sandwich he'd just taken. Thankfully, Mia intercepted before he had to answer.

"That's enough, Frances. Jack is a friend. That's all."

The look she gave him told a different story. Did he see hope spark in her eyes? He couldn't be quite sure. Any other date and he'd be running in the other direction. This time, running was the furthest thing from his mind.

Chapter Seven

Several days after their picnic in the woods, Jack woke in the middle of the night with the beginnings of what promised to be a terrible migraine. He got out of bed and dressed in a pair of old sweats and a t-shirt before he made his way downstairs to find some milk to take his medicine—or else he'd end up with another ulcer. He noticed a light coming from the kitchen along with an unusual scent wafting from the room. Mia was standing by the stove, stirring a pot of something dark green and watery. A stick of incense was burning in a wooden holder on the counter, a pungent and vaguely familiar scent.

"I hope I'm not interrupting anything," he said as he walked into the room.

She glanced up from the mixture in front of her. "Hi there."

"Hey. Why are you up so late?"

"I'm making an infusion for Mr. Jenson's skin, to help with the rash he seems to be getting from the trees around here."

Her smile slowly melted into a frown. "Why are *you* up so late? Is there something wrong?"

"Couldn't sleep. Headache."

She lifted the pot from the stove and set it on a potholder on the counter before placing a chrome teakettle on the burner. "Sit down for a second. I've got something that might help."

He shook his head. "No, really. I'm fine. It's mild."

And it was, for now. If he let it go, experience told him it would get worse.

"Sit, Jack." She took a small wooden canister out of a cabinet and scooped some of the dry mixture inside into a metal tea ball. When the kettle whistled she took it off the stove burner and poured the boiling water—or at least he *hoped* it was water—into a mug. She dropped the tea ball into it and brought the whole thing to the table.

"Are you upset that I didn't tell you about Frances?" she asked, taking him by surprise.

"No. I can understand that you wouldn't want a stranger to know about your daughter." Though he didn't like to consider himself a stranger to her, not after the intimate moments they'd shared.

"Good. I-I haven't been involved with anyone since her father died." She settled the mug in front of him and he took a sniff. It smelled pleasant, but familiar.

"What's in this?"

"Chamomile, mint, rosemary, and lavender."

He blinked at her response. "Is this tea, or the remnants of a bouquet?"

"Ha, ha. Trust me. This will help." She winked at him. "Have a little faith, Jack."

He hesitated before he lifted the cup to his lips and took a small sip. Surprisingly, he didn't feel the instantaneous need to vomit. That had to be a good sign. The flavor wasn't horrible, either. He sipped the tea while Mia sat across from him, enjoying the comfortable silence. When she darted her tongue out to wet her lip, though, he felt a tightening in his groin.

"Finish your tea, Jack," she told him, seeming to read his mind.

He did as she suggested, and was surprised to find that within a few minutes the headache had started to subside.

"Feeling better?"

Talk about psychosomatic. "Yeah, but I told you it wasn't that bad to begin with."

"Is it really that hard to admit that I might be right?"

"Yes."

She laughed. "Keep on telling yourself that. One of these days you might surprise yourself and concede a point to the other person."

That's the way he would have thought of an opponent. But he didn't think of Mia as an opponent.

That was probably where he'd gone wrong in most of his relationships. Knowing what he knew about marriage and divorce, he'd always gone in ready for a fight. But he didn't feel that way now. He could relax around Mia, because he didn't feel like she was going to suck him dry the first chance she got. He liked her open, honest personality—there wasn't a manipulative bone in her body—and she seemed to genuinely care about everyone, not just herself.

"Thanks," he told her, and not just for the tea. She'd gotten him to look at his life from a different angle, and to see that he needed to make some changes.

"For what? This is the kind of thing I do here. I would have done the same for anyone."

He wouldn't be surprised. "Well, thanks anyway. I'll let you get back to your infusion."

"It's done. It just has to cool overnight," she said quickly. Very quickly. Her tone made him even more hesitant to go back to bed—alone.

"Oh. Okay. Then, I guess I'll go and let you get to bed."

"You don't have to rush out. Stay here for a little while. I can make you another cup of tea. You know, just in case the first cup doesn't work completely."

She took his mug and refilled it, making one for herself before she joined him at the table.

"So, is this what your job entails?" he asked. "Staying up until all hours of the night to make herbal remedies?"

"Not always, but I couldn't sleep so I thought I'd get a head start."

He nodded, though he didn't understand as much as he'd like to. The closest he'd ever come to herbal healing was that cough syrup with the supposedly natural ingredients in it. But with the way that tea relaxed his head, he might consider trying it again.

She opened her mouth to speak, her expression questioning. He didn't feel like answering questions at this time of night, especially since the intimate talk they'd had that afternoon in the clearing in the woods. He wanted to change his old habits, and he did his best to make an effort, but he had to take small steps.

So instead of giving her the chance to ask more questions, he took advantage of her parted lips and kissed her. As always, a spark shot through him as soon as their lips met. The chemistry baffled him, but his feelings for her baffled him more. He wanted more out of this encounter than a one or two night stand. He wanted…everything. He wanted to bring her back to Boston with him, show her off, take her to Arizona to meet his mother.

His mother would love her. His colleagues would think he'd finally gone off the deep end. But none of that mattered right now. He could think about the consequences later. Now, as Mia's small hand rested on the inside of his upper thigh, all he could think about was his rapidly hardening cock and what he wanted to do with it.

He deepened the kiss, pulling her chair closer to him. She moaned softly when he would have expected her to push him away. Encouraged by her response, Jack cupped her face with his hands in a possessive gesture. Mia's hands flew to his shirt and fisted tightly in the soft fabric.

But just as suddenly as she'd accepted his touch, Mia broke the kiss and backed her chair away, standing up so fast she sent it toppling to the floor with a crash. "This is a bad idea."

He hadn't seen *that* coming. "Why?"

"I-I *work* here. You're a guest. That's not ethical."

"Aren't you the one who told me to go with my feelings?"

"That's different."

"No, it's not."

And then he understood. She tried to hide it, but the chemistry between them scared her as much as it scared him. Probably more, since she had a child to think about.

She sighed and tugged on a strand of hair before shoving it behind her ear. "Listen, Jack, this can't happen again. I won't deny that I'm attracted to you, but it would never work. I need more than a week-long affair."

What was it with women always thinking men were only out for a good time? "You know what? So am I. I'm so sick of flings and two-week relationships that I've given up on all of that. I want to build something with you. I don't want this to end."

And because he didn't know what else to do, he stood up, pulled her close and crushed her lips with his. His hands tangled in her hair and held her close. He didn't want to let her get away anytime soon.

Mia, apparently, felt the same way. She stood stiff for only a few seconds before she gave in to his kiss and wrapped her arms around his waist.

Chapter Eight

She couldn't believe she was going to let this happen.

She should stop him, find some excuse to get out of the kitchen — fast — before she let things go too far. But she wouldn't, because a small part of her had to admit that Jack was right. They had to let this thing take its course. It had been building since the first day they'd met, and she wanted to see where it would lead them.

When she broke the kiss, her breathing was ragged and her pussy soaked. Every nerve in her body screamed for him to take her, and take her *now*. Goddess, she needed that man more than she'd ever needed anything in her life. Tomorrow, she could worry about what would happen. Tonight, now, she'd take everything he offered.

When he pushed her robe off her shoulders, she didn't utter a word of protest. Instead, she reached for the hem of his shirt and pulled it over his head, tossing it on the table.

"Wait." His hands were at her shoulders, stilling her movements. He laughed when she uttered a sound of protest. "Not here. Too public."

She looked around, only just remembering that they stood in the middle of the kitchen — Clara's kitchen, where any of her family or the guests might have wandered down to find them. She blinked, not sure of how to proceed.

"We need somewhere more private," Jack continued when she remained silent.

"This way." She took his hand and led him through a door that led to the back hall and the owner's suites. "But be quiet, okay?"

He spun her around and pulled her back against him for a kiss. "I can't promise anything. I'll try."

She shushed him with a finger to his lips as she let them into her suite. "Frances is sleeping. You wake her up, you get kicked out. Understand?"

He laughed softly and kissed the top of her head. "Well, if you put it that way…"

"I do." She brought him into her bedroom, thankfully across the suite from Frances's room, and closed the door behind her.

A case of jitters struck hard as soon as she turned to face him. She wet her lips with her tongue. "Maybe this wasn't such a good idea."

"It felt pretty good to me a few minutes ago." Jack sat down on the bed and patted the mattress next to him. "Sit. Tell me what's on your mind."

She hesitated for a second before she joined him on the bed. It was hard for her to look at him—with his hair mussed and his shirt missing she didn't think she'd be able to keep herself from touching him again. But she had some things to say before this went any further. "I-I think maybe we shouldn't act on this."

"Why not? Whenever I touch you, your body gives me a different response."

And she knew it, too, but it didn't stop the fact that if she let herself get any closer to him, she'd be heartbroken when the time came for him to go home.

"You're leaving soon."

"Lousy excuse." He lifted her chin with his thumb and frowned down at her. "Come on. You can do better than that."

"I don't do affairs."

Jack's gaze turned hot and intense, burning a hole through her resistance. "You and I both know that this is so much more than a mindless fling."

"How can it be anything more? We're too different."

"It'll all work itself out in the end," he said, sounding suspiciously like Clara.

"How can you possibly know that? You'll go back to Boston soon, and I'll be here. We can't work through the distance."

"Trust me," he told her, repeating her earlier words to him. "Have faith, Mia."

Instead of giving her a chance to respond, he leaned in and kissed her.

She would have pushed him away, but her mind shut down as soon as his lips touched hers. He felt so good, so right, that she couldn't make herself let him go. Someday soon, she'd have to, but not tonight.

Tonight would be special. The moon cycle had finally come to a completion, and there was a new moon tonight. Time for changes, time for something new. Time to let herself do something she hadn't done in what seemed like forever.

Have fun.

Jack pushed her back against the mattress and covered her body with his. He kissed her deeply as his hand cupped her breast, his thumb flicking across her nipple. The flesh beaded under his touch, their skin separated only by her thin nightshirt. And then his pushed the nightshirt up and over her head and they were together, skin on skin.

"You're so beautiful," Jack whispered against her throat. "Perfect, Mia. Perfect."

His mouth found her bare, beaded nipples and he laved the skin tenderly. She moaned and arched into him, wondering how she'd gone so long without a man's touch. She threaded her hands through his hair as he trailed kisses lower down her body, stopping at the top of her underwear. With his teeth, he grasped the edge and moved them down her hips before using his fingers to tug them the rest of the way off.

"Do you remember what I said I want to do to you?" he asked, his breath hot against her mound.

She could only manage a moan as his tongue flicked across her clit. He used his fingers to spread her folds, and he traced his tongue over her pussy. She let out a panting gasp as he thrust his tongue deep inside her, in and out, bringing her higher than she'd ever been. She felt the orgasm building low in her belly only seconds before she came, drenching Jack's face with her juices. He gave her clit one last lap before kissing his way back up her body.

"Wow."

"You're telling me." Jack gently bit her shoulder as he rolled onto his back and got up off the bed.

"Where are you going?" She didn't want him to leave just yet. They'd barely gotten started.

He smiled as he stripped out of his sweatpants and dropped them in a heap on the floor. "Don't think you're going to get rid of me that easily. This time I plan to stay. I want to get inside you and make you come again."

She shivered, liking the sound of that. A lot.

But then Jack frowned. "Shit. I don't have any condoms. It's not like I came down here expecting—"

"I have some." When Jess had given her a box as a joke for her birthday a few months ago, she never imagined she'd actually find a time she needed to use them. She'd scoffed at the idea at the time, but she'd have to remember to thank Jess later. "In the top drawer of the dresser." She would have gotten them herself, had she been able to walk. But at the moment, her legs felt like jelly.

Jack found the box in record time and tore it open, ripping a packet off the strip. He rolled the condom on before he joined her back on the bed. "Are you sure you really want to do this? It's not too late to back out now."

She wrapped her hand around his cock and stroked, running her thumb over the tip. "I'm sure."

"Good." He smiled. "Come here." He rolled to his back and gestured for her to get on top of him. She straddled him, her legs hugging his hips, and leaned down to kiss him as he impaled her with his rock-hard cock.

She cried out as he filled her, stretched her almost to the point of pain. It had been so long, and she wasn't sure if she could take it. "Jack," she whispered, her voice strained.

"It'll be okay." He lifted his hips a little, seating himself further inside her, as he brought a finger to her mound and stroked her clit. "Relax."

Easy for him to say. Still, the more he stroked her sensitive nerves, the more she felt her body soften around him. Jack held back his movements, alternating the strokes of his fingers with gentle, steady pressure until she felt a second orgasm building. It was then that he gripped her hips and lifted her, bringing her back down on his cock.

With every stroke she felt herself getting closer and closer to coming. Her drenched pussy throbbed for release and she tightened her inner muscles around him. He groaned and pumped into her harder, slamming her down on top of him. Her orgasm ripped through her and she bucked on top of him, unable to control her movements.

In seconds Jack had her on her back, thrusting into her so furiously that the headboard banged against the wall. She dug her fingers into his shoulders as the aftershocks of her climax rippled through her. She felt Jack tense above her as he groaned with his own powerful orgasm. He collapsed on top of her and she clung to him, unable and unwilling to move.

"Are you okay?" he asked, his lips pressed into her damp neck.

"Mmm. Are you?"

He lifted up onto his elbows and smiled at her. "No. I don't think I am."

She laughed as he rolled onto his back and tucked her into his side. She'd lay with him for a few more minutes, but as much as she wanted to, she couldn't let him stay the night.

* * * * *

Mia woke up slowly and stretched her arms over her head. She stopped mid-yawn when she encountered something solid and warm in her bed.

Jack.

Her heart stopped and then started again with a thud. How could she have let him stay all night?

Voices outside her bedroom door caught her attention. *Frances.* She jumped out of bed and pulled on her robe, hoping Jack wouldn't wake up before she found a way to distract her daughter.

She found Frances in the sitting room, watching cartoons with Jess.

"Morning," Jess said when she saw her, a sly smile on her face.

"Good morning. Is something wrong?"

"Nope. I just came to return something you lost." Jess's smile widened as she gestured to a small table by the door. "Or, rather, your *friend* lost."

Mia's stomach clenched as she saw the item Jess referred to. *Jack's shirt.* She gulped.

Jess got off the couch and walked over to Mia. "Better put that away before the little one sees what it is," she mumbled before walking into the hall.

Mia followed Jess. "Did Clara see it?"

Jess shrugged, her expression amused. "Don't know. What exactly happened between you two, anyway?"

They stopped in front of the door to Mia's room, and she opened the door to toss the shirt inside. Jack stood there, rubbing his eyes sleepily. She shut the door on him and turned to Jess. "You need to leave."

"He's still here?" Jess shook her head, the smile on her face widening. "I never would have guessed. Not in a million years."

She didn't need this now, not with the repercussions of her actions to deal with. "Just shut up, okay?"

The bedroom door opened again and Jack stuck his head out. "I don't mean to interrupt or anything, but I need the bathroom."

Mia pointed down the hall and put her finger to her lips. "Jess, go, okay?" she repeated, her eyes never leaving Jack's retreating behind. She was hoping for more time alone with him. Too bad he'd put his pants back on—

What was she thinking? She'd just been caught by her cousin and possibly her daughter. She needed to get him out, not back into bed.

"Okay, okay. I'm gone." Jess turned to walk to the door. "Hey, Franny, do you want to come with me to the kitchen? I'll make you pancakes with strawberries and chocolate chips."

"Okay!" Frances jumped off the couch and ran to them. "Hi, Momma. Bye, Momma." She blew Mia a kiss as she followed Jess out the door.

Well.

Jack emerged from the bathroom a few seconds later. He smiled when he saw her, but his expression turned confused. "Please don't tell me you're going to spend the morning regretting what happened between us."

"Okay. I won't."

"Mia, come on. Don't do this."

A tear slipped from her eye, followed by another. She batted them away, refusing to let him see her cry over something so stupid. She'd gone and fallen in love with the guy. How that was even possible, she hadn't a clue. But there it was.

And he was leaving.

He took her hand and led her to the couch, sitting down and pulling her into his lap. "What's the matter now?"

"I don't even know where to begin."

Jack sighed. "You know if I could stay here with you, I would."

"You would?"

"Yeah. Of course." He ruffled her hair—which probably resembled steel wool after sleeping on it all night. "I can't leave my job, though. I have responsibilities. An apartment. Family."

"So do I," she said quietly. She couldn't leave. She couldn't pull Frances away from her family and friends and dump her into the middle of a big city.

"So where do we go from here?"

She shrugged and sniffled. "I wish I knew."

"Then let's take it one day at a time, okay?" He kissed her ear.

At this point, she'd take what she could get.

Chapter Nine

The morning for Jack's departure came way too quickly for Mia. She'd clung to the hope over the last couple of days that he'd change his mind and stay, but it hadn't happened. His bags were packed, and he was checking out as she sat waiting on the front steps to say goodbye.

He came out a few minutes later, his bags in his hands. Just the sight sent a hollow chill through her heart. She knew this would happen—that she'd be left alone and hurt in the end—but she hadn't done anything to stop it. She'd encouraged it, if she had to admit the truth. And it hurt more than she'd expected it to.

"So, this is it." She stood and walked over to him as he came down the steps. She tried to put on a brave face, but had a feeling she'd failed miserably.

"Not even close." Jack dropped his bags and pulled her into his arms. He kissed her hard, long and lingering, right there in plain view of everyone. "I'm not willing to let you go that easily."

She gaped at him until she could form a full sentence. What was he trying to pull? "But I told you before that I can't go with you. We're too different. It would never work."

He shook his head and cupped her chin in his hand. "We'll work something out. For now, let's take it slowly. I'll call as soon as I get back. Boston isn't that far away. I'll come up and visit on weekends. We'll talk on the phone every night."

A tear slipped out of her eyes and she wiped it away with the back of her hand. "Are you sure?" The one thing she didn't want right now was to drag it out. If he was going to walk out of her life, she'd rather it be now than two or three months down the road when she'd grown even more attached to the man.

"I'll call. I promise."

She said goodbye to him and watched him drive away, wondering if he really would call, or if he'd just been trying to ease her mind for a little while.

* * * * *

Jack drove home an hour later than usual, not looking forward to his empty, cold apartment. The one thing that brightened his day would be his phone conversation with Mia. He let himself into his apartment and collapsed on the couch, wishing he'd had a little more time with her in person. But what was he supposed to do? She wouldn't come with him, she'd made that quite clear, and he couldn't make a three hour commute every day to work. So...for now, they'd just have to take what they could get.

In the past two weeks, he'd realized why so many people said long distance relationships don't work. They spoke almost every night, and planned to visit this coming weekend, but it wasn't the same. He began to wonder if that vacation had been a terrible idea. At least if he hadn't met her, he wouldn't feel so lonely and empty all the time.

He picked up the phone and dialed her private number.

"Hey," he said when she picked up the phone.

He heard the smile in her voice when she spoke. "How was your day?"

"Well, let's put it this way. I'm glad it's over."

"I'm sorry."

"Listen, I was thinking," he said carefully, not sure how his suggestion would be received. He didn't want to hurt her, but he had to try one last time before he made a huge change that might not be necessary. "How would you and Frances feel about spending a few weeks here with me? If you like it, you might decide to stay even longer."

"Like forever?" Her tone turned frosty, and the whole tone of the conversation changed. "I already told you I can't do that, Jack. No matter how much you beg."

Beg? She made him sound like some kind of sniveling puppy. "Believe me, the last thing I want to do is beg. I just thought that maybe now that you've had time to think about it, you've seen how it's the best choice for us."

He realized his mistake in the stony silence that followed, but pride wouldn't let him take the comment back. He waited it out until she finally spoke.

"You know, I think the best *choice* for us would be to let go," she told him. "We never should have tried to make this work. This whole thing has been a terrible mistake. We're just too different. Goodbye, Jack."

He was left listening to the dial tone. He tried to call again, but she didn't pick up. He'd made a mess of things by not coming right out and saying what he'd wanted to say, and he just hoped it wasn't too late to fix his stupid mistake.

Chapter Ten

Mia sat on the porch swing, rocking slowly back and forth. In the days since she'd broken it off with Jack, she hadn't been able to pull herself out of a terrible funk. One week had stretched into almost two, and she still hadn't heard from him. As much as she didn't want to accept it, it was over.

And she was the biggest fool in the history of the world.

She looked up at the sky and her heart sank further into her chest. A new moon. There'd been a new moon the night she and Jack had made love. And now, she faced this one alone.

So much for Clara's ideas.

She'd learned the hard way that she didn't need changes in her life. What she needed, more than ever now, was for everything to remain exactly the same.

The sound of a car's tires crunching on the gravel driveway drew her attention. She looked up just as a little convertible came to a stop in the parking lot. Excitement welled inside her, but she warned herself not to get her hopes up. It could be a guest for late check-in. This was the last weekend the bed and breakfast would be open, and then they would all go back to the mainland until next spring.

At first she thought she must be seeing things when a man who looked like Jack got out of the car. And then she realized it *was* Jack as he walked up the steps toward her.

"Sorry I'm late." He told her. "I had to pick up something before I came, and the store was closed when I got out of work last night."

Late? *Late* was a few minutes. She hadn't heard from him in weeks. "You could have called."

"I can make it up to you."

She sighed. "That's really not necessary. I was just worried. You should have let me know you were okay."

"I have a good reason, if you're interested in hearing it," he said, smiling down at her.

"Fine. Sit. Tell me your reason." She tried to feign indifference, but couldn't quite manage it. "What kept you away for so long?"

He gestured to the star-filled night sky. "The moon."

"What about it?"

"It wasn't there." He sat down on the bench beside her. "Didn't you tell me that the new moon is the perfect time for starting something new?"

She nodded slowly, wondering where he was going with this.

He pulled a small jeweler's box out of his pocket. "Does that possibly include a new marriage?"

He opened the box and she looked down at the large brilliant blue Australian opal ring that sat in the black velvet.

"Oh, my."

"You don't seem to me like the diamond type. I saw this, and I knew right away it was perfect."

He was right. He couldn't have picked a more perfect ring—or a more perfect time.

"I love you. I don't know how this happened, but I wouldn't change it for the world. Marry me," Jack whispered against her hair.

"Are you serious?"

Her hopes were dashed as she thought about moving away. She didn't want to live in Boston, with a bunch of snobs she didn't know. She was perfectly happy here, as much as she loved him, she couldn't do it. "I can't, Jack. We talked about—"

"I quit my job."

"You *what*?" So much for Mr. Predictable.

"I quit my job. That's part of what took me so long to get here. I had a few loose ends. But I don't now. I don't have any ties." He smiled. "Except here."

"But I live on the island all summer. And the mainland isn't exactly Boston. Not even close. You wouldn't be happy here. It's so quiet, you're used to—"

He kissed her. Probably to shut her up, but at this point she didn't care.

When he broke away, he smiled down at her. "I don't care. I'll get used to it. And it's not like we're out in the middle of nowhere. I can open an office or something here. Maybe in the spring. For now, I've got plenty of savings."

Was this really happening? She shook her head and pinched her thigh, hard, to make sure she wasn't dreaming.

"So, will you marry me?" Jack asked again, his expression hopeful—and a little worried.

How could she say no when he'd quit his job just to be close to her? "Yes."

* * * * *

Jack's breath fluttered across her shoulder as Mia lay draped over him in her bed. "I was thinking."

"Hmm." She couldn't manage much more quite so early in the morning.

"I'm going to like living up here, but I think we should buy a bigger house on the mainland. You said you have a two-bedroom apartment. That's just not going to be enough."

"Why is that?"

He laughed. "My mother's already getting ready to visit, wanting to badger you about grandchildren."

"Does she know about Frances?"

"Yep. And she's planning to bring a suitcase full of toys for her. She can't wait to spoil the kid rotten. Is all of this okay with you?"

Okay? She'd never been happier. "I love you, Jack."

"I love you, too."

She rested her head on his chest, stroking his side with the tips of her fingers. Leave it to Aunt Clara to find her the perfect man, all because of a little wishful thinking.

Also by Elisa Adams:

Dream Stalker
Just Another Night
Dark Promises: Midnight
Dark Promises: Demonic Obsession
Dark Promises: Shift of Fate
Dark Promises: Flesh and Blood
Dirty Pictures
In Darkness
Eden's Curse

.

About the author:

Born in Gloucester, Massachusetts, Elisa Adams has lived most of her life on the east coast. Formerly a nursing assistant and phlebotomist, writing has been a longtime hobby. Now a full time writer, she lives on the New Hampshire border with her husband and three children.

Elisa welcomes mail from readers. You can write to her c/o Ellora's Cave Publishing at 1056 Home Avenue, Akron OH 44310-3502.

Why an electronic book?

We live in the Information Age—an exciting time in the history of human civilization in which technology rules supreme and continues to progress in leaps and bounds every minute of every hour of every day. For a multitude of reasons, more and more avid literary fans are opting to purchase e-books instead of paperbacks. The question to those not yet initiated to the world of electronic reading is simply: *why?*

1. *Price.* An electronic title at Ellora's Cave Publishing and Cerridwen Press runs anywhere from 40-75% less than the cover price of the <u>exact same title</u> in paperback format. Why? Cold mathematics. It is less expensive to publish an e-book than it is to publish a paperback, so the savings are passed along to the consumer.

2. *Space.* Running out of room to house your paperback books? That is one worry you will never have with electronic novels. For a low one-time cost, you can purchase a handheld computer designed specifically for e-reading purposes. Many e-readers are larger than the average handheld, giving you plenty of screen room. Better yet, hundreds of titles can be stored within your new library—a single microchip. (Please note that Ellora's Cave and Cerridwen Press does not endorse any specific brands. You can check our website at www.ellorascave.com or

www.cerridwenpress.com for customer recommendations we make available to new consumers.)

3. *Mobility.* Because your new library now consists of only a microchip, your entire cache of books can be taken with you wherever you go.

4. *Personal preferences are accounted for.* Are the words you are currently reading too small? Too large? Too...**ANNOYING**? Paperback books cannot be modified according to personal preferences, but e-books can.

5. *Instant gratification.* Is it the middle of the night and all the bookstores are closed? Are you tired of waiting days—sometimes weeks—for online and offline bookstores to ship the novels you bought? Ellora's Cave Publishing sells instantaneous downloads 24 hours a day, 7 days a week, 365 days a year. Our e-book delivery system is 100% automated, meaning your order is filled as soon as you pay for it.

Those are a few of the top reasons why electronic novels are displacing paperbacks for many an avid reader. As always, Ellora's Cave and Cerridwen Press welcomes your questions and comments. We invite you to email us at service@ellorascave.com, service@cerridwenpress.com or write to us directly at: 1056 Home Ave. Akron OH 44310-3502.

erridwen, the Celtic Goddess of wisdom, was the muse who brought inspiration to storytellers and those in the creative arts. Cerridwen Press encompasses the best and most innovative stories in all genres of today's fiction. Visit our site and discover the newest titles by talented authors who still get inspired - much like the ancient storytellers did, once upon a time.

Cerridwen Press
www.cerridwenpress.com

Discover for yourself why readers can't get enough of the multiple award-winning publisher Ellora's Cave. Whether you prefer e-books or paperbacks, be sure to visit EC on the web at www.ellorascave.com for an erotic reading experience that will leave you breathless.

www.ellorascave.com